g Love
REED

Big Love

"*Big Love* is a heart warming, heart breaking story about what it means to be gay in modern America."
—Divine Magazine

"*Big Love* gets 5+ stars from me.... I could probably write at length about why the book touched me so deeply, but simply put, Rick R. Reed writes from the heart."
—Gay Book Reviews

"I really enjoyed this book."
—Two Chicks Obsessed

"I was blown away by how good this book was and how it truly wound its way around my heart.... This is one of those books you remember years to come."
—Inked Rainbow Reviews

"*Big Love* is definitely one of my new all-time favorite books. It's about love, family, and helping someone who seems unable to help himself. I can't recommend it enough."
—On Top Down Under Reviews

Bigger Love

"A tone of authentic tenderness and yearning, completely without artifice, suffuses Reed's engaging Appalachian tale of high-school gay love."
—Booklist

By RICK R. REED

Published by DREAMSPINNER PRESS

www.dreamspinnerpress.com

BIGGER LOVE
RICK R. REED

WITHDRAWN

Published by
DREAMSPINNER PRESS

5032 Capital Circle SW, Suite 2, PMB# 279,
Tallahassee, FL 32305-7886 USA
www.dreamspinnerpress.com

Bigger Love
© 2018 Rick R. Reed.

Cover Art
© 2018 Reese Dante.
http://www.reesedante.com
Cover content is for illustrative purposes only and any person depicted
on the cover is a model.

Mass Market Paperback ISBN: 978-1-64108-064-4
Trade Paperback ISBN: 978-1-64080-622-1
Digital ISBN: 978-1-64080-621-4
Library of Congress Control Number: 2018934235
Mass Market Paperback published November 2018
v. 1.0

Printed in the United States of America
∞
This paper meets the requirements of
ANSI/NISO Z39.48-1992 (Permanence of Paper).

For big sissies everywhere...
and the men and women who love them.

"Where there is love, there is life."
—*Mahatma Gandhi*

"We are born of love; Love is our mother."
—*Rumi*

"Let men see, let them know, a real man,
who lives as he was meant to live."
—*Marcus Aurelius*

PROLOGUE

On a shore somewhere, two boys embrace, clinging, their bodies not pressed so tightly together out of desire, but from a need for comfort, for knowing that this moment is one to savor, because it may never come again.

Nearby... wind rushes through trees, and a thousand tiny voices lament the boys' parting.

Nearby... stars twinkle in an impossibly black sky, not shining down exactly, but providing a jewellike backdrop for this unfortunate and drawn-out farewell.

Nearby... water rushes, slamming a shore in frustration at the separating of a pair who'd, once upon a time, proclaimed, "forever."

Eyes meet. Lips touch. Minds and hearts meld, knowing that tomorrow nothing will ever be the same again.

CHAPTER 1

"THERE'S A man in your room. I can smell him."

Truman Reid confronted his mom, Patsy, in the kitchen. Early morning sun streamed in brightly through the kitchen window over the sink, making Truman long for the relative freedom of summer that was about to be put to rest that very day.

Patsy glowered at him from the stove where she was scrambling eggs. She didn't often get up to make him breakfast, but Truman had figured—at least at first—that she was doing so because this was Truman's first day back at school. He'd be a senior at Summitville High. First days of school had always been a source of high anxiety for Truman, who'd been bullied and teased mercilessly throughout almost the entire four years. But now Truman wondered if Patsy had risen early to fix bacon and eggs because she was hiding a man in her room. You know, to distract him.

This wasn't a usual experience for his mom, Truman was sure, and he wondered if he'd embarrassed her. But he couldn't help but wonder how a man in her room might affect his exclusive hold on her. Would he still get her undivided attention, you know, if this was a "thing"?

Of course, Patsy, lovely, diminutive, with curly black hair and wide eyes, had every right to have a man in her room. Even if that man smelled of cigarettes and motor oil. But she didn't have the right, Truman opined, to keep secrets from *him*. A mother should never keep secrets from her boy, right? Wasn't that one of those unwritten laws?

"That may be. Or may not be," Patsy said, giving the eggs one final push-around with a spatula before dumping them on a plate. She sighed and eyed him. "I have a right to my privacy. You don't need to be privy to every detail of my life. I show you that respect and expect the same in return."

She's reading my mind. Again. "Oh, I didn't mean to pry, Mama. I just wanted to say it's okay if you did have a man sleep over. It's not like I would mind. It's not like we're not both adults around here. We have separate bedrooms and separate lives." Truman almost choked on the words.

Patsy set the plate of steaming eggs before him. Truman saw, to his delight, that the eight pieces of bacon Patsy had fried up before the eggs were all for him.

Patsy smiled, but there was something just a tad bit evil in it. "Thank you, sweetie. I'm so glad to have your *go-ahead* if I want to whore around." She chuckled and returned to the counter where she'd left her mug of coffee. She leaned against the counter, mug in hand, and took a sip. Patsy was all of thirty-four years old but looked at least ten years younger in the dappled morning light, and Truman felt a rush of love for her. The bond they had was kind of a you-and-me-against-the-world one. Truman felt he could say just about anything to Patsy, and he knew she felt the same; witness the "whore" comment. What kind of mother said that to her son?

Truman wasn't sure, but he was glad he had one who did.

Besides, between raising him, which could be, um, challenging at times, and working at the Elite Diner in Summitville's tiny downtown, she had little time for romance. Given that Truman's father was still a mystery to him—and to Patsy—he assumed that, once upon a time, she did have her whoring-around days, but he'd seen little evidence of them.

Until this morning.

"So who is he? Can I go take a peek? Is he hot?" Truman laughed.

Patsy answered the three questions in short order: "None of your business. No you can't. Yes. Very." She took another sip of coffee and tightened the sash of her white chenille bathrobe. Truman noticed she was wearing a little makeup this morning—mascara, some blush, a hint of lip gloss. She hadn't overdone it. Truman would say she looked "dewy" if she asked. "You need to eat up and get in the shower, young man. The bus will be here—" She turned to look at the wall clock on the soffit above the sink. "—in twenty minutes. I know you need your primping time."

Truman dropped his fork to the table. "Seriously? Only twenty? Good Lord." He wrapped his bacon up in a paper towel and headed for the single bathroom. Patsy blocked his way. "Since when do we leave our plates on the table? What? You think I'm your servant?"

"Mom!" Truman whined. "You know I need time to get ready. Please, please, please take care of it for me. I'll love you forever!"

"Okay. This *once*. And sweetie, I'd thought loving me forever went without saying. But you cook *and* clean up tonight."

"Deal."

Truman rushed to the bathroom, wondering if Patsy would use the time to sneak her man out of the house. Too bad the only window looked out on the backyard. It was frosted glass anyway.

He hoped his mom *had* found someone to love.

He hoped his mom *hadn't* found someone to love.

It had been just the two of them for so long, Truman didn't know if he could cope with someone else vying for Patsy's affections. He felt a little sense of violation at the thought.

In the bathroom, Truman laid out on the counter all the stuff a boy would need to make a suitable senior-year debut:

eyeliner,

clear mascara,

blush,

and the lip gloss that added no extra color to his lips but made them shine.

He stepped into the shower after brushing, flossing, and exfoliating his face.

WHEN HE emerged, breathless, in what he thought was far too little time, Patsy rolled her eyes and then smiled. "The bus is waiting outside. I signaled Fred to hang on for you, but I think he may be losing his patience. Didn't you hear him honk? Three times?"

"I heard him." Truman, ever observant, noticed Patsy's bedroom door, just off the kitchen, was open. It had been closed before. Patsy had hastily made up the bed, from the looks of it. He thought about mentioning it to her but decided to give her some slack. After all, one day he might want a little privacy, although he still didn't know how he felt about his mom's newfound secretiveness. Or why it was even necessary.

Besides, he didn't have time to interrogate her. A honk sounded outside—again.

Patsy kissed him on the cheek and handed him his lunch in a brown paper sack.

"There's no carbs in this, right?" Truman asked.

She side-eyed him. "What do you think? Celery, carrots, ham-and-cheese rollups, and a Honeycrisp apple. You worry about carbs but have no problem wolfing down eight slices of bacon!"

"Thanks, Mom." He snatched the paper-towel-wrapped packet of bacon he'd made earlier off the table. "Bacon doesn't have carbs, or hardly any. Carbs are what make you fat."

"Whatever."

The bus horn sounded again.

Patsy slapped Truman's ass. "Scoot!"

Truman hurried to the door. When he had it open, she called after him, "Love you, son."

He waved over his shoulder and called back, "Love you more."

WHEN HE boarded the bus, there were whispers. There were snickers. Someone said, "Get her!" which caused an eruption of laughter as Truman headed for the back of the bus.

He was used to it. There was a time when he would have been devastated by the laughter and the remarks, but now? *Just another part of the school day*, he told himself. Truman knew it was important that they didn't know they could get to him. So he took a little bow, left, then right. He forced himself to smile at the other kids, who gawked at him. "Please. No special ruckus for the likes of me."

Once upon a time, he wouldn't have dared say such a thing. He would have hurried to his seat, face burning and head bowed. That was before he knew the power of claiming your own identity, however different it was. That was before he stopped believing he was worthless because he wasn't like everyone else. That was before he'd caught on to the lie that being different somehow made you less. Often it made the reverse true.

He headed toward a pair of empty seats near the back of the bus, knowing every eye was trained on him. For his first day of school, he'd paired black skinny jeans with a hot-pink-and-black polka-dot button-down shirt—he'd raided Patsy's closet for the blouse. Black Chuck Taylors completed the ensemble. He thought the look had kind of an eighties vibe, back in the olden days when his mama was born. For Truman, today's outfit was dressing down. For everyone else on the bus, well, he knew they were stupefied into silence by his ensemble. He couldn't imagine why.

He'd been dressing this way—a style he'd come to term *gender-fuck*—since freshman year, when the bullying and teasing had reached a tipping point, driving him to the literal edge. He'd almost jumped off the roof of the high school after a particularly humiliating and cruel prank.

What he'd learned that year was *not* to hide who he was but to claim it—to get right up in the faces of those who dared challenge him, in effect saying, "Fuck you, sister. This is who I am. If you don't like it, that's *your* problem, not mine."

It took a while, and many days of daring, to come to school in thrift-store treasures that played with the idea of gender with a mélange of male and female options, a little makeup to highlight his handsome yet waifish appearance, and an attitude that one might be tempted to say he'd borrowed from someone like RuPaul. *Fierce.* When he began saying, with his outward appearance and attitude, that he *was* different, and that this difference was his right, the bullying and teasing continued but slowed dramatically. It was hard for someone to call him a "sissy," a "fag," or a "piss-willy" if he first claimed those terms for himself. It became difficult, if not impossible, for the bullies to challenge what they thought of as his effeminate ways if Truman himself not only didn't hide them but celebrated them.

Of course, inside, Truman was always terrified he'd be pummeled, teased unmercifully, spit on, or worse, but he tried his best to never let that fear show. He discovered, after a long time of practice, that one could be quivering with fear on the inside while his outside could exude a calm radiance.

No one knew he was shaking in his boots if they couldn't see it.

Though the bullying and teasing never quite came to the halt Truman dreamed of, it slowed increasingly over the past three years of Truman's high school career. For this, he was grateful. Yet he always harbored a little anxiety that the front he projected would one day come tumbling down, things would go back to the way they once were, and he'd find himself again on his knees in the dark of his bedroom praying tearfully to God that the hurt would stop, if only for one single day. He'd spent too many nights in the past like that, even wishing his very identity away.

Just like Pinocchio, he'd once been desperate to be a "real" boy.

But Truman, through hard-won self-acceptance, realized he was just as real as any other boy... or girl.

For now all he had to do was stare out the window and wait for the bus to transport him to Summitville High. It was his final year, the year when seniors ruled the school. What would these nine or so months hold for him?

Truman couldn't wait to jump the hurdle of this final year and get out. He knew that once he put Summitville behind him, with its small minds and judgments, he could really begin to *live*. He could be the person he was meant to be—somewhere with bright lights, skyscrapers, cosmopolitan drinks, and cosmopolitan people....

He took his gaze away from the view out the window, the sun-dappled foothills of the Appalachian Mountains, and opened the book he'd started a week ago—*Letters to a Young Artist* by Anna Deavere

Smith. The book was fast becoming his bible; it deepened his faith that something bigger lay in wait for him beyond the tree-covered rises of this provincial valley.

Near the last stop before they got to the high school, Truman couldn't prevent a grin from spreading across his face, because he spied his best friend waiting there beneath the shade of an old maple. Like Truman, Alicia Adams had endured her fair share of teasing over her school years. She'd tell you herself she was fat, black, and sassy, and if you didn't like it, you needed to get over yourself, because that's just the way God made her. Hey, if Ms. Oprah Winfrey could claim those same attributes and be adored by the masses, well then, by God, so could she.

One day.

Like Truman, Alicia put up a brave front but had been tormented a lot—especially in elementary school—until one day a group of mean girls pushed her past her breaking point and she lashed out with fists, claws, and a brick. Alicia wasn't proud of how she'd sent two of the mean girls to the emergency room, at least not in retrospect; but she was proud of how her actions, decidedly not compassionate or kind, had afforded her a measure of fear-based respect she used to her advantage from about the sixth grade onward.

She and Truman had become pals when she became his first defender and supporter. She knew what it was like to be different, and she celebrated Truman's courage when he'd shown up one day at school in a "Sissies Rule" T-shirt and makeup. Her defense, and his gratitude, had forged a bond—one that allowed each to be vulnerable around the other. That was something neither could claim with almost anyone else.

A dark shadow crawled in front of the sun when Truman thought of Alicia's brother, now playing basketball at Ohio State. Darrell. Truman closed his eyes for a moment, thinking of him, of the warmth of his eyes—and his arms. He'd thought they were in love. And, in his naïve way, he'd supposed Darrell would forgo a full-ride scholarship to stay in town and close to Truman. He knew it was horribly selfish to expect such a thing, but Truman read a lot of gay romance, and his thoughts were clouded by their easy visions of happy-ever-afters.

He forced his mind away from the image of Darrell, the two of them pressed close, their contrasts of skin color, height, and weight not mattering. He realized toward the end of that summer after Darrell's senior year, he had no choice other than to let him go, to wish him well at school. He could still harbor the belief that one day Darrell would come back to him.

He'd gotten disabused of the notion, though, once Darrell was really gone to that metropolis of Columbus, Ohio, and a school with five times the population of Summitville. The fact that their love affair had ended all too quickly became easier to endure as a figure stepped out from behind Alicia. A figure that caused Truman to forget, if only for a moment, all about Darrell.

Wait. A. Minute.

Damn.

Who is *that?* Truman wondered.

The boy, young man really, was one Truman had never seen before. He'd know if he had! Good God, this one was unforgettable.

There was something about the guy that set Truman's heart to racing, that erased every logical thought from Truman's mind as all the blood in his body rushed south.

It wasn't only the fact that he was gorgeous—which he was, with cropped black hair and a five o'clock shadow—but there was something about him that called to the nurturing side of Truman. Even at a glance and from this distance, there was something dark and brooding about him. It set him apart, making him both mysterious and alluring. For just a moment, everything around Truman silenced—the chatter and laughter of the other kids on the bus, the grumble of its engine, the whine of its brakes as it slowed to a stop, and the pneumatic whoosh of the doors opening.

Truman knew, somewhere in the back of his mind, that these sounds *should* be there, but for one brief, shining moment, all that existed was *the boy*.

He was at least six feet tall, probably a couple of inches above that. Broad shoulders. Beefy. To use one of Patsy's terms, he was "strapping." Unlike Truman he dressed *not* to attract attention to himself. He wore only a pair of faded Levi's, a plain white crewneck T-shirt that had seen many washings, and a pair of very basic black canvas tennis shoes. Slung over one shoulder was a battered and faded red backpack.

Mesmerized, Truman watched as he made his way to the bus and then disappeared from view for an instant as he boarded. Truman snapped out of his reverie as he realized Alicia was staring at him as she stood a few people back in line. She stuck her tongue out as their eyes met. Truman chuckled. And he went right back to searching for just one more glimpse of that face.

And then *he* was on the bus, passing close enough to Truman to touch. Truman swore his heart stopped. Their eyes met, and Truman was nearly bowled over by how crystalline blue they were, bluer than Truman's own, with an icy paleness from which it was impossible to look away. The lashes fringing those eyes were as black as the hair on his head—which, by the way, contrasted wonderfully with the pale blue—and long enough to cause a twinge of jealousy and desire to flare up in Truman.

Truman swore he felt something pass between him and the boy in that smallest exchange of glances. Something charged. Truman actually felt the downy hair on his neck rise, tingling. He would be hard-pressed to say just what that something was, but he knew for certain that a kind of communication definitely took place.

For the fearful, teased boy who still lived somewhere inside Truman, there was a supposition that the good-looking boy met his glance because he was appalled by what he saw. Through those self-hating eyes, Truman would see a boy dressed all wrong, a boy with makeup who should be ashamed of himself. He wasn't a *real* boy. Through that lens, Truman saw disgust.

And it made his blood run cold.

But the other—and ever-growing-even-stronger—part of Truman hoped that what had passed between them was recognition, a kind of kindred-souls thing. Maybe a little interest?

Dare he hope for attraction? Even lust?

Alicia plopped into the seat beside him with a sigh. She punched him, hard, in the bicep, which drew his reverie to a close. Frowning, Truman looked over at her and began rubbing at his upper arm. "Ouch! That hurt!"

"Dude! Where were you?"

"What do you mean?"

"Honey, you were *not* on this bus. You were someplace far, far away. Over the rainbow, maybe?" Alicia snickered as she settled into the seat, spreading her stretch-pant-clad legs and crowding Truman. Some things never changed.

"Very funny." Truman had a lingering thought, yearning, about the black-haired boy and had to fight the impulse to turn and look for him in the seats behind. "I was just thinking about the year ahead."

"I know, right? Seniors. Can you believe it?" Alicia settled her stuff on her lap—her phone, a spiral-bound notebook, and one of those clear plastic organizers that seemed so old-school, which had an assortment of pens and pencils in it.

"It should be an interesting year," Truman said and thought *Especially if he's in some of my classes.* And then he chastised himself. *Jesus, pull yourself together. Next you're gonna be doodling his name in your notebook, right in the middle of a big red heart. Whatever his name was…. Heathcliff? Gage? Hunter?*

"Interesting?" Alicia made a huffing sound. "That's a good word for it. There's way too many days ahead of us until graduation, and we can finally break free from this shithole one-horse town."

"And be the superstars we are meant to be?"

"Damn right." Their heads canted toward each other as they laughed. "Who you got for homeroom?"

"Mr. Bernard! I am so grateful." Dane Bernard, although old enough to be Truman's dad—and could be, for all Truman knew—had come out almost simultaneously with Truman during Truman's freshman year. That connection helped negate a thirtysome-year difference in their ages. They'd forged a special bond. Truman considered Mr. Bernard, and his new husband, Mr. Wolcott, friends as well as mentors and role models. He and Patsy had even been honored to attend their wedding at the beginning of last summer.

"Lucky," Alicia said. "I'm stuck with some chick goes by the name of Ms. Waggle."

Truman cocked his head. "Who dat?"

"I don't know. She's new. First job out of school from what I hear."

"So that means go easy on her. Behave yourself," Truman said, knowing what he was asking for was hopeless.

"Right. Sure thing." Alicia snickered. "You know how easy I go on everyone."

They sat, for once, in silence for the rest of the ride to Summitville High.

Truman didn't know what Alicia was thinking about. For one, he supposed she was preoccupied with what kind of year it might turn out to be. Remarkable? Devastating? A year in which she might finally find herself a boyfriend, maybe? Would she pull good enough grades to get into a decent college, like her brother, with his basketball full-ride scholarship? Alicia's family, like Truman's, could never in a million years afford to send a kid through college, even one of the cheapest state schools, without help. It was reaching for the stars.

He supposed all or none of those things might be cycling through Alicia's mind. Maybe she was simply thinking about what color to paint her nails. Or nothing at all.

As for Truman, his mind was filled with one thought.

That boy.

CHAPTER 2

TWO WEEKS into the school year and Truman had pretty much forgotten all about *the boy*, because he'd yet to see him a second time. Of course, he'd looked and looked for him at Alicia's bus stop every day for at least the next six mornings, but then he got involved with homework, fear of gym class, and the routine of his school days. The boy slipped from the prominent place he'd held in Truman's head. *Almost.* Once in a while, especially if Alicia was late and missed the bus, he'd picture him all over again, imagining him coming aboard the bus, replaying the first day of school in his head. In Truman's fantasies, he'd sit next to Truman, even though there were other seats available. And, with a smile that would melt granite, he would meet Truman's gaze and shyly say, "Hi." They'd ride the rest of the way to school together, their legs barely touching, but intent on that touch and the heat generated by something as simple as two thighs pressed together.

But most mornings lately, there was gossip to attend to with Alicia. There was last-minute homework to read or write. There were taunts and jeers to deal with now and then.

But it was *this* morning, near the end of September, that would transform a ho-hum senior year into a remarkable one. And the change was brought about by something as simple as a flyer tacked to the bulletin board opposite the main entrance to the school.

CASTING CALL, the flyer shouted out in bold all-capital lettering.

It went on to say:

The senior class play this year is a classic. Harvey by Mary Chase is a comedy about Elwood P. Dowd and his best buddy, an invisible six-foot-three-inch tall rabbit (called a 'pooka') known as Harvey. The play won the Pulitzer Prize!

There are a total of twelve roles available, six male and six female.

Auditions are next Wednesday immediately after school in the auditorium. Mr. Wolcott will direct and cast the play. Email or see him for an audition package. He'll give you sample scenes and a synopsis of the play.

All roles will be cast by Thursday, and rehearsals will start directly after school the following week. The play is scheduled to be performed the first and second weekends in November.

Please come and try out! Note: the role of Harvey will be played by an invisible actor. LOL.

Below the announcement was a drawing of a pair of rabbit ears.

Cute, Truman thought. He walked away from the bulletin board, thinking not about the play but about his first-period class, the hated geometry with Ms. Rosemary Hissom, who lacked even the slightest sense of humor. Truman wished she were more likable, because he harbored a sneaking suspicion she was a lesbian, and anyone on the LGBTQ rainbow really needed to be fabulous and not a drone like Ms. Hissom. In class he daydreamed about her getting up to all sorts of shenanigans with other female teachers in the teacher's lounge. She was a mistress of depravity everyone called Butch.

And then, as though he'd been tapped on the shoulder by an invisible rabbit, Truman was seized by a thought that came completely out of nowhere but was so irresistible that he couldn't ignore it.

You have to do it. The play. You simply have to.

The thought wasn't so surprising, because Truman had secret dreams about being an actor and had since he was about six years old, but the insistence and unexpectedness with which this current thought came was, well, kind of shocking.

It was as though it was imperative that he try out. As though the universe, and not his own subconscious, was speaking to him….

TRUMAN RUSHED from his last class the following Wednesday to get to the auditions early. He wanted a chance to grab a seat at the back of the auditorium to see who his competition might be. Last week he'd dropped by Mr. Wolcott's room to pick up the audition package.

Truman loved Seth Wolcott. Not in *that* way, of course, but more as someone to be looked up to and admired. Unlike poor Dane Bernard, Mr. Wolcott had never—at least as far as Truman knew—struggled with coming out and being gay. He was simply out and proud, confident in who he was. Being gay was just an integral part of him, neither good nor bad, and Truman admired how he never made it central to his being. He looked up to the man and hoped one day he could be as easygoing about his own orientation.

Plus, if he were being totally honest, Truman would be forced to admit to maybe the tiniest of crushes. With his tight, fit build, curly hair, and fondness for jeans and sweater-vest combinations, he always put Truman in mind of Mr. Schuester from *Glee*, which Truman had watched faithfully growing up.

"Which part should I try out for?" he'd asked Mr. Wolcott.

"That's hard to say," Mr. Wolcott told him as he handed him a sheaf of stapled pages. "Read through the audition scenes I put together and see which one speaks to you the most. A good actor can find an 'in' to almost any part."

Truman wanted to ask him other questions, things that might give him an edge, but Mr. Wolcott was preoccupied. His next class was starting up in just a few minutes, and already the students for that class were streaming in, skirting Mr. Wolcott and Truman as they headed for their seats.

Now, as Truman sat in the cool dark of the empty auditorium, he tried to psych himself up for his

audition. He was going to read a scene from almost
the end of the play, when a taxicab driver talks about
how the fares he brings to Chumley's Rest, a sani-
tarium, are changed for the worse. Going to, they're
easy, happy, big tippers. But coming back, they're
"normal;" they don't tip, they've got no time. He even
says what "stinkers" normal folks are. There was a
kind of yearning about the taxicab driver's speech that
Truman identified with—in his own humble way, the
driver celebrated being different, being an outcast, following the beat of your own drum. Truman identified
with that.

It also gave him his best chance, he believed, to
show off his thespian skills. The winsome longing the
driver displayed for a more easygoing world would
be, he hoped, riveting, profound. The speech was one
of the best, too, from the sample scenes Mr. Wolcott
had put together.

And speaking of Mr. Wolcott, he was just now
coming into the auditorium. Truman sucked in a
breath, realizing he didn't see him sitting there in the
shadows.

Mr. Wolcott wasn't alone. Mr. Bernard, his husband, walked beside him, one hand on his arm. They
were laughing and whispering. The couple still didn't
realize Truman was sitting there in the dimness of
the last row, which was why, Truman thought, grinning, they felt free to have a totally inappropriate
conversation.

"Both kids are gone tonight," Mr. Bernard said.
"We have the whole place to ourselves."

"Oh? Whatever shall we do?" Mr. Wolcott pulled
Mr. Bernard close, hand wandering down to his ass.

Truman bit his lip. He wished there was now a way for him to discreetly draw attention to himself, or that he could put on a cloak of invisibility for just a moment and slip soundlessly from the room.

"Yeah. Think we can shake up the routine a little bit?" Mr. Bernard yanked Mr. Wolcott even closer and kissed him.

The kiss didn't last long.

Mr. Wolcott was eyeing the double doors to the auditorium over Mr. Bernard's shoulder. "Maybe we can christen that new dining room table that was delivered over the weekend," Mr. Wolcott said, a little breathless, breaking away.

And then he spied Truman sitting there.

Mr. Wolcott leaped back even farther, putting at least a foot between himself and Mr. Bernard. "Truman! Buddy, I didn't see you there." He gave Truman one of the most sheepish smiles Truman believed he'd ever seen. It made him want to laugh. It made him want to cringe in empathy.

Even in the dim light, Truman could see that Mr. Wolcott's face was beet red, the flush rising from his neck on up to his cheeks. "Clearly," Truman said. He laughed. "Don't worry about it. Your secret is safe with me."

As he said the words, two more kids, a boy and a girl Truman was only vaguely acquainted with, entered the auditorium. They were giggling, the girl shoving the boy.

Mr. Wolcott hurried to the wall and flipped several light switches. The stage illuminated, along with the sconces along the wall.

"I'll see you at home!" Mr. Bernard called. "I'll stop at the deli and pick up some of that rotisserie chicken you like, some Jo Jo potatoes, and a salad. Okay?"

Mr. Wolcott first glanced over at Truman, as though searching for approval on the menu. "That sounds great. I should be home no later than six thirty."

God. Please eat before *you put that dining room table to other uses.* Truman suppressed a snicker at the thought. He started to let his mind wander to an extremely pornographic image, one in which Mr. Wolcott's legs were astride Mr. Bernard's shoulders, but he forced himself to stop. The swelling in his loose-cut pants would be far too apparent when he stood.

Mr. Bernard left, and about twenty other kids milled into the auditorium in groups of twos and threes. Truman searched in vain for Alicia, who'd said she was going to come to try out for the ingénue role of Myrtle, but she must have gotten cold feet.

He pulled his phone from his pocket and texted *You coming?*

She immediately texted back. *Nah. Theater is for sissies and losers. Like you.*

Very funny, Truman keyed in, then turned off his phone because Mr. Wolcott had moved to the front of the auditorium and clapped his hands a couple of times to get everyone to settle down.

He cleared his throat and said, "I'd like to thank all of you for coming today. It's great to see so many familiar faces. We're going to get started right now, because I don't want to draw the process out any longer than we have to. As you may or may not know, each of you will have five minutes to audition, whether you read from my suggested scenes or not. I'll be making up my mind and casting tonight. Tomorrow,

I'll post the cast list on the main bulletin board. It looks like we've got more folks than parts, but rest assured everybody here can do something in the show if they want to, whether you're onstage or behind-the-scenes. Next to the cast list I put up, I'll also add a sign-up sheet for stage crew."

Truman rolled his eyes. If he didn't get a part, no way was he being reduced to stage crew. If he couldn't be in the spotlight, he wouldn't be caught dead off-stage operating that same spotlight for some other kid. It would simply be too cruel, too hard.

Besides, he'd get a part. He just knew it.

He glanced down at the scene he planned to do again. He read it over as Mr. Wolcott answered questions about—again—how long they'd have to read, when they'd know if they got a part, would there be understudies, and so on. Hadn't anyone read the flyer… or even better, listened to Mr. Wolcott as he spoke?

No, they were probably busy looking at their Facebook feeds or texting on their phones. Truman was convinced his generation would have permanently downturned faces from staring at handheld screens all day.

Just as he had that thought, his phone vibrated in his pocket. *Probably Alicia.* He resisted the phone's siren-call imperative and let it remain in his pocket, especially since he'd just been mentally chastising his peers for their obsession with smartphones.

"And is there a difference in pay between a leading and a supporting role?" Jason Abner asked, snickering.

"Yes," Mr. Wolcott replied, his face and expression serious, earnest.

Some of the chatter died down. There was pay involved?

"Leads get double the amount that supporting players will receive."

The chatter started up again.

"Who can do a little math?" Mr. Wolcott asked.

Stacy Timmons raised her hand. She was a dark-haired girl who put Truman in mind of a young Natalie Wood. He knew most of his generation didn't even know who Natalie Wood was, but he had several DVDs of her movies at home: *Gypsy*, *This Property is Condemned*, and his favorite, *Splendor in the Grass*. Poor Alicia, Truman thought, would never stand a chance against Stacy Timmons for the female lead.

"Stacy?"

She nodded.

"Can you tell me what zero times two is?"

Truman smirked. The poor girl actually had to think about it. Then she grinned and rolled her eyes. "Oh, okay. Zero."

Mr. Wolcott nodded, smirking. "So let's get started. Who wants to go first?"

Everyone shifted in their seats, almost in unison. Almost also in unison, everyone stopped talking. The silence went on until it felt like an unwelcome extra presence in the auditorium.

Truman stared down at the floor, noticing the subtle pattern in the brown-and-beige tiling. He was ready, but he wasn't so ready that he'd volunteer to go first.

He breathed a sigh of relief when Stacy Timmons, at last, raised her hand.

"Stacy!" Mr. Wolcott clapped. "Thank you for stepping up to the plate. Make your way on up to the stage." He watched as she mounted the set of stairs at the side of the stage and then turned to the kids assembled in the third and fourth rows of the auditorium. "You guys? If you're afraid to get up and audition, how are you gonna get out in front of a whole bunch of people when this theater is filled to capacity? Because it will be. Your families alone will guarantee that." He chuckled. "So, I expect no hesitation when Stacy's done with her reading." He smiled, looking at each of them in turn. "Okay?"

He turned his back on the crowd and sat down. "Stacy? If you're ready, go ahead."

Truman looked at the young woman standing in the spotlight. She was obviously terrified, and in a way that made Truman feel better. A whole fleet of butterflies had taken wing in his gut, now that this process was becoming real. She coughed. Shifted her weight from one foot to the other. Flipped a mass of dark hair over one shoulder. Peered into what Truman knew was only darkness beyond the stage lights.

"Go ahead," Mr. Wolcott urged in a soft and gentle voice.

Truman thought Stacy had nothing to worry about. Like Natalie Wood, she was stunning, with thick mahogany hair and big brown eyes that seemed larger than the average person's. She was petite yet had an exuberance about her that almost made her glow, made her seem larger than she probably was, which Truman would guess was around five one or five two, weighing in at no more than a hundred pounds.

Truman surmised that, no matter how good or bad she was, she'd get a part, maybe even *the* part, that of Myrtle Mae Simmons, a young debutante. Stacy's beauty was mesmerizing, and Truman was young, but old enough to realize the treasures the world bestowed on the young and beautiful.

Stacy began to read, and as she read, Truman realized she had something. She stumbled over a couple of words and kept her head bowed over the script pages a bit too much, but a small transformation took place as she read—she became Myrtle Mae, a little older than Stacy's actual years, maybe not even as smart, caught up too much in appearances, with a kind of vintage charm about her.

The thing Stacy managed to do—and what Truman hoped *he* could do when his turn came—was that she made you forget where you were, made you forget too she was a teenaged girl reading a part from some old play that had originally debuted long before his mother was born, maybe even before his grandma was born.

He was surprised when she finished.

Everyone in the auditorium applauded, and Stacy smiled. It wasn't a smile full of guile, as though she were getting the accolades she deserved, but one of genuine surprise and gratitude. She walked quickly off the stage to Mr. Wolcott's words, "Thanks, Stacy. Very good."

He stood again. "Next?"

And again, it was as though he were asking who would be next to mount the gallows. No one raised his or her hand, and it also seemed no one could be bothered to meet Mr. Wolcott's gaze. Truman couldn't allow the poor man to suffer again, not when he knew what Mr. Wolcott had waiting for him at home.

And Truman was *not* thinking of Jo Jo potatoes!

So he stood up. "I'll go."

"Thank you, Truman." Mr. Wolcott sat down as Truman headed toward the stage. His spine stiffened a bit as he very clearly heard someone whisper— someone anonymous, it was always someone anonymous—"Who's *she* trying out for? Veta Louise?"

There was snickering, and Truman tried to pretend the cutting remark didn't bother him. But it did—it always did, no matter how secure he became in his own skin. It wasn't so much the assault on his masculinity that hurt—even Truman had to admit he was about as masculine as Miley Cyrus—no, it was more the fact that it felt like someone *wanted* to hurt him. On purpose.

Why? Why do they want to do that?

Now's not the time, Truman. Get up there and do the one thing you need to do—act well your part.

A hush again fell over the cavernous space as Truman approached center stage. He cleared his throat and tried to relax. He knew the paper with the lines he was about to say quaked, right along with his trembling hand.

He allowed himself the luxury of shaking out his arms, wiggling his fingertips.

"Whenever you're ready, Truman."

"Or Tru-woman," someone shouted out, to snickers.

Mr. Wolcott shot up and turned around. "Mr. Keller, you can exit through the rear doors." He paused for a moment, and when nothing happened, he said firmly, "Now."

Truman, because of the bright lights shining in his face, couldn't see anything, but he heard quick foot-falls, the slam of the auditorium door.

Mr. Wolcott said, "Sorry, Truman. Even in the theater, we do not escape idiots. But at least we can have a say in whether or not we tolerate them."

"Thank you," Truman said, feeling unexpectedly choked up. He drew in a quivering breath.

From out of the shadows, a female voice: "Go, Truman! You got this."

And now Truman was ready to burst into blub-bers. Kindness, when it was simple, genuine, and real, never failed to touch his heart. He turned away for a moment, trying to compose himself, and then began his audition, looking up a little as though he was thinking, and started talking about how he'd been driving this route for fifteen years.

When he finished, there was silence for several long seconds, which the scared Truman interpreted as a sign of failure.

But then, as he walked off the stage, the applause erupted, and someone even whistled. *Should I bow? Should I acknowledge? No, this is a tryout, for crying out loud.* Still, the clapping warmed his heart.

He hurried from the stage, and his performance was quickly eclipsed by the next person waiting to audition.

LATER, THE sky was beginning to darken just a tiny bit as dusk fell. Truman looked up to see how it was navy blue high up, but as his gaze came down, he took in the change of colors as the sun set behind the hills. There was gray, then lavender, and the tops of the hills were touched with a kiss of tangerine.

Beautiful. Sometimes, Truman thought, living in this little burg wasn't so bad after all. He still longed to get out to bright lights, excitement, some city that never slept, but in moments like these, with the hush, the cool breeze, the silhouetted hills and trees against the darkening sky, he believed Summitville might not be such a bad place to return to when he came home to see Patsy.

He reminded himself to never forget that his roots were here. *There's no place like home....*

"You did great," a voice called from behind, startling him. Truman tensed, not so sure he wanted company on the long walk home. But a nice compliment like that deserved to be acknowledged, right?

He turned. Stacy Timmons stood there, just above him on the long drive that sloped downward to the valley. The school was situated on a hilltop, from which one could view the whole little town and the brown-green Ohio River as it snaked through, dividing Ohio from the northern panhandle of West Virginia.

He didn't really know Stacy, other than being as familiar with her face and her name as he was with the other faces and names of the one hundred and three other kids in his class. She'd always been on a different plane—one of the popular kids, a cheerleader, National Honor Society, student council. She was never without a posse of cool kids around her.

She was from a different world, one Truman didn't exactly aspire to, but one in his weaker, lonelier moments he envied.

She'd never given him attitude, never teased him. Yet Truman was surprised she'd spoken to him, because he wasn't even sure she knew he existed.

She hurried down the hill toward him. When they were face-to-face, Truman smiled slightly and bowed his head a bit. "Thanks." He stared for a moment into those wide brown eyes and then told her, "You were great too."

She curled a lock of hair around one finger, let it go. "Oh, I don't know."

"Get out! You were!" Truman said. "For a while I completely forgot who you really are. You, uh, what's the word? You *inhabited* the role."

A smile spread across her features. "Wow. Thank you. That's high praise. I appreciate that."

Truman vainly hoped she'd say the same about him, but those hopes were quietly dashed when she said, "Are you walking home?"

"Yeah, all the way down to East End. I live down by the river." He rubbed his arms and shivered, hoping she'd get the message he wanted to be on his way.

"I know where you live." Stacy started walking, and Truman joined her. It was getting dark fast. He honestly had no idea where *she* lived. Maybe one of the old mansions that lined Park Boulevard?

"You do?" Truman couldn't imagine why she'd know that. And immediately he felt a little embarrassed. Their house was tiny, run-down, and right now it seemed like the best description of it would be a shack. He knew Patsy did her best to make their little home presentable, and Truman wanted to kick himself for the momentary shame he felt when he realized Stacy knew where the house was.

Surely Stacy lived under much grander circumstances, although he had no basis for the belief.

"Sure. The cute little house up the hill from the river. You always have such nice flower beds out front in the spring."

They continued on down the hill. A cool breeze picked up. Stacy said, "I hope you don't mind my walking with you. It's scary for a girl, especially at night."

"Not at all." Truman was quiet for a moment, and then he couldn't resist. "I have to ask. How do you know where I live?"

Stacy giggled and elbowed him. "Come on, Truman! There's—what?—nine thousand people in Summitville? Everybody knows where everybody lives."

Truman blurted, "I don't know where *you* live."

"I'm about ten blocks from you. I'm in the green-and-white two-story on Ohio Street."

Truman knew the house. It was right at the bottom of the highest hill in town—and on the busiest street. People exiting off the bridge over the Ohio would race down that hill way faster than they should go. Stacy's house was big, on a corner lot, but it was run-down, with rusting aluminum awnings over the door and picture window at the front, weeds choking the brick sidewalk outside, a dirt driveway at the side of the house, and at least four broken-down heaps, a mix of trucks and cars, flattening what grass there was in the side yard. But all Truman did was nod and say, "Okay."

"Besides," Stacy said. "My grandma lives just two doors down from you."

"Lula Stewart?"

Stacy nodded. "Yeah, didn't you know? I've been over lots of times." Stacy laughed. "I used to watch you on your front porch, playing Barbies."

Scalding heat rose to Truman's cheeks. Truman had a flash of the black patent leather trunk he kept the Barbies and their clothes in—and how Patsy, bless her heart, had never once given him shit about wanting them. And then he realized something—there was no trace of ridicule or judgment in Stacy's voice either when she mentioned him playing with dolls. He expected her to snicker, but her face and voice stayed impassive. In fact, if he had to guess, he'd say there was a touch of envy in her voice; she might have wanted to join him.

"Oh God, that was a long time ago." They were now away from the school, and Truman led Stacy down the road that would come into the valley where they both lived, gallantly keeping her on the wooded side of the road so she wouldn't be at risk from the cars whizzing by. There were no sidewalks leading down to their neighborhood.

It was now full dark.

"Your grandma's nice," Truman said, thinking of the woman with the dyed jet-black hair who always sat out on her porch on an ancient aluminum glider, simply watching the world pass. Her husband, Welcome, had passed away when Truman was ten. He'd drowned in the Ohio. Lula contended to everyone he was swimming, and everyone nodded sympathetically, but they all knew it was suicide. Who went swimming in the Ohio in October?

"She's sad," Stacy said. "She's never gotten over Pap's death."

They were quiet for a bit, and then Stacy said, "But at least she's not quite as lonely anymore. Her boy moved back in with her a few weeks ago. George? He's a mechanic at the Shell station downtown? He and his wife got a divorce last summer. *His* boy, Mike, lives with his mom, over on First Avenue."

"My friend Alicia lives on First."

"Then you've maybe seen Mike. He lives just a couple houses down, in the duplex? Big boy, dark hair? Gorgeous."

And Truman's mouth got dry. Could Mike be the boy he'd seen on the first day of school? The handsome, quiet boy?

Truman pressed her. "Is he, uh, like really tall? Kind of football-player build? Black wavy hair—" Truman stopped himself before he blurted out "And the most beautiful blue eyes."

"That's him. Do you know him?"

I wish! "Nah. I just saw him at the bus stop that first day of school." Truman shrugged like he didn't care. And realized he was acting. "I haven't seen him lately, though."

"He's terrible. He oversleeps all the time. Misses the bus every single day. His mom? Carly? Well, I shouldn't talk, but she's a little, um, loose? And she's, well, let's just say she's not often home in the mornings to get her boy off to school. Mike pretty much has to fend for himself. He's real quiet. My uncle George is trying to get custody."

Truman wasn't sure what to say. He was thinking that if Uncle George got custody of Mike, then Mike would be his neighbor.

"I think this is where you and I have to part ways." Stacy stopped abruptly. She pointed down Ohio Street to where Truman now knew she lived. "I'm down there." She smiled. "Sorry I talked your ear off. I tend to do that when I'm nervous."

Truman laughed. "You don't need to be nervous around me." The thought that anyone would be nervous around him was just about incomprehensible.

"Well, you should come sit by me at lunch or something sometime. I liked talking."

And you can tell me more about Mike. "Thanks. I'll do that." *It'll save me from hiding out in the library at lunch.*

"Well, bye, Truman. I hope you get a part."

Truman had almost forgotten about *Harvey* in his excitement over learning about Mike.

"Yeah, I hope you do too."

"Oh, I doubt it," Stacy said. "But I appreciate your nice words."

"They weren't nice words. They were the truth. You're a shoo-in."

"Thanks, Truman." She turned and walked away. Truman stood in silence as she grew smaller and smaller in the distance until she disappeared into the run-down house at the bottom of the hill.

Maybe he wasn't as alone as he thought.

CHAPTER 3

THE FIRST thing Truman noticed was the smell of cigarette smoke wafting in through the kitchen screens. Patsy hadn't smoked in years, so long ago Truman could barely imagine her with a cigarette, so he wondered who might be out on the back porch. He could hear the little Bluetooth speaker he'd gotten for Patsy last Christmas, playing her favorite Pandora station—Al Green. Right now "Oh Girl" was playing, by the Chi-Lites. If it weren't for Pandora, Truman was sure he would have never heard of the band or the song. But he had to admit he liked it, and it didn't sound dated at all.

The second thing he noticed was his dog, Odd Thomas, gingerly hopping down from the couch to greet him. Odd was getting up in years—he'd be eleven his next birthday in December—and the dachshund/bulldog mix was showing it. There was a stiffness about his movements that didn't used to be there, and lately, all he seemed to do was sleep.

But still, him making the effort to come and greet Truman at the door brought a big smile to Truman's lips. He went down into a squat as Odd neared, stump of a tail wagging, snorting and grunting. People had actually had the nerve to tell Truman that Odd Thomas was one of the ugliest creatures they'd ever laid eyes on and that his name fit him. Truman agreed that the name did indeed fit, but the ugliness? Well, that was in the eye of the beholder. Truman had had the old boy most of his life and, right about now, couldn't imagine a sweeter or more beautiful sight than Odd lumbering over to cover his face with stinky kisses.

"Oh! I didn't hear you come in. I was just about to take him out for a little walk." The slam of the screen door heralded Patsy's entrance.

"'Little walk' is right. About all he can manage these days." Truman stood to grab Odd's leash and harness off the hook by the front door. "I can take him." He squatted back down to get Odd "suited up." When he was ready to open the front door, he paused. "Got company?" It wasn't just the music and the smoke, but Patsy looked particularly lovely tonight, in a pair of jeans and simple white lace cropped top. Her hair was pulled away from her face, and she wore sterling silver hoop earrings.

Patsy giggled, and Truman could have sworn she blushed a little bit.

"Yes. I want you to meet him. I think it's about time."

Truman nodded. Odd tugged at the leash, wanting to get outside. With age had come a lack of control, so

Truman knew he should heed the dog's urging. "So this isn't one of the girls from the diner?" Patsy sometimes had one or two of the waitresses over from the Elite for a beer and gossip.

"Not quite." She gestured toward Odd, who was waiting by the half-open front door, whining. "You better get him outside."

Truman and Odd stepped out into the night. They walked around to the side of the house, where Truman could look down the bluff at the Ohio River flowing just below. The moon, a shimmering silver crescent, spread out on the black water. Truman remembered when he used to walk Odd Thomas down to its banks, cutting through woods. He used to love to chase sticks and sniff the detritus that had washed up on the river's sandy banks. The two of them would spend hours down there. In summer they'd even brave the river's admittedly dangerous current and swim out to the little tree-covered island in the middle. Truman smiled as he remembered lying in the sun on the island's pebbled bank, Odd Thomas snoring at his side.

But now all Odd Thomas could manage was a quick trip around the house to take care of business and then back inside, usually to lie down once again on the couch or on his worn fleece bed. Truman sometimes wondered how much longer he had left with his friend. Then he'd push the idea away because it made him sad.

Mission accomplished, Truman headed back inside with Odd Thomas. For a reason he couldn't quite put his finger on, Truman was nervous. He felt like he was poised between now and then. And yes, he knew we are always poised on that particular point, but it felt as though something momentous was about to occur, something that just might upset the balance of Truman's world.

He hung up Odd Thomas's leash and harness and rubbed his sweating palms on his thighs. He took a few steps toward the kitchen and the back door. There was low laughter underneath the music, which was now Al Green himself singing "Take Me to the River." Truman had a sudden urge to take *himself* to the river, to sit alone on its moonlit banks and ponder both the future and the past. Fragile things that never seemed to remain still....

"Truman?" Patsy's voice floated in through the open window over the sink. Truman noted the dirty dishes stacked there, along with Patsy's cast-iron skillet. A plate, covered in foil, presumably his supper, waited nearby. He wondered what was underneath. He hoped fried chicken. Patsy made the best.

"Honey. You want to come outside for a minute?"

Truman swallowed and briefly considered pleading hunger. Could she wait until after he'd eaten? But even he knew how rude and immature that would be. Still, what was keeping his feet rooted to the floor?

"Truman!" He recognized the peeved tone.

He hurried outside. It took a minute for his eyes to adjust. There was a little concrete slab out there, with a redwood picnic table and a Weber grill arranged on it. The only light came from a flickering citronella candle.

"Hey, honey," Patsy said. Truman edged nearer and could see the man at the table. His first thought was that he looked familiar, yet he couldn't place him. "I want you to meet someone. This is George Stewart."

The man looked up at him and nodded. Truman, even in the dark, could make out the pale ice blue of his eyes, framed with long black lashes.

George rose to extend his hand. Truman reached out to shake, and his hand was practically swallowed up in George's grip. Truman feared his joints might be crushed. When he spoke, George's voice was raspy and deep, maybe from too many cigarettes. "How you doin', son?"

"Good. Pleased to meet you, sir." Truman drew his hand away and looked to Patsy, hoping she'd hear the pounding of his heart, would understand, and say something along the lines of "George here was just leaving."

He suddenly, desperately wanted his mom all to himself. The want was that much stronger, simply knowing this particular wish wouldn't be granted any-time soon.

Truman backed toward the door, knowing how sheepish his grin looked and wondering if the want and worry were obvious.

"C'mon and sit down, Truman." Patsy patted the bench next to her. "You can tell George and me about the play tryouts. What was the show again?"

Barely finding breath to put behind his voice, Truman said, "*Harvey*. It's about an invisible rabbit."

George nodded. Truman noticed his thick, curly dark hair, cropped close to his head. He eyed Truman as he lit a Marlboro Red. On his exhalation of smoke, he asked, "Wasn't that a movie? With Jimmy Stewart, maybe? I think I saw it a few weeks ago on TV."

Truman shrugged. "I dunno. Maybe." *Why are you acting like you don't know the movie?* He looked away from George and directed his gaze at Patsy. *What do you see in this guy, Ma? He smokes! He's a big lug! I bet he doesn't have the brains God gave a squirrel! You deserve better.*

Patsy cocked her head. "You feelin' okay, sweetie? You look—a little pale."

Truman tried to smile, fearing it came out as more of a grimace. "Just tired. And hungry. I saw a covered plate in there. Was that for me?"

Patsy nodded. "Barbecued chicken, potato salad, and baked beans." She looked away from Truman to glance at George. "All homemade." She smiled.

Truman was almost to the screen door. "Well, sounds better than the usual leftovers from the diner."

He ducked inside before Patsy could admonish him.

He took the foil cover off the plate and looked down at the perfect char on the chicken breast, the bowl of baked beans, and the mustard potato salad— all his favorites—and didn't feel hungry anymore.

"Just nuke the chicken and beans for, oh, like a couple minutes, Tru." Patsy's voice drifted in through the window.

"Sure, Mom."

He took the plate and went toward the front of the house and ducked outside to the porch, where they had a glider. He sat with the cold plate in his lap, thinking of standing up, walking to the back, and just pitching it over the embankment toward the river.

Odd Thomas, probably aroused by the smell of chicken, scratched at the screen to be let out. Truman sighed, put his plate down at his side, and went to comply. Tail wagging, Odd immediately went to the food. Even though he knew it probably wasn't good for him, Truman moved the plate down onto the porch floorboards. The chicken breast was boneless, so Odd Thomas should be okay. But the beans, the barbecue sauce, and potato salad? Truman shrugged.

"Enjoy it, dude," he whispered, leaning over to scratch the dog behind his ears. He was wolfing down the food as though, at any moment, someone would yank it away. "Because after you eat all that, it's gonna be diarrhea city around here."

Truman snickered as he thought of Patsy cleaning it up.

And then immediately felt a deep wave of shame roll through him. *What's wrong with me? Don't I want Mom to be happy?* He reached down and snatched the plate away from Odd Thomas. "Sorry."

And then it hit him why the guy out back was familiar. He looked exactly like the gorgeous, quiet boy, Mike, from Alicia's bus stop on the first day of school.

Why, they could be father and son. And at that thought, Truman smiled and then shuddered.

TRUMAN WAS just drifting off to sleep, Odd Thomas curled up under the covers in the crook of his knees, when the creak of his bedroom door opening woke him. A slant of light fell on the braided rug next to the bed.

Patsy crept into the room in her bathrobe.

Truman rolled over, rubbing his eyes, feeling a little disoriented. He'd been dreaming of traveling with Patsy in a car, something new and relatively luxurious, and the two of them had just crashed through some bushes at the side of a road and were airborne above a bluff. The weird thing wasn't that Truman felt terror at the prospect of crashing down hard on whatever was below, but the contentment he felt, the *lack* of fear. They were flying… and it was okay.

"Honey?" Patsy whispered. "You awake?"

Truman got up to a half-sitting position. Odd Thomas crawled from beneath the covers, shook himself, farted, lay back down, and continued snoring.

Patsy sat down on the bed. She was so little that her presence barely registered. Truman, although he only weighed about a hundred and fifteen pounds, realized he now weighed more than his mom.

She squeezed his calf.

"Is he still here?" Truman blurted, unsure from where the question even came.

Patsy sighed. She removed her hand and then folded her arms across her chest. "Yes," she said.

Truman crossed his arms. "Is he going home soon?"

Patsy sighed and didn't say anything for a long while. "If 'soon' is first thing in the morning, then yes." Patsy lay down next to Truman and played with his hair for a minute. Truman closed his eyes, basking.

She turned to him, and he opened his eyes to peer back at her, her face less than a foot away from his in the dark. How many conversations had they shared—just like this—over the years? Too many to count, Truman was sure. He felt a little lump in his throat as he wondered if all that was about to change.

Quit being such a baby! You're almost eighteen years old!

"You don't like him, do you?"

"Who?"

"Tru," Patsy admonished. "Come on…."

"I don't know him well enough not to like him. I'm sure if I did, I'd hate him." He laughed, but Truman wasn't sure how much truth there was in the joke. "Was he the guy who was here a few weeks ago?"

"Yes." Patsy rolled over on her back and stared up at the ceiling. "And he's been here several other times. You just didn't know."

"Slut."

"Brat." Patsy chuckled. "I really like him, Truman. I might even be falling in love. Can you imagine?"

I can imagine all too well. I just don't know how I feel about it. "Yeah, I can imagine. Even with the very, very limited exposure I've had to the two of you, I can sense it. Love is in the air." Truman laughed, or maybe it was a choked sob? "Or maybe just gas...."

"He's a good guy, Truman."

"He smokes," Truman said, and then felt lame. "This is going somewhere, then?"

"It already has."

Truman rolled over toward the wall. He felt all of seven years old again. He drew in a deep breath, reminding himself to be the young man he knew he was becoming and not a petulant child. He knew he should be happy for his mother, his pretty, charming mother, who'd done nothing but work her fingers to the bone all her young life in support of him. His lovely and loving mother, who, he knew for a fact, had turned down many a man so she could stay home with him and eat frozen pizza while they watched *Project Runway* or played Yahtzee at the kitchen table.

He thought of an old Diana Ross song he'd heard recently on Pandora, and thought it applied here—not to him, but to Patsy. The song? "It's My Turn." It was

Patsy's turn now, to not only find someone to love, but also to find someone who would love her in a reciprocal, grown-up way. His head said he hoped Patsy had found joy; his heart hoped this relationship would come to an abrupt end—sooner rather than later.

Truman turned back to Patsy and touched her cheek. She really was so beautiful—with her dark hair, porcelain skin, and fine-boned features. "I'm happy for you," Truman whispered, the words coming out a little breathless and broken.

Patsy smiled. "No, you're not." She ruffled his hair. "But I hope you will be."

They lay there like that for the longest time, not saying anything.

And then Truman heard George get up and pad to the bathroom between their two bedrooms. He could hear him peeing and then the flush of the toilet.

"I should be getting back." Patsy rose from the bed, and Truman had to resist the urge to hold out his arms, to beg her to stay with him.

But he lay there, still, on his back, waiting to hear her walk away, bracing himself.

Patsy stopped at the door and turned. "Truman?"

"Yes, Mother?"

"You know I'll always love you best, right? You know that?"

Truman couldn't speak. He was too choked up, too overwhelmed. He sniffed. Odd Thomas got up and rearranged himself closer to Truman's pillow. Truman hugged him.

"I know you know," Patsy said. "Because nothing is truer."

Truman wanted to say something, wanted to tell her how much he loved her, but if he did, he'd sound like a baby, speaking through broken sobs.

Patsy closed the door softly behind her.

CHAPTER 4

GEORGE WAS gone the next morning.

When Truman awoke, it was to the smell of pancakes and coffee. He struggled out of bed around the furry, lumbering, snoring mess of Odd Thomas, stood, and stretched. He picked up a T-shirt from the foot of his bed and pulled it over his head.

Sunlight, like golden honey, streamed through his window. Today was going to be good, he told himself. Not only were there pancakes—his favorite food in all the world, despite the copious carbs hiding in them— but today was the day Mr. Wolcott would post the cast for *Harvey*.

What part would he get? Dare he hope for the lead, Elwood P. Dowd? The cabdriver near the end had a great speech, pivotal, but it was such a *teensy* role. The old saw about there being no small parts, only small actors, popped up in his head. *And that saying probably came from someone who only got small parts.*

He padded out to the kitchen barefoot. As he left the bedroom, he listened for Odd Thomas to follow, but all he heard were snores. Such was the new normal with his senior best friend. He glanced back at the dog, stretched out on his side, and a rush of love for the creature coursed through him. Each day with Odd Thomas was becoming more and more precious as Truman witnessed his time-lapse aging process. There was a very sad day in the near future, Truman knew.

Oh, stop it! Enjoy your time with your dog! Don't ruin it by being maudlin over what's to come. For all you know, he may mourn your death sometime soon. The thought gave Truman a chill, which he tried to quickly dismiss.

The kitchen was flooded with sunlight. Dust motes danced in the air. Shafts of pale smoke lingered, testimony to recently fried bacon. He felt both pleased and guilty at the knowledge that Patsy knew how vulnerable he was feeling and wanted to make it up to him. To show him, in effect, rather than tell him, that he was her number-one man.

Truman didn't wait for Patsy to serve him. Those days were long past—so long, in fact, he couldn't even remember them. He piled a plate up with four pancakes and six pieces of bacon, poured himself a cup of coffee and a glass of orange juice, and—artfully balancing it all—seated himself at the table.

"Good morning!" Patsy entered the kitchen wearing a pair of dark jeans and a gauzy white top. She'd pulled her hair up on top of her head in a casual knot. "I have to go in to the diner for the breakfast shift, and

I'm already late, of course! But LaVonne needed me to cover for her, and she's covered for me so many times in the past, I just couldn't say no."

Truman shifted a mouthful of pancake to one side of his mouth. "Thanks for taking the time to make me breakfast. You didn't have to."

She waved his thanks away with a flick of her hand. "I know I didn't have to. But number one, I know you'd probably just leave here with a cup of instant coffee in your belly and *maybe* a bowl of Froot Loops if I left you to your own devices. And number two, um, well, I just wanted you to know how much you were loved." She tousled his hair.

"Don't make me lose my appetite, Ma. This Mrs. Butterworth's is sweet enough as it is."

"Oh, shut up." Patsy grabbed her bag and keys from the kitchen counter. At the door she turned to Truman. "Is it today you find out if you got a part in that play? What was it called? *Henry*?"

"*Harvey*. And yes, Mr. Wolcott's supposed to post the list today."

"You think you got something?"

"Of course I did, Mother." Truman patted the back of his head and sat up straighter. "How could I not?"

"Well, they'd be fools not to cast you. I'm sure you were far and away the best."

"Thanks. Praise like that coming from one's mom always means a lot."

"Yeah, yeah. Text me and let me know what part you got."

"I will."

Patsy started out of the door.

"Mom?"

She turned, a little patient smile on her face. "I'm late…."

"I know. I'm sorry. Just a quick question—does George have any kids?"

Patsy grinned, and Truman thought she was glad he was showing some interest. "Um, yeah. He has a boy, about your age, I think. Mike. Mike Stewart. Do you know him?"

I wish, Truman thought, both intrigued and weirded out by the coincidence of his mother falling in love with the father of the boy Truman was falling in love with—if *falling in love* wasn't too strong a descriptor. "Nah. Not really. I might have seen him at the bus stop."

Patsy nodded. "By Alicia's?"

"Yeah."

Patsy nodded. "He lives over that way with his mom. You probably won't cross paths. He's in the vocational program. Wants to be a woodworker or somethin'."

I bet he's good with his hands, Truman thought lasciviously. He was a little disheartened that Mike wasn't college preparatory like Truman. The vocational kids were in a separate building down the hill from the main school. Truman was a little ashamed suddenly that even he looked down on those kids, not that they gave a rat's ass what Truman Reid thought about them, he was sure.

Lost in thought—and bacon—he didn't even notice Patsy had left. Just as he was finishing up, Odd Thomas wandered in, and Truman leaped up from the table to take him outside. In the early morning sun, the dog squatted—he couldn't lift his leg like he used to—and let go. Truman watched and encouraged him with a "Good boy."

They went back inside, and Truman glanced at the clock. If he didn't get a move on, he too was going to be late. And he had to clean up, feed Odd, and, most important, decide what to wear.

He wondered how long it would be before Mr. Wolcott posted the cast list.

CHAPTER 5

Mr. Wolcott posted the cast list at the end of the day, after the last bell, when everyone was rushing outside to get in one of the yellow buses assembled in the parking lot. "Great timing," Truman grumbled, rolling his eyes.

He backtracked to the bulletin board, where several people had already gathered around, checking to see what parts they got—or didn't get.

Stacy Timmons was directly in front of him. She squealed with glee. As she turned away from the bulletin board, she saw him. "I got the part I wanted. Myrtle Mae! Can you believe it?"

Yes, Truman could believe it and had actually foreseen no other outcome. But he was touched by her excitement and her genuine modesty. It was sweet.

A couple of kids moved away so Truman could finally get up close to see what part he'd gotten.

Harvey Cast

Myrtle Mae Simmons.... Stacy Timmons
Veta Louise Simmons.... Amber Wolfgang
Elwood P. Dowd.... Rex Lucas
Miss Johnson.... Megan Schmidbauer
Mrs. Ethel Chauvenet.... Maryalice Frederick
Ruth Kelly, RN.... Lori Moynagh
Duane Wilson.... Michael Burt
Lyman Sanderson, MD.... Craig Kennedy
William R. Chumley, MD.... John Soldano
Betty Chumley.... Tiffany Gilpin
Judge Omar Gaffney.... Sam Mainhardt
EJ Lofgren.... Kirk Nizer
Understudies.... Jessica Stringfellow, Tommy Blevins

Truman's heart dropped with a thud to his gut, which was suddenly swirling with acid. He read the list over once more, sure his eyes had deceived him.

I had to have gotten a part! Even EJ Lofgren, the cabdriver! A small—but important—role, at least. And I nailed the audition. Nailed it. This has to be a mistake. Truman tried to swallow but found no spit in his dry mouth. He wanted to cry and felt a lump the size of a tangerine in his throat threatening to cut off his air supply, but he wouldn't yield to the tears of disappointment lingering within him. God, it was embarrassing enough not to be picked, let alone crying like a two-year-old in front of everyone.

He noticed someone had moved close, just by his left shoulder. He turned and looked at Stacy, standing there. "You're going to do great. I can't wait to work with you on this."

What? Now this bitch is gonna have the nerve to rub it in? He was just on the verge of channeling Alicia and cutting Stacy down with some genuinely mean snark when he thought he should double-check just what the *hell* the girl was yammering about.

His brows furrowed in confusion as he stared at her. He reminded himself to shut his open mouth. "What? I *didn't* get a part." It cut like a knife to say this, to make it real in his head all over again.

"Silly. Did you read the whole thing?"

"Well, no. I just stopped after I saw I wasn't cast."

Stacy put her hands gently on his shoulders and turned him toward the bulletin board. He scanned the lines of type below the cast, and there it was, his name.

Student Director.... Truman Reid

The notice went on to say that rehearsals would start in the auditorium directly after school the following Monday. There was also a sign-up sheet posted to the right of the cast list for stage crew. The message at the bottom of the cast list went on to add that, if anyone had questions or second thoughts, they should talk to Mr. Wolcott immediately.

Truman sniffed. *Sure. Student Director. Probably because I'm not manly enough for any of the male roles. Mr. Wolcott took pity in me. He doesn't need a student director, for God's sakes.* He said none of this aloud. What he did say was, "*I* have questions. *I* have second thoughts."

"What do you mean?" Stacy asked. "You're the director!"

"*Student* director," Truman corrected. "A meaningless title, a consolation prize. I wanted to act, not direct, not that I think I'll get the chance to do much directing anyway." He stared down at the floor and then looked back up at Stacy, whose big brown eyes were alive with concern.

"I don't know why you'd say that," Stacy said. "Mr. Wolcott sees something in you, something great. He wants you to help him *run* the show." She punched Truman's shoulder hard enough to make him gasp. "You big silly! You should be proud."

Truman considered for a moment, thought of repeating he'd wanted to act, then closed his trap. Weren't actors always claiming what they really wanted to do was… *direct*? Maybe he shouldn't be so quick to dismiss this. Maybe it wasn't a slight after all, but a compliment, even. Still, it was hard to quell the disappointment, like a dark shadow lurking, deep within him. He'd been so sure he'd get a part.

Let it go. You did *get a part. You just won't be on stage. But you'll also have the reins. Or at least the co-reins. You can really make this play into something!* Truman tried to console himself. And he had to grudgingly admit it was beginning to work—already. He gave a little half grin to Stacy. "I guess it could be fun, provided I'm given some leeway."

"You're gonna do great, Truman. I'm really looking forward to having your guidance. God knows I'm gonna need it! I've never acted before."

Truman didn't tell her that neither had he. Why undermine her confidence in him? After all, he *was* the student director. And he already had some ideas about how she could play the role, ways she might go a little opposite of what was on the page to make the part unusual, funny maybe. He squeezed her shoulder and quipped, "Stick with me, kid. I'm gonna make you a star!"

Stacy giggled. "Are you walking home today?" She glanced out through the plate glass front doors. "I think we just missed the bus."

"I guess I'm walking home, then. Care to join me?"

Stacy slipped her hand under Truman's arm, and the two of them departed for East End.

Truman couldn't wait for Monday to come. He'd spend the whole weekend reading the play over and making notes. If he was going to be student director, he was going to be the best student director Summitville High had ever seen.

CHAPTER 6

THE FIRST week of rehearsals was just sitting around the stage on folding chairs, reading aloud from the scripts. The following week, they'd begin blocking—and building the set. Truman wasn't quite sure how that would work. How were they supposed to act with the stage crew hammering and hollering and moving things around?

Use your imagination. It's an actor's—and a director's—job to fully immerse in the world they're creating and rise above distractions.

But that first week, he couldn't be too concerned with what was to follow. Now he needed to assert his leadership role, which was something new. In spite of the makeup and flamboyant clothes, Truman was shy, a victim of a paradox—he both wanted to be noticed and didn't want people to look at him. He wondered if other people, famous people, in the spotlight could possibly also face this introvert paradox.

So, as a leader he expected pushback, ridicule maybe, people rolling their eyes if he dared to actually try to direct them. He didn't have much confidence that people would listen to him, let alone respect him. *Of all the nerve*, he could hear them thinking, *Truman Reid trying to tell me what to do. Not gonna happen!* Thoughts like these made him quiver inside.

He was surprised to find, though, that most everyone in the cast laid their undivided attention at his feet with hope in their eyes. They actually *wanted* him to lead, to show and tell them what they might do to make their turns on stage the best they could be. They ascribed to him knowledge that they didn't know he didn't possess. But that was okay; what they didn't know wouldn't hurt him. If they wanted to assume he knew all about acting, diction, movement, and so on, so be it. Truman didn't have to admit to them that he was doing his own acting as he sat next to Mr. Wolcott, earnestly listening as people read their parts aloud. Truman didn't have to admit he was winging it and faking it until he made it.

And Mr. Wolcott was fully on board with letting him be an equal partner in directorial duties. In fact, he'd said that every Thursday night would be Truman's turn to fully take the reins. Mr. Wolcott wouldn't even be around on Thursdays.

Near the end of the latest rehearsal on Friday, Mr. Wolcott turned to Truman and asked, "So, Truman, after a week of reading the script aloud, how do you think we're doing? Any notes?"

Truman had been largely silent during the rehearsals that first week, allowing Mr. Wolcott to take the lead while he scribbled madly in a leather-bound notebook upon which he'd pasted a black-and-white still of Jimmy Stewart as Elwood P. Dowd in the movie version. The notes he made, he dutifully turned over to him before homeroom every morning. It did Truman's heart good to see Mr. Wolcott earnestly incorporating those notes during each subsequent rehearsal.

"Johnny, you need to speak up, project more. Aim for the last row in the theater," Mr. Wolcott would say, for example, taking that "last row" comment from Truman's own advice, advice Truman himself had stolen from the internet.

"Lori, be willing to take some chances. Loosen up. Don't be afraid to be someone you're not. Think about how you'll look in one of those old-time nurse's uniforms with the little cap. *Be* that nurse."

"Amber, Veta Louise is a society matron, nose in the air. Go ahead, put on airs."

And so on. So much so that Truman was beginning to feel he actually was directing the play, but from the back seat. He looked forward to when they started blocking in earnest and making the play real instead of sitting in this confounded circle. And he really anticipated Thursdays, when he could be in charge, if only for the night.

But back to Mr. Wolcott's question. What overall thoughts did Truman have? This would be his first time truly speaking to the cast, although he had tossed out a bit of advice here, some snark there, a laugh after a certain line.

"Well, I think you're all doing a really good job." He forced himself to look at each of their expectant faces in turn. "I can see that some of you already are well on your way to having your parts memorized. And that's impressive after only a week." He eyed Kirk Nizer, who had been cast in the part Truman used for his audition, that of the pivotal cab driver, EJ Lofgren. Nizer had never lifted his head from the script, not once. And sometimes he even seemed to stumble over his lines, as though reading didn't come easily to him. Why on earth had Mr. Wolcott cast him? Truman thought his own cabdriver had stood head and shoulders above this boy's. He'd have to work extra hard with Kirk, which wasn't such a daunting prospect because he was kind of cute, with red hair, freckles, and green eyes, which made him appear boyish, yet the worked-out, ripped bod and the six-foot-four height was all man.

Maybe, it suddenly occurred to Truman, Mr. Wolcott wasn't so stupid in his casting choice of Kirk—he'd be eye candy. There was a reason Hollywood was filled with beautiful people, some of them vapid and talentless but famous nonetheless.

Anyway....

"One thing overall I don't see you guys doing, though, is *interacting*. You're all acting, or trying to, and that's painfully obvious." He looked at Mr. Wolcott and saw that maybe he'd crossed a line, at least this early in the process. Mr. Wolcott gave him a sort of wincing expression, which Truman interpreted to mean "Tone it down. Be more diplomatic."

"I mean, I'm impressed at how you guys are going all out to *be* your characters." Truman smiled.

"But, as I said, what we need to see more of is *interacting*. Sometimes it's not what's said that makes an impact, but what's left *unsaid*."

"And by that you mean…?" Mr. Wolcott asked.

"I mean you guys need to relate to each other more. You need to *listen* and react. See, from where I sit, I see you all taking turns reading your parts. Dutifully. You wait patiently—and graciously—for each person before you to finish, and then you read your part."

Stacy piped up, "So?" Her eyebrows furrowed. "What are we supposed to do? Cut each other off?"

"No, no. Of course not, but remember that listening is equally as important as speaking. Sometimes you might do your best acting just by being silent." Truman scratched at the top of his head, suddenly realizing everyone was not only staring at him but hanging on his every word. Heat rose to his cheeks. He was used to being the center of attention because he was the only boy in school who dared to wear a little makeup and, sometimes, clothes pulled from the women's department, but he wasn't used to being respected.

This was a new thing.

"Your reactions to each other are just as important as the actions you make and the words you speak," Truman said quietly. He glanced at Stacy, who was taking notes in the margin of her script. "It's really the *opposite* of cutting each other off, because when you cut each other off, you're *not* paying attention. And what I want you to do is pay closer attention to what your scene partners are saying and doing."

Mr. Wolcott clasped Truman's shoulder, squeezed, and let go. "Truman's right." He stood up and stretched, signaling everyone else to do the same. "I think we're about finished here for tonight. Everybody have a great weekend. We'll hit it again on Monday."

Truman stood next to Mr. Wolcott as he watched the cast file out. Maybe it wasn't so bad—this student director gig. He was learning something and, wonder of wonders, establishing a place for himself in the high school hierarchy, even if he was only a minnow in a very small pond.

As he left the auditorium, Truman found himself actually looking forward to the long walk home. Autumn was in its last throes. The air, finally, had a real nip to it. Truman picked up on the scents of woodsmoke and moldering leaves on the breeze.

Ah! There was Stacy, just ahead. He thought to catch up with her. They'd walked home from rehearsal once before that week, and Truman was starting to like her. Before, he'd thought she was stuck-up, another popular kid, a cheerleader—someone who wouldn't ever give Truman the time of day. Instead, he found someone who was warm, interested in him, and just as nervous about doing well as he was. And this was another thing he never would have expected: she came from similar financial circumstances. Unlike Truman, though, she didn't even have a single parent to call her own. She lived with her great-aunt Sarah, whom she called Aunt Sus, the reasoning for which remained unclear to Truman. Aunt Sus was nearly eighty years old and was much more interested in reality TV and her Bible than she was in her great-niece.

Besides, he hoped especially to walk home with her tonight because he wanted to ask her about her cousin, Mike. He didn't know *what* he wanted to ask, because really, what could he ask? What's he like? How did he get to be so damn sexy? Was he a "friend of Dorothy"? Truman smiled. He knew he could never ask any of those questions of Stacy. For one, he didn't have the nerve. And for another, asking such questions would probably nip their developing friendship in the bud.

"Stacy! Hey! Wait up." The roar of a loud muffler, the deliberate kind and not like the one on his mom's car that needed to be repaired, drowned him out. Truman was left waving his hand in the air ridiculously. With some exaggeration he tried to morph the unacknowledged wave into patting his hair into place, just in case anyone was looking.

He glanced behind him. No one was. In fact, Truman and the driver of the souped-up vintage Trans Am that had just pulled up in front of Stacy were the only people around this long after school had let out.

Truman stepped back into the shadows of a large maple tree as he watched Stacy approach the car idling at the curb. He didn't quite know why, but he felt nervous about being seen. There was something illicit about what he was observing. Something secret. Truman could practically smell it in the chilly autumn air.

Stacy flicked her dark hair over her shoulder and leaned into the driver-side window. Truman could hear muffled laughter, flirtatious, coming out of her. And then a man's voice—definitely not a boy's—deep and raspy, as he talked to her. Truman couldn't make out any words, but he caught the timbre and tone and could hear the persuasion being attempted.

Truman was about to step out into the light when Stacy turned and peered around her. Instead of stepping forward, he went back a little so he was more hidden. Stacy, he thought, looked guilty, as though she was checking to make sure she wasn't being observed.

Truman thought he should let her know. What kind of stalkerish friend spied as he was doing? Before he had a chance to announce himself in some way, though, Stacy hurried around the front of the car to slide into the passenger seat. He heard the clunk of the door close. He tried to get a look at the man, but saw only the glow of a cigarette in the dark.

They roared off.

Truman stepped out from the shadows, feeling unaccountably shaken.

The whole scene simply looked *wrong*. There was a sense of guilt about Stacy as she peered around. The car, and the man—even though Truman couldn't really see him—seemed too old for her. Plus, there was the weird fact that Truman felt a completely illogical stab of jealousy. Of course, he didn't like Stacy in *that way*, but he was growing toward thinking of her as a friend. He was on the verge of asking her to come by his house some night after rehearsal, just to hang out.

But now he felt shaken, inexplicably a little nauseous. It seemed to Truman he'd witnessed someone doing a bad thing, something they didn't want anyone else to see. Truman appreciated secrets, understood most people's need to have them, but when he was forced to witness one—as he thought he was tonight—it just felt, well, *weird*.

Maybe he didn't know Stacy as well as he thought.

Or maybe he did. Truman thought back to once upon a time when he'd carried around his own secret life—there was a boy who used to meet him on the banks of the Ohio, a popular boy with whom Truman thought he was in love. Truman had mistaken being used as a come receptacle as being loved. It had been a very rude awakening. Thankfully, he now had enough distance from that experience to see that it had taught him a life lesson, even though the result of that lesson had been a broken heart. He'd thought it would never mend—but it did.

Truman wanted to hurry home, be in his little house with Patsy, where he felt safe.

He started down the hill toward his East End neighborhood.

To keep himself company during the long, dark walk by the side of Parkway Road, he fished his cell out of his pocket and called Alicia.

She picked up on the first ring. "Oh, so you finally called? I thought you were getting too big in your britches for the likes of li'l ole me, motherfucker. Mr. Student Director!"

They both laughed. It was good to hear her voice. They had no classes together this year, and somehow they were always missing each other in the mornings. Alicia could just as easily walk to school from her house, so she wasn't often at the bus stop. Hers was the last stop before Summitville High's front doors.

Plus, Truman knew how tough it was for her to get ready in the morning—she had to share a single bathroom with a mom, dad, and two little sisters, all of whom needed to get out before 8:00 a.m.

"Oh hush," Truman said as a pair of headlights rose up behind him, as though he were being spotlighted.

He heard the familiar bass thrum of a muffler. A Trans Am whizzed by him. Although he couldn't make out any faces in the car, he knew it contained Stacy and her mystery man.

"Do you know Stacy Timmons?" Truman asked.

"White bitch? From the rich part of town?"

Truman laughed. "That's what I thought too. Come to find out she lives just down the street from me in East End. She's poor white trash—like me."

Alicia snorted. "Well, she could have fooled me. Why you askin' about her?"

"I don't know. She's in *Harvey*—plays the young ingénue part. I just saw her go by."

"Where you at?"

"Walking home from rehearsal. On Parkway."

"You be careful. There's no sidewalk on that road, and folks go *way* too fast."

The mention of folks going way too fast reminded Truman of the Trans Am. What he was about to say wasn't provable or maybe even true, but he blurted his supposition out to Alicia, who loved gossip more than anyone he knew. "I saw her go by in a Trans Am with some older man." He frosted the cake with even more made-up details. "Much older. Like, thirty. It just didn't seem like the girl I was getting to know. You know?"

"I *don't* know, Tru. I don't know the bitch." Alicia paused, and he could hear the crunch of something, maybe potato chips, as she chewed. "What do you care if she has a daddy figure in her life? I *know* you ain't jealous." Alicia let loose a high-pitched twitter.

Truman explained how he saw her get in the car with the guy—how she looked guilty.

"Well, we all have our little secrets, don't we?"

Long ago, Truman had confided in Alicia about his "boyfriend," Kirk Samson, the quarterback at Summitville High, a young man so deep in the closet he probably would have committed suicide if his secret got out. This was all before Truman had met—and begun a relationship that lasted through the spring of freshman year and the summer following—with Alicia's brother, Darrell. What a pair they'd made, truly the long and short of any romance!

"I guess," Truman said. "Although neither of us seem to have any lately."

"Are you asking?"

"No. It's none of my business."

"You're right. We've both become kind of boring. I keep waiting for senior year to heat up so I *can* have some secrets, like a rich white boyfriend."

"You and me both, sister!"

They laughed.

Alicia continued, "What's also none of your business is what this Stacy girl is up to on her own time."

"Are *you* telling *me* to keep my nose out of other people's business? Queen of Gossip at Summitville High?"

"Honey, you the only queen I know at our school."

"Hush, girl."

They teased each other for a while more, long enough for Truman to get near his own house. They eventually hung up, with Alicia promising to meet Truman in the morning for breakfast at the Elite Diner. Part of the diner's charm, for both of them, was that their breakfasts there would be free, compliments of Patsy.

"Oh… and Alicia?"

"Yes?"

"Give Darrell my love."

Alicia chuckled. "I will, but I hate to break it to you. He's got a boyfriend, another B-baller. Irish guy from the south side of Chicago named Keith. He's hot."

"Oh, I know all about Mr. Keith," Truman said. "Girl, the guy is all over your brother's Facebook page. I'm happy for him."

"Sure you are. Listen, I gotta run. See you in the morning!"

Truman stepped up onto his front porch. Odd Thomas must have heard him because he began scratching at the front door. Truman opened it and let the dog out into the front yard. Truman sat on the stoop as Odd made a circuit of the yard, sniffing the front hedge, nose to the ground by the gravel driveway, and finally squatting to pee almost out of view. He called the dog back, and the two of them went inside.

As he made himself a sandwich, he thought of Alicia's comment, "Sure you are."

He knew Alicia supposed Truman was simply pining away for Darrell.

In truth, Truman thought, settling down on the couch with his chipped-ham sandwich and Fresca, he *was* pining for a boy—just not Darrell.

He closed his eyes for a moment, envisioning the ice-blue eyes, jet-black curls, and broad shoulders of Mike Stewart.

Then Odd Thomas jumped onto the couch beside him and snatched the sandwich right off the paper plate in his lap.

CHAPTER 7

TRUMAN STIRRED, rolling over and shifting to move his cramped legs away from Odd Thomas. What had awakened him? Had he heard rain tapping against his window? No. That couldn't be. Just before heading to his room earlier, he'd taken Odd out for his final walk, and Truman recalled the night sky was brilliant with stars, completely clear. He could even make out the Big Dipper.

The tapping sounded again, and this time, to him, it sounded more like sleet than rain. He sat up in bed, more awake, more alert. Odd Thomas lifted his head to peer up at him from the foot of the bed. He made a snorting sound, then laid his head back down and picked up his snores right where he'd left off.

Truman glanced over at his window, expecting to see it rain-smeared. Instead, a dark figure stood just outside. Truman let out a little gasp, moved back toward his headboard, and then slowly leaned closer to get a better look.

Stacy Timmons rapped again on the window with her fingernails.

Truman picked up his phone off the pile of books he used as a makeshift nightstand and checked the time. It was just past 2:00 a.m.

What the hell?

He got up from bed and, rubbing his eyes, approached the bedroom window wearing only his boxers.

He opened the window and leaned out a little. Cold night air rushed in, raising goose bumps. "What are you doing here?" he asked, the last vestiges of deep, middle-of-the-night sleep still clinging to his voice.

"Can I come in?" Stacy managed to get out. She was crying. "Please."

"What's wrong?" Truman asked.

"Can I just come the fuck in, Truman?"

Truman wanted to ask more questions. He barely knew the girl, after all. "Gimme a sec," he said, still sleepy. He closed the window because the air coming in wasn't just chilly, it was cold, maybe even the first harbinger of winter. He found the jeans he'd worn earlier on the bedroom floor and slid into them. There was a Cher T-shirt on the ladder-back chair by his bedroom door, and he pulled that over his head.

Barefoot, he padded to the front door, casting glances over his shoulder in the gray semidark, expecting Patsy to throw open her own bedroom door at any moment. The last thing she'd expect to see, Truman thought, bemused, was her very out and proud gay son sneaking a girl into the house in the middle of the night.

He opened the front door, shoulders hunching up and wincing as it creaked, to find Stacy standing outside. She had her arms crossed around herself, shivering.

"Come on in." Truman opened the door a little wider and stepped back. "Before you freeze to death. What's going on?"

She followed without answering. He led her toward his bedroom after putting a finger to his lips to indicate she should keep quiet—at least until they got to his room.

He switched on the little sock monkey night-light he'd had since he was five, and the room filled with a warm, dim glow. Odd Thomas sat up and stared at Stacy, panting.

"Aw, poor puppy." Stacy scratched Odd behind his ears. "You're so ugly, you're cute."

"People have said the same thing about me."

"Oh, they have not. You're gorgeous. In your own way." Stacy moved the socks, black with pink polka dots, off the ladder-back chair and plopped down in it heavily, as though carrying the weight of the world on her shoulders. She stared down at the floor for a long time, her dark hair a curtain hiding her face, not saying anything. Truman was just about to break the silence by asking to what did he owe the pleasure of this call, or at least repeating his earlier question about what was wrong.

Just as he opened his mouth to speak, Stacy's head fell more, down to her open palms. Her shoulders trembled with sobs. This was no casual cry but genuine grief, full-on, nose-running weeping.

Odd Thomas beat him to the act of showing concern. He got down with some difficulty from the bed, went over to Stacy, and laid his head in her lap. She removed one hand from her face to pet the dog.

Truman followed suit. He edged close to Stacy and placed an awkward hand on her shoulder. In a soft voice, he asked, "What's the matter? You can tell me."

She looked up at him then with wondering, puffy eyes. Her face was wet. Truman reached over her to grab a tissue from the box on his dresser. "Can I?"

He handed her the tissue and then squatted down beside her. "Of course you can."

"I mean, can I *really* trust you?" She looked away, then back. "Most kids at school love nothing more than spreading rumors and gossiping. And Facebook and Twitter help them with it!"

Ah, so she does have secrets. And I bet, ten to one, they have to do with the man in the Trans Am.

He felt a pang of guilt over gossiping earlier about Stacy with Alicia. He was better than that, wasn't he? "Listen, Stacy, anything you tell me goes no further than this room. That's a promise."

"Good." She hiccupped out a final little sob, blew her nose, and wiped impatiently at her eyes. "I somehow just know I can trust you. You're not the same as most of the kids at school. You're more mature than most of them, especially the boys. You're an old soul, you know?"

Truman didn't know. So he just said, "You can trust me. Consider this room the confessional. And I'm as gay as any priest, Lord knows. Now tell me—what's going on?" Truman eyed the closed door. He expected his mom to burst into the room at any minute.

Stacy paused for a long time. And then she blurted out some of the worst news a girl in high school could have. "I'm pregnant."

The words hung in the air for a moment, like something unreal or out of a bad teenage soap opera.

"What?" Truman asked. "Are you sure?"

She nodded. "I did a home pregnancy test and everything." She sniffed. "Besides, I haven't had a period in three months. And I never miss."

Truman moved to his bed and plopped down on it. He wasn't sure what to say, so he tried, "What can I do?"

"Oh, Truman, I wish there *was* something you could do. But honestly, tonight I just need someone to talk to. Can you, maybe, I don't know, listen?"

Truman nodded. He patted the bed next to him, and Stacy came to sit beside him. After a moment she put her head on his shoulder and started talking. "At the beginning of the summer, I met this guy, Ryan, out at the lake?"

Truman nodded. Lake Keller was on the outskirts of town. It was really just an old quarry that had filled in with green-brown water, but it was a place where the popular kids and the bad kids came together to drink, smoke weed, and make out.

Truman had never been.

"Okay," he said.

"He was older than me. Twenty-five, a real bad boy with his own car—an old Trans Am! He was sexy as hell, with buzzed hair, a beard, lots of tattoos. I knew I shouldn't go near him, but he drew me like, like—" Stacy groped for the right image.

"Like a moth to a flame?" Truman filled in.

"Right!" Stacy stared ahead for a long moment, and Truman imagined her visualizing this Ryan person. He visualized himself and found the image made him feel a little aroused. He tried to suppress the feeling, throwing a black screen over that mental picture of a muscular man with tattoos and a beard, oozing danger and raw sex. A bad boy. Bad boys were always so intoxicating, despite, or maybe because of, their warning labels. He put the bad-boy chatter out of his head. He needed to be present for Stacy right now.

"He wasn't anyone I ever thought I could see myself with, Truman. I hang out with the National Honor Society kids and my girls from cheerleading. The wildest we get is maybe sharing a beer somebody stole from their parents' fridge." She lifted her head a little to glance at him. "Until Ryan, I was a virgin."

"Really?" Truman asked, maybe sounding a little too surprised, he feared. The idea that someone could reach the ripe old age of seventeen or eighteen with his or her virginity still intact was a surprise, though. Truman had lost that distinction himself when he was only fourteen, to Kirk Samson. He shook his head, remembering those passionate—and very, very secret—nights down on the banks of the Ohio, just below this very house.

And Stacy was so pretty! He couldn't fathom why she'd choose to "save herself." What was the point of that? Where was the fun? Truman mentally shrugged. He guessed not everyone grew up with such a freewheeling and open mom as Patsy. Sexuality had always just been one more topic for conversation around their house, neither good nor bad, just a literal fact of life.

"Yes, really, Truman," Stacy said, sniffing a little. "I was a good girl. I planned on saving it for marriage."

Truman cocked his head.

"Why?"

"You're not Catholic, are you?"

"Good Lord, no. We're not anything." Truman had actually been to a church about three times in his whole life, all at the behest of his grandma, who lived in Pittsburgh and seldom spoke to Patsy. Patsy, Truman knew, had been raised Methodist. But she considered herself nothing at all these days. And she'd brought him up with a healthy skepticism of organized religion.

"If you were Catholic, maybe you'd get why it was important to me to save it for my husband." Stacy toyed with a thread that had come loose from Truman's quilt. "I always believed that my first time would be with someone special, even if I didn't quite make it to marriage." She smiled sadly.

"Okay…," Truman said, not sure he understood. He'd known a few Catholics, male and female, in his day. And honey, none of them were saving it for marriage!

"Anyway," Stacy said as she let herself fall backward on the bed. "Whatever. None of that matters now, because here I am, seventeen and knocked up." She stared up at the ceiling. "This wasn't exactly what I had planned, you know? My dreams were all about finishing school, going to college, maybe Kent State or OU, getting out of *here*, anyway. I'd get a degree in education, teach elementary school. Somewhere through all that, I'd meet a nice guy, a blond, straight-arrow type who was also a nice Catholic boy, and we'd fall in love, have a long courtship, and finally get married. We'd live in a split-level and have a bunch of kids, a Labrador retriever, an SUV, and a compact car."

"Oh God," Truman said. "I'm sorry, but that sounds like the most boring life ever." For everything she'd said, he'd imagined almost the opposite for himself. He pictured himself moving to a big city, New York, LA, or Chicago, working to sustain his creative dreams, living somewhere edgy and free, where he could be "gender-fluid," as he liked to think of himself, and no one giving even a single fuck about it.

"To you, maybe. But it was my dream." She drew in deeply, let the breath out in a long, quivering sigh. "And then I met Ryan. And it all went to hell. Or heaven. I guess it depends on your perspective. I never thought a hot guy could make me completely lose my mind. Oh my God, Truman, he swept me right off my feet." She bit her lip as though considering something. "I shouldn't tell you this, but I gave it up to him the very night I met him—right in the back seat of that damn Trans Am of his." The ghost of a smile, irrepressible, whispered across her features. "Do you think I'm terrible?"

"No, no, of course not. We've all got our inner sluts." *Oh God, that probably wasn't exactly the most comforting thing to say!*

Truman expected tears of guilt, shame, and regret. "It was awesome!" She laughed. "He was—is—just so hot. A real man. I couldn't resist. Not then and not a thousand times more the rest of the summer."

"A thousand?" Truman gulped, feeling queasily jealous—and not of Ryan.

"At least," Stacy said. "Let's just say I had quite an education over the summer." She rubbed her tummy. "But, as I knew in the back of my head, the tuition for that education was high." She was quiet, and Truman had the wisdom not to cut in. He had to resist the urge to ask impertinent questions about positions and the size of Ryan's cock, even if he was dying to know. What kind of friend would ask such questions, especially at a time like this? Now if it was Alicia lying there next to him—no problem.

Stacy caught his gaze and held it. Her eyes were growing shiny again with tears. "What am I going to do?" Her voice came out all whispery and quivering.

"Have you told him?" Truman asked. What was the protocol here, anyway? Shouldn't Ryan offer to marry her and make an honest woman of her? Or at least pay for an abortion, if that was what Stacy thought best? Although Truman believed Stacy had every right to go for that choice—and at her tender age, it made perfect sense—he couldn't help but think of Patsy with a rush of gratitude that she hadn't opted for that same choice eighteen years ago.

It occurred to him then that Stacy had underlined her Catholicism, so abortion probably wasn't a likely option for her.

"Of course I told him! Silly. What do you think I was doing tonight? Why do you think I'm so upset?" She let out a little sob and pressed the backs of her hands to her eyes.

Truman gently removed the hands. "You don't have to stop yourself from crying, sweetheart. You're safe here with me."

She allowed herself to weep for a couple of minutes.

"I take it that, when you told him, things didn't go well."

"That's putting it mildly." She shook her head. "He was mad! Can you believe it? He raged at me, all about how he thought *I* was 'taking care of things,' which I guess means he thought I was on the pill or using a diaphragm or whatever." Stacy laughed bitterly. "What? Just because I'm the one who can get pregnant, it's all on *me*?" She sighed. "I was just as dumb, though. I should have taken responsibility, I guess." She giggled, sounding a little hysterical, which Truman supposed she probably was. "He told me he had a latex allergy and couldn't use condoms. But he would pull out every time, I swear!"

Truman had to bite his lip to keep from asking, "And how did that work out for you?" Instead he said, "I know you didn't mean for this to happen." *But really, what did you expect?* "And he was a real dick to you. So what's he gonna do?"

"What's *he* gonna do? What's *he* gonna do? He's already done it, my dear." She stared up at the ceiling for a minute or two, almost as though she was at a complete and utter loss. "He broke up with me. He was *nice enough* to drop me off in front of your house. And you're right about the dick part—he even had the nerve to ask if I was sure the baby was his. Unless it's the virgin birth come again, there's no one else's it could be, and I told him that."

Truman felt out of his depth. Other than being the child of a single mother who'd had him as a teenager, Truman gave little thought to a consequence of sex being the start of another human being. Sex to him was something enjoyed by two consenting males. This whole male/female business and the complications that came built in were slightly repellent, although he did acknowledge the necessity of such couplings to produce more boys he could love.

"But, but.... Did he offer to marry you?"

Stacy snorted, first laughed, and then sobbed again. "Yeah. Like that would happen. Oh, what am I saying? Even if he did propose, I don't want that. I'm seventeen! He was hot, granted, but I don't think I loved him. No, I never did. Looking back, I can see it was all lust."

Truman scratched his head. "Well, he has to do *something*, right? I mean, he can't just drop this problem at your doorstep and walk away, scot-free. Can he?" Truman honestly didn't know. What had the mysterious man who'd fathered him done, way back when?

"He did offer to take me up to Pittsburgh to have it 'taken care of,' as he put it." Stacy shook her head. "I could never do that, Truman."

"I get it." Although he really wasn't sure if he did.

"He said if I didn't want to do that, I was on my own." Her face became impassive, kind of blank.

"What will you do?"

"I suppose I could go off somewhere and have it? I'd have to leave. I don't want everybody and her sister here to know about it." Stacy looked away for a moment. "Maybe give it up for adoption?" And these questions started Stacy's tears up again. "I don't know if I could do that." She turned away from Truman, curling into a little ball. She covered her face with her hands again as she wept, as though she thought tears were a sign of weakness. Patsy had always encouraged Truman to cry and told him tears were not an indication of weakness, but of strength. Truman edged close to Stacy's back and held her until they both drifted off to sleep.

PATSY'S VOICE awakened him before the diffused sunlight seeping into the room early that Saturday morning had a chance to. "Do my eyes deceive me? Has this young lady managed to do the impossible? *Turn* my son? Oh my God!" Patsy moved to Truman's window and opened the blinds. The morning light was pale gray, almost pewter. Clouds hung low over the horizon.

Truman sat up, rubbing his eyes at the sudden light, even if it was muted. "Mom," he grunted. Stacy stirred next to him, and he could practically feel her staring at Patsy, who stood by the window in a chenille bathrobe, hands on hips, grinning.

Odd Thomas gingerly got down off the bed with a little wince and wandered over to Patsy. He paced at her feet, looking up first at her, then over at Truman.

Patsy bent down to pat the dog. "You better take this fella out. Then you can tell me all about your miraculous conversion to heterosexuality. Praise the Lord!" Patsy padded barefoot from the room, snickering. She mumbled to herself, "And I didn't even have to pay a dime for conversion therapy."

Stacy got up on her elbows. "Your mom's pretty. She looks like she could be my age."

Truman glanced over at her. "She was just a little younger than you when she had me."

"Is she mad?"

"Did she sound mad?"

"Not unless you mean 'mad' in the sense of crazy." Stacy let out a short laugh.

"Well, we're all certifiable around here. Get used to it." Truman swung his legs out of bed and told Stacy, "Gotta take Odd here for a little walk. I'll be back shortly. You like coffee?"

Stacy nodded.

"Mom will make us some. Go out and be friendly. She won't bite."

"Oh, I don't know. Can I just wait here until you get back?" Stacy sat up in bed and drew her legs up to her chest.

Just then Odd Thomas let out an impatient whine, and Truman said, "I better go. Yeah, sure, wait for me." And he hurried to the bedroom door. "C'mon, boy." He slapped his thigh.

"I didn't mean to fall asleep!" Stacy called after him.

"It's cool. Don't worry about it."

Truman, with Odd Thomas trailing behind, passed Patsy in the kitchen where she was, indeed, making coffee. He met her gaze and smiled. "It's a long story. I'll tell you all about it later."

"So I'm not gonna be a grandmother?" Patsy pressed the button to start the coffee brewing and laughed.

Truman shook his head as he opened the back door. *If you only knew....*

Outside, it now felt like full-on autumn. It was cold!

There was a haze of silver on the grass, and the wind, out of the north, felt wintry. Truman stood shivering, rubbing his goose-pimpled arms up and down, wishing Odd Thomas would hurry up. But the old boy seemed to enjoy the crisp morning, taking his time to sniff just about everything that crossed his path before finally getting serious and taking care of business.

"Come on!" Truman cried impatiently, turning toward the door. "Don't you want your breakfast?"

The dog, obviously invigorated, trotted after him, to Truman's great relief.

When he returned to the kitchen, he was pleased to find Stacy must have found her nerve, because she was in the kitchen with his mom. Patsy had put her to work, and she was whisking eggs in their big blue mixing bowl. Stacy glanced over at Truman, and her brown eyes looked happy, as though she might be grateful to be here.

"I see you two have met."

"Yes, we're just comparing notes on teenage pregnancy." Stacy was at the kitchen counter, next to his mom. She was finished with the eggs and was now removing slices of bread from a plastic bag.

"Wow. You didn't waste any time." Truman was stunned that Stacy had shared her news so quickly.

Patsy looked at him, her eyes sympathetic. "One of the drawbacks of our little castle here is it's pretty easy to overhear. Not that I was eavesdropping!"

Stacy patted Patsy's shoulder. "It's okay. I'm glad you know." She put four slices of bread in the toaster and pushed down the bar to start the heat. "You understand, which is more than I can say for my aunt Sus."

"That's who she lives with." Truman got out the bag of kibble, poured some into a bowl for Odd, then went to refresh his water bowl. The dog would be done with his morning meal in minutes, and then he'd go back to bed for a nice long nap. Such was the life of a senior....

"She knows my living situation. I already told her."

Truman sat down at the kitchen table. "And did you tell her your aunt is a Catholic nut? Kind of like a fundamentalist, only blessed by the Pope?"

Stacy eyed Patsy for a moment and then looked away. "No."

Patsy rubbed at the tension Truman could see causing Stacy's shoulders to rise up, stiffening. "Is it gonna be hard to tell her, hon?"

"She'll go ballistic. Probably throw me out." Stacy looked around the homey yellow kitchen. Truman had always thought of their home as white trash, poverty level, a hillbilly haven, and other disparaging terms, but seeing it through Stacy's eyes, he saw that their humble little kitchen was actually warm, comfy, and welcoming. It was a place where people lived—and loved. And he knew that Stacy, facing the very real chance she might be thrown out of her own home, most likely saw it as a sanctuary, a haven.

Patsy nodded. "I understand. My mom *did* throw me out. Didn't think twice about it. I was no longer her daughter, she said, and so a slut like me had no place under her and Dad's roof." A sad smile whispered across Patsy's features as she remembered. "It's why I didn't get to finish high school. I had to get a job!"

Truman felt a deep pang within. He'd never given all that much thought to what Patsy had to sacrifice to have him. He just accepted her hardship as his due. *Isn't that the way*, he thought—he hoped—*all*

*children think? Or at least like to think? That their
parents are there for them and really have no other
lives of their own?*

Patsy had been younger than he was right now
when she'd had him. How scared she must have been!
Truman couldn't imagine what his life would be like
now if he were forced to not only go out and support
himself, but a kid as well. It seemed impossible.

Yet Patsy had done it. And never complained—at
least, not to him.

He stood and went to Patsy. From behind, he
wrapped his arms around her and hugged her, laying
his head for a moment to rest against the top of her
head.

Patsy laughed. "What's that for?"

"For being there for me—always."

Patsy moved away from Truman and stood looking at him for a moment. She touched his cheek. "I
wouldn't have had it any other way," she said softly.
"It's been a bitch, I won't lie. But I have no regrets."
They were all quiet for a moment, and then Patsy
laughed and turned to the cupboard to draw down
some mugs for coffee.

She glanced out of the corner of her eye at Stacy.
"Sweetie, just remember: I am not a role model."

Stacy nodded, and Truman could see the admiration in her eyes for his mom, despite Patsy's
warning.

Over breakfast they discussed what they would
do, especially about Stacy's aunt Sus. She'd called her
aunt the night before, to let her know she was staying with a friend, and the news, according to Stacy,

had barely registered on old Aunt Sus, who'd been half-asleep.

In the end, Patsy agreed to come home with Stacy after her shift at the diner so they could break the news to her aunt together.

CHAPTER 8

Truman's heart was in his mouth that Monday afternoon.

It all began with Mr. Wolcott clapping his hands together to get everyone to quiet down. Truman had noticed a cluster of kids sitting as a group in the back of the auditorium when he first came in. He didn't pay them much mind because he was eager to get started on rehearsal, which would be the first that would incorporate blocking, or movement, on the stage.

They would be freed from sitting around in a circle on folding chairs. Things could finally start to come to life, even if everyone still needed the help of his or her script in hand.

"I want everyone to meet our stage crew! We got a great turnout from the sign-up sheet I posted, so I didn't have to go and hunt anybody down, draft 'em. And these guys are gonna be terrific. They'll create the world we'll all live in for the next couple of months," Mr. Wolcott said.

For a moment, Truman had hoped Alicia had maybe relented and would join the stage crew. But she would have told him, wouldn't she? He glanced back at the group and saw only one girl, and she was white. And over six feet tall.

"Everybody." Mr. Wolcott motioned with his hand, "Come on down to the front so we can get a look at you. And thanks again for stepping up to the plate."

The group, almost as one, hoisted themselves from their seats and lumbered down the red-carpeted aisle.

That's when Truman's heart leaped to his mouth, because one of the crew stood out so stunningly that everyone else faded into a blur. Mike Stewart, in all his quiet masculine glory, was part of the group making their way to the front of the auditorium. He wore tight, faded jeans, a black T-shirt, and tan steel-toed boots. All he needed was a hard hat to look like the construction worker from that old band from the 1970s, the Village People. It felt, for a moment, like Mike's blue eyes connected with Truman's, and Truman felt like fainting. He'd never fainted before, but if light-headedness and a weird feeling of being levitated from the ground were precursors, well, all Truman could think was that Mr. Wolcott had better have the smelling salts on hand. It was like that moment on the bus when Truman first saw Mike, when their eyes met. Objectively he couldn't see it was anything more than a couple of pairs of eyes meeting for a moment. But intuitively there was more—a connection that went far deeper than a casual glance.

I'm going to die. Right here and right now—just from the sight of him, the very sight of him. Truman sank down in his seat, certain everyone could see the erection tenting the front of his pale yellow slacks, sure everyone could read his mind—his filthy, lust-filled mind. They knew what he wanted from that boy was a kiss—for starters. Yes, they were right. A kiss would indeed make for a very good start. Truman imagined Mike's lips seeking his own, their softness and wetness. As their faces pressed together, Truman would feel the delightful sandpaper scratch of Mike's dark stubble against his own soft skin.

Magic.

The stage crew, all six of them, lined up by Mr. Wolcott, shuffling their feet and staring down at the floor. It was obvious why they chose to be behind the scenes and *not* in the spotlight. Every one of them stunk of shyness, of an almost fierce desire to be invisible.

Mike towered over everyone else. Well, not so much the six-footer girl, who Truman had seen around but never really talked to. All he knew about the gangly blonde was that people called her "Stretch" behind her back and that she was the star center of the girls' basketball team. She'd be pretty, Truman thought, if it weren't for the black horn-rims and, maybe, if she'd work a little on her posture. *Shoulders back, chin up, girlfriend! You're not Sasquatch! Pretend you have a stack of books balanced on your head.*

Mr. Wolcott mentioned her name, Tammy Appleby, Applegate, Appledorn, or something like that. Truman wasn't really listening. Mr. Wolcott called out several other names: Blake, Jeremy, Dylan, Jake... a bunch of boys Truman had been in school with and been humiliated in front of in various gym classes over the years.

But none of them really stood out. He understood suddenly the old romantic cliché "I only have eyes for you," because it was how he felt about Mike. He couldn't stop staring.

Okay. Now I gotta stop. Truman felt fiery heat rise to his face, burning, because Mike obviously had gotten wise to all the intense stares Truman was throwing his way. He looked back at Truman with his thick brows furrowed and head cocked, as though to ask, "What the fuck, dude?"

Truman cast his eyes to the floor. His stomach churned. *Oh God, he caught me. If he didn't already know I was the school fag, he does now—what with me making eyes at him like some silly, lovesick teenage girl. And all that bullshit about this magical connection between our eyes? Wishful thinking. Mike's too straight to be interested in the likes of me. Even if he did lean toward playing for my team, he still wouldn't want a sissy like me.*

Truman hazarded one more glance at Mike. Mike stared back, a grin playing about the corners of his mouth.

He's laughing at me!

Truman wanted to run from the room. Once outside, he knew the apple, carrot sticks, and tuna he'd had for lunch would come right up. In fact, bile splashed against the back of his throat, warning, threatening. Truman forced it back down. *I have shit to do here.*

And then he noticed Mr. Wolcott calling his name. He must have been trying to get his attention for a while now, because he was employing that trusty standby phrase used by teachers nationwide when they caught some poor, unfortunate soul daydreaming.

"Earth to Truman. Earth to Truman."

Giggles all around.

Truman cleared his throat and sat up a little straighter. "Um, yup."

More laughter.

"You want to clue our crew here in on your thoughts about the staging and the set?"

No. Not really. What I'd like to do is run home and hide under the covers, Odd Thomas at my side. "Um, okay…."

"Come on, Tru, you gave me notes on what you thought the set should be like when we first started out. And I loved your ideas." Mr. Wolcott had his arms crossed and, frankly, looked a little peeved. Great. *Now one of the few people in this school who respect me is pissed at me. This is shaping up to be the perfect day.*

"Tru?"

"Uh, yeah, sure, Mr. Wolcott." Truman stood and tried to recall exactly what his ideas were for the set. Right now his mind was a wide white canvas, blank, or maybe imprinted with a sort of afterimage glow of Mike Stewart's face.

Truman dove in, figuring if he just started talking, his thoughts about the set would come to him. "Uh, yeah, first of all, thanks, you guys, for being a part of the show and volunteering to build the set and light it. I know you'll make sure all our props are in the right place at the right time."

He dared to look at the crew. They were all staring, expectant. Even Mike. The grin of ridicule was wiped off his features, and he was once more brooding and oh-so-handsome. Truman had to force his gaze away. *What's wrong with you? That boy's as straight as they come. As Queen Elsa sang, "Let it go."*

"Anyway, my thoughts for the set. Yes." Truman paused, clearing his throat.

Mr. Wolcott prompted. "Minimalist. Simple."

"Right!" Truman shot him a smile of gratitude. "So, what I was thinking is that we'd just have *suggestions* of things for each of the two sets—the Dowd mansion and Chumley's Rest—the nuthouse, if you will. Like, for the mansion, maybe a column, or a fireplace painted to look like marble. Maybe we could do a doorway or something and make it look ornate. We could probably find thrift-store furniture we could gussy up with some throws or something. For the rest home, insane asylum, really, we just need a reception area. Keep it simple. Stark. A few chairs. A desk… and the usual props. If we could score some kind of cabinet that could pass as an old-time doctor's cabinet, that would be really cool."

Mike spoke up. "We got an old entertainment unit at home we don't use anymore. It's in the garage. I could haul it in with my pickup, and we could sand it down, paint it white—be really cool for the chest." He smiled, a little sheepish when he noticed all eyes on him. "Be really cool."

"That sounds perfect," Truman said, amazed to be exchanging words with the guy. His voice was so deep, like gravel and velvet. So sexy it almost made Truman shiver. *And he drives a pickup? Great Lord Almighty!* Truman's fantasies were springing to life left and right. He squelched the urge to ask Mike about his power tools or if he was good with his hands. "Bring it in next time?"

"Sure thing, bud."

Bud! He called me bud. Truman felt like fainting again.

Mr. Wolcott took over. "And this idea brings up something I wanted to talk to all of you about, cast and crew alike. As you know, we have a very limited budget. As in shoestring. As in zilch, nada, zero." He cocked his head. "So we're kind of on our own here as far as our set, our costumes, and our props go. So as we rehearse, and the set, as Truman described it—" He interrupted himself to ask Truman, "You can sketch up your ideas, right? So these guys can get started with their hammers and nails."

"And two-by-fours," Truman added, although he had no idea what two-by-fours even were. But the concept sounded correct.

"Right," Mr. Wolcott said. "So, sketches?"

"I'm on it." Truman held up a spiral-bound notebook that contained his notes on *Lord of the Flies*, which Mr. Bernard was teaching in his college-prep advanced literature class. But Mr. Wolcott didn't have to know that.

Mr. Wolcott continued on, his voice a drone as he talked to them all about seeing what props and furnishings they might persuade parents and other relatives to loan to the school for the play. Truman interrupted to tell them they'd need to run any clothes they were planning on wearing for costumes by him first.

The whole rehearsal went very well, save for one glaring absence—Stacy hadn't shown up. Mr. Wolcott asked Truman about it after it was clear she was apparently blowing this rehearsal off.

He knew she was planning on talking to her aunt with Patsy at her side. He hoped it hadn't gone too horribly.

In the meantime, Truman shouted her lines from the front row so people on stage would have something to *react* to.

CHAPTER 9

TRUMAN MISSED Stacy that night after rehearsal as he headed down the hill toward home—alone. He'd been getting used to having her by his side in the darkness as they each headed home. He sure hoped she was okay!

The night was cold and clear, and the stars above him shone like diamonds cast on black velvet. The nip in the air renewed his energy and made him even more eager to get home and back to Odd Thomas and the leftover mac and cheese with ham and peas he knew Patsy had left in the fridge.

He also wanted to see if there was any news about Stacy. Maybe Patsy had left him a note? She certainly hadn't called or texted—he'd checked his phone. He'd worried off and on about Stacy throughout rehearsal. He hoped her fears of being thrown out had turned out to be groundless. Surely her aunt loved her like a daughter and wouldn't cast her out?

Truman shook his head. If only…. His own mother had been cast out herself, by a mother upon whom she'd probably once relied and believed loved her. *How can parents do that to their kids? Isn't love about accepting? Loving people as they are, faults and all? God knows nobody's immune from making mistakes!*

It was Patsy's night to work late at the diner. He'd have the house to himself. For Truman, that meant two things. One, he could stream whatever he wanted on TV, which was usually some old three-Kleenex weeper like *Imitation of Life*, *Madame X*, *A Summer Place*, *Stella Dallas*, or even *Valley of the Dolls*. And two, he could jack off with impunity. Ever since he'd turned twelve, being alone in the house meant jacking off. It was almost imperative—the deed *needed* to be done, whether Truman was in the mood or not. But what teenage boy was ever *not* in the mood? So he "took matters into his own hands," sometimes two or three times, with every home-alone chance he got. If he didn't, he'd mourn the lost opportunity forever. Good thing he didn't have much chance to mourn that particular loss!

As he was thinking about putting to use a particularly filthy website he'd discovered that contained all the porn Truman could handle, his thoughts were interrupted by the low idle of an engine.

Someone was slowing down on the roadway beside him. Truman nearly came to a stop, nerves tightening. Paradoxically he was already wondering how fast he could run. He'd been conditioned to know that the sound of a car decelerating on a lonely road at night beside him could only mean one thing—teasing, bullying, or worse. Fortunately for Truman, he'd never been attacked, but he'd had his share of cars coming almost to a standstill when they spied him. A window would roll down. There'd be whistles, catcalls. A nearly anonymous voice would drift out of the vehicle to accuse him of the crime of "sashaying" or "traipsing." He'd been called "fag," "fairy," "girlfriend," and once even "pretty lady." He'd been asked if he was in the mood to suck some cock. Cowardly snickering voices from inside a car or truck had wondered aloud if his ass was sore.

So Truman's whole body tensed, and he poised himself to flee, if need be. He knew that just to his right, the embankment sloped down sharply to a little creek. Growing up, Truman had spent hours playing by himself next to that creek, which, back then he called a "crick," so he was familiar enough to navigate it even by starlight. He also knew that farther down there was a drainage tunnel he could hunch over and creep through, even if that would mean wet shoes and spiders in his hair.

If necessary, escape was possible.

"Hey," a masculine voice called out from the idling truck Truman now spied in his peripheral vision. Truman rolled his eyes, bracing for the suggestive remark, the name-calling. Worse, the truck could pull over, blocking his path. And he pictured several guys jumping out of it, swinging baseball bats. He'd read of such things happening in Pittsburgh to the east or Youngstown to the north.

These days, he was pretty much left alone at school despite what some might call his "flamboyant" ways—the girl's clothes, the touch of makeup—but he knew that out here, by himself on a virtually empty road, all bets were off for being left alone. Darkness coupled with Truman being alone could be very empowering for a coward like a bully—some folks might do things they'd not otherwise consider during the light of day or when others were around to judge.

Truman nervously took a quick glance over his shoulder. He couldn't make out the face in the dark cab of the pickup, which had now rolled almost to a complete stop. Its tires crunched on the gravel at the side of the road. "Hey," Truman said back, cursing the feminine lilt to his voice even in that single word. He tried to swallow and discovered his mouth was dry.

"You need a ride, buddy?"

Truman stopped, drew in a deep breath, and even though everything inside him was screaming *Run!* he moved a little closer to the truck to peer inside. "I know you?"

Before he could even make out features, though, the driver identified himself. "It's me, Mike Stewart."

"Oh my God, it's you!" Truman squealed before he could even think to censor himself, to speak in a deeper register. But why should he bother doing that anyway? Still, he felt heat enflame his face, despite being "out and proud."

Mike chuckled. "Yeah, it's me. You need a ride or no? I know you live over by my grandma's place. Lula?"

Truman let out a breath of relief. "I know her. She's a sweet lady," Truman said, even though what he really thought of her was that she was a sad, depressed mess. Some tragic heroine out of Tennessee Williams….

"Yeah, my pop's staying with her until he can get his own place. I'm supposed to come by for supper. Fish sticks, my favorite. Which reminds me, I'm gonna be late if I don't get a move on. So, you wanna lift or no? No skin off my ass either way."

And as Truman contemplated that same glorious ass, he happily opened the truck door and hoisted himself inside. Soft country music, Patsy Cline singing "Crazy," came out of the radio's speakers.

Mike took off down the hill. The ride was bumpy, the exhaust noisy. It was just what Truman was used to. Patsy had always been lucky enough to have a car, just not one younger than ten years old or with fewer than 100,000 miles on it.

Truman sniffed. "You smoke?" The interior of the truck smelled like an ashtray.

"Nah, not me. Pop. This was his truck originally. He gave it to me when I turned sixteen. But I could never get the fuckin' reek of his Marlboros out. Sorry."

"It's okay. Just wondered." Truman stared out through the windshield at the night. He noticed a hairline crack running across the top of the glass.

"Rock."

"What?" Truman asked.

Mike pointed at the crack. "Rock did that. It was just a little ding to start with, and then it started to spread. Pop's hunting around in the junkyards to see if he can find a replacement windshield before this one blows in on me."

"Cool," Truman said. Sitting next to this guy in his pickup, their thighs almost touching, should have been a wet dream come true for Truman, but suddenly he was very nervous. Or not worthy, or something.

He couldn't think of a single thing to say. He turned his head to stare out the window. They'd reached the bottom of the hill. There was the old American Legion hall, closed now for a couple of years, the Brew and View drive-through, which specialized in beer, cigarettes, and once upon a time, movie rentals. And a bunch of run-down houses—rusting aluminum siding, peeling paint, weed-choked front yards.

Home sweet home, Truman thought, promising himself for the one-thousandth time that he had to get out of this place. Summitville was the poster child for dying rustbelt towns. It was sad, really, because the area had such an abundance of natural beauty.

And then an obvious topic of conversation came to him. "I think your dad is seeing my mom."

Mike snorted. "Really?"

Was Truman not supposed to say anything? Mike seemed surprised at the news.

"Yeah, Patsy Reid?"

"Oh, I know who your mom is. I eat at the diner where she works once or twice a week. My ma, she don't cook much. So she gives me a few bucks and sends me on my way, which is fine by me, because Ma can't cook worth shit." He laughed, and Truman noticed how deep and melodious it was. Mike's laugh actually warmed him a bit, made him feel a little more at ease. "But, uh, I didn't know my dad was seeing her." Mike stared out the windshield, and Truman wondered what was going on in his head, what was causing those bushy eyebrows to furrow. "She's pretty. Your ma."

"As far as I know, it's only been going on for a little while." Truman hoped minimizing his mom's relationship might make Mike feel better. He decided Mike didn't know that Mike's pop, George, was now spending a night or two every week at Truman and Patsy's house. Why *didn't* Mike know that? Truman guessed it was because he lived with his mom.

They rode in silence the rest of the way to Truman's neighborhood. Mike pulled up right in front of Truman's house. *He knows where I live?* Truman's heart skipped a beat.

But then Mike pointed to Lula Stewart's house, just down the street. "Gram's," he said.

"Yeah, I know."

Mike laughed. "Of course, you would. You always live here?"

Truman met his eyes, which shone icy blue, even in the yellowish light from the streetlamp shining down on them. "All my life," Truman said. He ventured, "I would have thought we might have crossed paths before, what with your grandma being so close by."

Mike shook his head. "Nah. I just moved here middle of the summer."

"From where?"

"Shoreline, Washington."

"Wow," Truman marveled. "A long way away." Truman couldn't begin to imagine the Pacific Northwest, beyond what he'd seen in the *Twilight* movies.

"Yeah, close to Seattle."

"Didn't Frasier live there?" Truman cursed himself. Not everybody had pop culture references for geography.

"Frasier who?"

"Never mind. So what made you move all the way here?"

Mike shrugged. "I didn't want to, but when my parents were busting up, they decided, for whatever reason, to come back to their hometown. Who knows why? I know my dad wanted to be close to his ma. She's getting up in years, and ever since Pap-pap killed himself—" Mike stopped suddenly and corrected himself. "Ever since my grandfather died, she's been pretty low. He's stayin' with her."

"I know."

"You do? Oh, that's right. My dad's seeing your mom. Wonder why he never told me? If he thinks it would hurt my feelings or something, he's sadly mistaken. Or if he thinks I'm like some little kid hoping Mommy and Daddy will get back together, well, dude, I have news for him." Mike turned away to stare outside the driver's-side window. "No skin off my ass if he has a girlfriend." He snorted with laughter, but Truman detected a bitter edge. "Anyone's gotta be better than my ma."

"Do you have one?" Truman asked, a little nervous, thinking the question made it all too obvious that he was interested in Mike, who from all outward appearances was as straight as they come. Looking as he did, Mike could have his pick of any girl at Summitville High.

"What? A girlfriend?" Mike laughed. "Fuck, no. Who has time for that shit?" He looked away from Truman, staring out the window.

"Yeah, who has time?" In the dark, Truman grinned.

"Listen, I gotta get to Gram's. She'll be holding supper for me."

"Oh sure," Truman said. "I didn't mean to keep you."

"No problem." And with those words, Mike reached across the seat and grabbed hold of Truman's shoulder and gave it a squeeze. Truman all but melted at his touch. *I will never wash this shoulder again.*

"Hey, Truman. I, uh, don't really have any friends here. That's why I signed up for the play thing." Mike swallowed, and Truman noticed that he seemed a little nervous, which had its own charm. It made Truman feel like they were on the same page. "You maybe wanna hang out sometime?"

This guy, this gorgeous butch guy wants to hang out? With me? This was a once-in-a-lifetime moment for Truman. *Well, not so much. Once upon a time there was this butch guy who liked hanging out with me down on the riverbank. But he was a user....* Truman forced the thought—and the images it brought on— right out of his head. He attributed Mike's interest to being new in town, otherwise why would he give any attention at all to a big sissy like Truman? *Now that's just the kind of thinking that makes you feel less-than, makes you feel down! Even Mom says that you're just as good, just as lovable—more so, in her opinion—as anyone else.*

"Sure," Truman said. "Anytime." He barely got the words out on account of his heart being in his throat. He thought of Elwood P. Dowd in *Harvey* at that moment. He liked the way the gregarious, head-in-the-clouds fellow would always pin folks down when they suggested getting together. So he tried the technique now, guessing his heart was about to be crushed. Of course, Mike had only made the suggestion to be nice.... But in for a penny, in for a pound. "Um, when are you thinking?"

Mike turned his head to smile at him. "How about tonight? After supper? Since I'm already here and parked? Sometimes I couch surf at Gram's."

"Tonight?" Truman tried to play it cool, to pause for a moment as though he were considering. But inside his heart was going *rat-a-tat-tat-tat* like a machine gun. It almost hurt. "Sure," he said, grinning back at Mike. "No skin off my ass," he added, then felt like a fool, sure Mike would pick up on Truman's appropriating his catchphrase.

"Cool. Well, gotta go." Mike turned off the engine and hopped out. He looked back in at Truman sitting on the passenger side, a small smile turning up the corners of his lips. "Bud? Need you to get out of the truck. This is the last stop. End of the line. All passengers must disembark." Mike grinned.

"Oh! Sure thing." Truman got out and hurried up his front walk. He turned. "See you in a bit."

He wasn't sure Mike had heard. If he did, he made no indication as he jogged toward his grandmother's weathered red-and-white house with the big wraparound porch and swing. Truman paused in his yard to watch Mike as he lumbered up the front steps, looking at least twenty-five years old and at least seven feet tall. He was a giant, Truman thought, a little breathless and wondering what Mike would feel like on top of him. *Cut it out!* Truman admonished himself. *If you think the day or night is coming when you'll know the answer to that one, you've got another think coming.*

Truman took a few more steps toward the cinder blocks that passed for front steps—and even darker shadows—and watched as Lula opened the door and gathered Mike up in her arms. Even from over here, he could hear her sobbing as she hugged him hard.

"Come on, Gram. It's not like you didn't just see me a couple days ago. Pop here?" Mike broke away from her, and before Truman could hear Lula's reply, she had pulled her grandson inside and then closed the door behind them.

Truman took that as his cue to get his own butt inside. Odd Thomas groaned as he got down from the couch and waddled over to him. Truman squatted to reward him for his efforts, scratching him behind the ears and trying not to show how much he wanted to recoil at the dog's bad breath. "You wanna go outside?" he asked, trying to inject some excitement into his voice. He could remember a time when the very question would elicit excited barks, perhaps a bit of tail chasing, and a run to claim his leash if it was within in his reach. Now the old boy simply stared at Truman as he put his harness on him.

He took Odd outside, thinking that the leash and harness were simply old habit. He didn't really need them for the dog anymore. For one, even if Odd Thomas did try to run away, he wouldn't get too far too fast because he just didn't have the same speed he once did. He'd passed from the canter stage to the trot stage when Truman and Patsy hadn't been looking. For another, Odd seemed to have lost interest in the outdoors—trips to the yard and beyond were just another chance to use the bathroom and nothing more. He couldn't wait to get back to his side of the couch, worn from his weight and furry from shedding. Truman sadly recalled a younger Odd, of whom he once thought that if he ever got off-leash outside, he'd never be able to catch him.

As Truman waited for Odd to finish up, he realized he was no longer hungry. No, he was busy thinking he should try to grab a shower before Mike arrived, maybe slip into something a little less obtrusive than the school clothes he wore. Could he get away with just pajama bottoms and a T-shirt? Was that being too forward? Whatever. He'd decide when he got out of the shower.

He could still heat up the mac and cheese and offer some to Mike.

What would he and Mike do, anyway? Truman wondered as he took Odd back inside. Should he see if there were any sports on TV? Perhaps the Steelers were playing? Truman was clueless. He only knew Mike would probably *not* be interested in the things Truman enjoyed watching, things like *Project Runway* and *Little Women LA*. And he certainly would have no interest in Truman's collection of old tearjerker movies made even before Patsy had been born.

Do we have any common ground at all?

It would come together. He shouldn't worry so much. To hang out tonight had been, after all, Mike's idea.

Truman took a long, hot shower, soaping every nook and cranny he could reach and letting the extra-hot water sluice over it all, even if he knew Mike probably could care less if Truman had even showered at all.

When he came out and dried off, he decided pajama bottoms, sans underwear, would be the right choice. God help him if he got a boner! He topped off the striped flannels with a black T-shirt that had a caricature of Grace Jones on the front he'd found at a rummage sale at the Catholic church down the road last spring.

He was debating putting on just a hint of eyeliner and maybe a bit of blush when he heard the roar of an engine outside.

He hurried to the window and watched, mouth open, as Mike pulled away from the curb. The truck backfired once and sent out a plume of blue exhaust as it headed away.

Truman, a lump in his throat, threw himself on the couch, endeavoring to make himself believe Mike was just going to a store or something and would be back within minutes.

But he didn't come back. And even Odd Thomas licking his clean, clean face didn't make him feel better. He must have sat for over an hour on the couch, TV off, just staring. Waiting.

He finally gave up and went to bed. Maybe he'd misunderstood?

CHAPTER 10

MIKE DROVE off into the night, not allowing himself to look back at Truman's ramshackle house. He tried to force the image of the place out of his mind, what with its dry-cleaner plastic over the windows and how the paint was practically worn off, making it appear sad, depressing, as though a good wind could blow it right off its bluff into the Ohio River below. It was hard to believe the gray hole-in-the-wall could contain a force of light that shined as brightly as Truman did.

Truman. Now there was an image Mike couldn't seem to erase from his mind. Ever since he'd first laid eyes on him, Mike had been transfixed. There was a weird blend of delicacy and strength in Truman that appealed to Mike, that made him want to touch, to caress, to kiss. The harder he tried to force these longings away, the more they persisted. It was like trying to get rid of them actually made them stronger. Truman was there with him when he woke in the morning, when he fell asleep at night. He'd even avoided riding the bus to school, just so he wouldn't see him. He reasoned that if he didn't see him, he could pretend Truman didn't exist. It didn't work. Nothing did. He was hopelessly attracted.

And tonight, picking him up off the side of the road like some forgotten treasure, Mike had gone against all his good intentions. But again, he couldn't resist. And he'd heard somewhere that what we resist persists. The idea of being alone with him in his house was too much to bear, though. Mike wasn't ready for it. He didn't know if he could trust himself. Didn't know if he was ready to let this secret side of himself, at least so far in this new place, out.

Speeding away from the house like something guilty and ashamed, Mike wanted to slap himself, scream at himself. He knew he was the one who'd made plans with Truman. Idiot move! What would Truman think when he didn't show? He'd probably hate him.

And maybe that's for the best.

Mike told himself he was doing the right thing. What good could come from hanging out with a boy like Truman Reid? The kid was, like, the poster child for the LGBT community, and who the hell needed that? Especially when you're trying to establish a reputation for yourself in a new place? Mike scoffed, shaking his head.

He drove up to Jackman Park, at the crest of the biggest hill in town. The park had been there for centuries, and its serpentine road and trails wound up and down through copses of maple, black walnut, paw-paw, mulberry, and buckeye trees. In the dark of night, as it was now, the place could be kind of creepy, Mike had learned. It wasn't hard to imagine a werewolf or serial killer lurking within the bushes' deep shadows. But creepy also meant deserted, and Mike, in his short time living in this little godforsaken town, had learned it was a good place to come and think, even if those thoughts might occasionally be interrupted by the hooting of an owl or a rustle in the bushes as some-thing unidentified moved on through.

Now the truck bounced over potholes in the cin-der block parking lot at the park's entrance just off Park Boulevard, Summitville's only street with real mansions. He turned off the ignition and sat, not think-ing and just listening to the *tick-tick-tick* of the over-worked engine as it died down into silence.

After it was quiet for a minute or two, Mike grabbed the keys from the ignition and then got out of the truck. The air smelled good, clean, and if he closed his eyes, he could imagine he was back in Washington State. He thought he'd live in the Pacific Northwest forever! How rude to rip him away from school when he was just about to go into his senior year. He'd had a life there. People knew him for his true self.

Moving here, it was like the real Mike had van-ished. He didn't know who he was anymore.

But his parents had wanted to come back, clear across the country to Nowheresville, eastern Ohio. Mike shook his head. *Why?*

He wandered down a grassy slope. He discovered an old fence post on which to perch and pulled out the can of Budweiser he'd stolen from his pop's stash. It was still cold, although the can was damp with condensation. He pulled the tab, lifted the can to his lips, and took a long swallow.

The beer tasted good. He'd been drinking a lot of Pop's beer lately, so much that he was pretty sure he'd be called out soon on the missing cans.

But the beer was a kind of comfort, putting a haze over things like how alone he felt these days, how he missed the life he'd made for himself back in Shoreline. He felt justified in grabbing a little oblivion for himself.

He belched and stared up at the stars. The night was clear, and he was able to make out some of the constellations. Back when times were good, when they were a family, his dad had shown him where the Big and Little Dippers were. The stars made him long not only for Shoreline but also for his family. Sure, his ma and pop were still around, but what they were, the family—that was pretty much gone.

Stop thinking about this crap. It doesn't change a thing.

He let himself slide back in time and found himself once more on Richmond Beach on Puget Sound, staring up at the same stars. *These ones here, they couldn't be the same, could they, though? They don't seem to shine as brightly, twinkle as fiercely as the ones back home. Stop it now. That place over there to the west, all the way across the country? That's not home anymore. You gotta face reality—this is home now, whether you like it or not.*

Mike drained the beer and crushed the empty can. He briefly considered chucking the can into the woods not three feet away from where he sat, but that wasn't him. He'd save it, take it back to the truck with him, at the very least find a garbage can, if not a recycling bin.

The air had a crispness to it that Mike didn't associate with home, er, Shoreline. Crispness? Hell, it was downright cold! Mike shivered, rubbing the arms of his jean jacket, wishing he'd stolen two beers instead of just the one.

Why did you do it? Why did you make plans with the kid and then run out on them—and him? Mike hopped down from the fence post and began pacing the grass bordering the woods. He still hadn't summoned up the courage to go into the woods after dark, although his rational mind told him they'd be no different than they were during the day, when there was nothing Mike liked better than aimlessly wandering those same trails. The trees formed a cover that made it almost dusky-dark, the trail dappled here and there with patches of warm golden light.

He didn't want to face the answers to his self-imposed questions. He'd noticed Truman Reid the first day of school when Mike had gotten on the bus. Their eyes had met for only the briefest of moments, but there had been something there, some connection. Understanding, maybe? Recognition? Attraction? *Hey, you're alone now. You can admit it.*

Mike let out a long and low sigh. Recognition of what? Like to like?

He snorted. Put Truman and him in a room together and no one would see any similarities save for the fact that they were both male, and even that part was questionable when it came to Truman. *Now, now, that's not nice.* But objectively speaking, it was true—they were so different they might as well be from separate planets, universes even. Truman couldn't begin to hope to hide from the world who he really was. And Mike? He was so deeply hidden no one would guess who he really was.

Mike glanced up at the star-crowded night sky again. *Silly. The stars shine just as brightly here.*

Mike got back in the truck and rolled up his window because he'd begun to shiver. He wasn't quite ready to go home yet. If the house he shared with his mom could even be called home. The fuckin' two-bedroom, one-bath shithole was fully furnished with someone else's broken-down furniture. There was nothing there that felt familiar, that gave Mike any comfort, made him feel any sense of *home*. Add in that his mom was hardly ever there—she'd sure learned to make friends fast, all of them male—and Mike didn't wonder for long why he wanted to spend so little time there.

Much as he tried to steer his mind away from him, all Mike could think of was Truman. How knowing him just wasn't a good idea. But good idea or not, Mike couldn't keep thoughts of the blond kid out of his head. He was small but solid. There was a fierceness to him that Mike liked, admired even. *Truman* wasn't hiding who he was.

And you're not either, Mike told himself. *You're just being selective about who you share yourself with. Nothing wrong with that. This is a small town. You've heard how the guys talk about Truman behind his back.* Mike felt a hot rush of shame wash over him as he remembered, just the other day in woodshop, how Art Hoyle had said something about how Truman Reid loved a hot drill bit in his mouth, how he couldn't resist getting "drilled" just like his mom, only Truman was a lot tighter. The guys gathered around had laughed as though Art was some kind of Louis CK, come right here to eastern Ohio.

And Mike had laughed too, right along with the other guys.

And hated himself for it.

He should have stood up for Truman.

And what, expose myself? This is why, Mike thought, he was better off keeping his distance from the big sissy. Guilt by association.

Still, Mike touched himself through his jeans, rubbing as he thought of touching Truman's silky blond hair, of the feel of those full lips on his own….

It was hopeless.

Mike opened his pants. With Truman's smiling face across from him in the dark doing the same thing, he finished himself off.

And then Mike drove back to the house in which he lived with the woman he called Mother.

CHAPTER 11

"Everything's changed," Truman said softly into the phone. Alicia, withholding judgment and being supportive, Truman guessed, listened with none of her usual sass. For a moment, it even seemed the never-without-a-snarky-comment Alicia was speechless. Silence hung between them for perhaps longer than it ever had.

He sat outside the school auditorium, on a bench next to the big trophy case, arms wrapped around himself for warmth. It was a week and a half into October, and Summitville High's production of *Harvey* was coming along relatively smoothly. The sets—black-and-white line drawings on big painted boards cut to resemble things like furniture, doorways, and window frames—were almost complete. The lighting had been set up, with everything in place well ahead of opening night. Most of the cast, save for one notable exception, had made amazing strides in memorizing lines.

Rehearsal was due to start in twenty minutes, and Truman figured he could count on this time to be alone with his thoughts—and with Alicia. He needed to talk to *someone*, and she was, as she reminded him when he first called after not having spoken in a week or more, his BFF and he should never forget it.

"What's wrong?" Alicia finally asked.

"I don't know. It's just like nobody notices me anymore." He was thinking mainly of his chief heart-ache—Mike. Since the night he'd driven Truman home and then stood him up, he'd been moody and distant, not saying anything at all to Truman. Even when, once, Truman had in desperation asked Mike what happened that night, the guy had only shrugged and mumbled something about how their plans had never been definite. Truman had wanted to argue, wanted to tell Mike he'd hurt him, made him feel like a fool, but he was fairly certain Mike would have told him that none of those things meant any skin off his ass. So Truman let him walk away—maybe forever.

There was nothing, only an empty ache where once hope had lived.

Truman tried not to take Mike's morose silence personally. That was easy to do, since the guy barely opened his mouth to speak to anyone else, even his fellow stage-crew members. He followed directions. He worked hard. He kept his head down and, most of the time, eyes averted. And when rehearsal was over, he was simply gone, as though he'd never been there in the first place. He was like a hunky ghost.

Personal or not, Truman couldn't help but wonder if he hightailed it out of there to avoid Truman. Or was he flattering himself in thinking he mattered that much to Mike? Maybe the simple truth was that Mike just wanted to get home. Or he had some girl to meet at one of the make-out spots along the Ohio River.

Truman went on, fearing he was whining but needing to vent. "At first it was like I was on equal footing with Mr. Wolcott as director of the play, but now it seems like he's taken over. He's used *all* my ideas for the set, for how things should be lit, for what everyone in the cast should wear, but now that it's down to the nitty-gritty and the performances are getting, you know, nuanced, it's all him. I just sit like a lump next to him, keeping time."

"Well, you're the prettiest lump I know," Alicia said. "And pretty is as pretty does."

"Thanks." Truman looked around the empty lobby. Still no one had shown up. It was getting dark earlier and earlier these days. Already the sky outside was a deep shade of violet, which Truman knew would last only for a moment or two before full dark descended. He dreaded the long days of winter, when they'd go to school in the dark and come home in dusky twilight. It was like they didn't have as much time, even though there were still twenty-four hours in each day.

Alicia said, "Truman, it sounds like you *have* been a big influence on how this play will turn out. To me it seems like you're not giving yourself enough credit for all your work. But that's par for the course for my little buddy." Alicia paused. "We need to get together soon. Have a girl's night out. Or in."

"Put on our cha-cha heels, play some records," Truman said, laughing. "Listen, hon, I gotta go." Truman could see Mr. Wolcott approaching the heavy glass front doors of the field house. He was wearing a navy peacoat and a red muffler, and if he wasn't a teacher, Truman would have flirted outrageously with him.

"Truman!" he called when he got inside, stamping the snow that had just started coming down off his boots onto the black rubber mats just inside the front doors. "I'm glad you're here early," Mr. Wolcott spoke as he walked closer. "There's something I want to talk to you about."

He sat on the bench next to Truman, and Truman could smell something woodsy on him. Sandalwood, maybe?

Mr. Wolcott unbuttoned his coat and removed the muffler. He side-eyed Truman, smiling. There was a high blush to his cheeks from the cold outside that only served to make him sexier. Mr. Bernard was a lucky man, having *this* to curl up next to every night in bed. Almost involuntarily, Truman's gaze went down to Mr. Wolcott's left hand, where a black wedding band adorned his third finger. The reminder had its intended purpose, in that it jolted Truman back to respectable reality.

"Oh?" Truman asked. "I didn't think there was much left to talk about. It seems like all we need to do is keep things on track. This train is rolling effortlessly into the station."

"Truman, you're ignoring the obvious."

Truman knew immediately to what he referred. Stacy. He hadn't seen her since the night she had crept into his bedroom and shared her secret with him. He knew that Patsy had gone, the very afternoon following that night, to see Stacy's aunt with her, to help her break the news. According to Patsy, the aunt was a basket case, far too old to understand how to talk to a young girl in trouble, and far too Catholic to show even one iota of compassion. Patsy said she all but had to pull the aunt off Stacy. Before she did, the aunt had slapped the poor girl's face a couple of times and, according to script, called her a *puttana* or "whore."

Patsy had tried to intervene, suggesting that Stacy could come and stay with them, even though they could ill afford it in terms of space or money, but the aunt would not be dissuaded—Stacy needed to be sent away. There was a Catholic girls' home for unwed mothers just outside nearby Youngstown, and it was there Aunt Sus insisted her great-niece go to wait out her gestation and then, in her aunt's words, to give up the baby to "decent" people.

Truman didn't even think such places existed anymore. And if they did, he guessed they were little more than prisons.

"Stacy. I know," Truman said, thinking for a moment of her wide brown eyes, her innocent smile. He hoped they were treating her okay in that home…. "You haven't found a replacement yet? Doesn't somebody want that role? It's a juicy part!"

"Well, I kind of do have a replacement in mind." Mr. Wolcott eyed Truman. Truman grinned and scratched the back of his neck.

Ever since Stacy's disappearance from town, Truman had been reading her lines to keep rehearsals moving. He had them all memorized now. "You do?"

"I do." And before he could get the absolutely in-sane idea out of his mouth, Truman knew he needed to stop what Mr. Wolcott wanted to propose.

Truman held up a hand. "Don't even go there."

"Truman. Why not? I can't think of a more per-fect solution."

"Oh Lord, Mr. Wolcott, don't you think I have enough trouble heaped on my shoulders without *that*?" Truman stared down hard at the floor, feeling the pan-ic rising in him like some winged thing, trapped, with no escape. "You put me up on stage as a girl—no, a young lady—and I'll be not only the laughingstock of the school, but also of this whole town. Do you hate me that much?"

And yet the idea of donning the dotted-swiss dress, black and purple, he'd found for the character in a thrift store, and the wide-brimmed straw hat he'd swiped from Patsy's closet, had a certain appeal. Ap-peal that was, paradoxically, causing a wave of panic so severe to rise within him he feared hyperventilat-ing. *All I need is a pair of white lace gloves and some white kitten heels....*

Mr. Wolcott smiled, his gaze taking Truman in and looking, Truman thought, a little sad. "You don't really think I hate you, Tru, do you? After all we've been through?"

Truman could see the fear on Mr. Wolcott's face and thought if he answered his question in the affir-mative, he'd just about break the poor teacher's heart.

"I like to think of myself as your greatest cham-pion around here. Dane and me." Mr. Wolcott stared ahead, his voice soft but steady.

Truman thought of his freshman year, when things had gone so horribly wrong he'd literally wanted to throw his life away by leaping from the school's roof, and how both Mr. Wolcott and Mr. Bernard had stepped up to the plate, counseling him and letting him know life was worth living. No, more than that, that life was worth living on Truman's *own* terms. That there was nothing wrong with who he was, and he didn't need to change a thing simply to suit a sometimes cruel and often misunderstanding world sitting in judgment, a world where men were men and women were women and woe be it to anyone who dared to mess with those definitions.

Uncharacteristically and perhaps a little boldly, Truman reached out and took one of Mr. Wolcott's hands in his own and squeezed it. "Of course you don't hate me. You guys saved my life. You showed me it was okay to be me, no matter how whack *me* turned out to be." Truman gave him a small, sad smile. "I love you—and Mr. Dane—for that. I always will." Truman had to look away, the rawness of his admission pretty much ripping his heart open.

When he looked back, Mr. Wolcott stared at him with something that, to Truman, looked an awful lot like admiration in his eyes. "You may not realize it," he told Truman, "But you are one of the bravest men I know. I look up to you."

Truman laughed. Brave? Him? Truman associated bravery with butch, macho types. People like cops and cowboys, construction workers straddling beams thirty stories above some hazy cityscape. And yet…. And yet, the idea that he was brave caught Truman up short because he suddenly felt, deep within, the truth of it.

He saw himself looking into a mirror, mouthing the words, "I am brave." And he wasn't laughing.

Anybody can blend in with the crowd. It's what most folks do. It's where they're comfortable. In truth Truman envied them. But on the other hand, it did take a kind of courage to be different, to stand out starkly from everyone else. Truman knew he had little choice in the matter, but that didn't make him any less brave.

Still, this thing Mr. Wolcott was about to propose…. It was outrageous! He hadn't really even said the words yet, but Truman was 99.9 percent certain he was going to ask him to take on the role of Myrtle Mae Simmons. Truman had to admit he already had over the past several weeks. Even though he only sat on the side of the stage in a folding chair and pretended to read from the script—he had every one of Myrtle Mae's lines memorized and had done so from so early on; they were now second nature, a hybrid of himself and this rather silly and naïve young woman mooning over some sort of insane asylum orderly—he had let himself become *her*. He'd added in a little laugh that he thought suited her, sort of a musical titter. He had a way of talking that was high and a little breathless, sort of like how Marilyn Monroe spoke in those old movies Truman loved watching on rainy afternoons.

"Truman. I know it seems crazy, but when you think about it, it's the only logical choice. You're already playing her. And it's a stellar performance, I might add."

"Logical?" Truman snorted, imagining himself sashaying around on stage in a dress and picture hat.

He could hear the laughter now, and it made him sick to his stomach. It made him break out in a cold sweat. Even though in reality, he'd probably be blind to the audience when he was on stage on account of the lights, he could see them in his mind's eye, clutching their bellies, breathless with laughter.

The idea was terrifying.

And yet he wanted it. In a strange way, he knew he could play the hell out of the part and do it way better than anyone else could have, even Stacy. In fact, he'd wondered how he'd feel when Mr. Wolcott did find a replacement for Stacy and Truman would have to give up the part. He knew he'd be jealous of whatever female classmate got the role. He also knew how silly such jealousy would be, because any other alternative, i.e. Truman as Myrtle Mae, was just impossible.

"Yes. Logical. You know the lines. You know the blocking. And come on, I've listened to you. You've got the part down pat. You're not just reading lines to keep the flow of the play moving; you're *becoming* her, inhabiting her. It's been beautiful to watch, Truman. And that's okay. It's what *acting* is all about. It doesn't make you 'less than' anything if that's what you're thinking, beating yourself up about. Think of Dustin Hoffman in *Tootsie*, or John Travolta in *Hairspray*, or Robin Williams as Mrs. Doubtfire." Mr. Wolcott touched Truman's cheek lightly, forcing Truman to look at him. "You want me to go on?" He smiled. "I have more examples."

"Nah. You don't need to. Tyler Perry as Madea, and that classic pairing, Jack Lemmon and Tony Curtis in *Some Like It Hot*. Although you could argue those last two weren't really playing women. Well, none of them *really* were. They were just guys in drag."

Mr. Wolcott mussed up Truman's hair, and Truman had to fight an urge to right it.

Mr. Wolcott said, with great admiration in his voice, "Your knowledge amazes me. You're probably the only kid in school who can keep up with me on pop culture. And you're deliberately missing my point." He looked away for a moment and then back. "So? What do you think?"

Truman wasn't aware, until this very moment, of the power of a single idea to both terrify and excite at the same time. "I don't know," he whispered. Although he did. Yes, he did. From the top of his head to the tips of his toes....

Before he could say any more, several of the cast came in, laughing, shoving, swearing. A gust of frigid air rode in with them. And Truman felt he'd been caught in a compromising position with Mr. Wolcott. By the way he rushed to his feet, a big stupid grin on his face, Truman knew Mr. Wolcott probably felt the same way.

"Hey, guys," Mr. Wolcott called, his voice bright and overly cheerful. "All set to go?" He moved away from Truman a bit as he headed toward the auditorium to switch on lights and begin the process of transforming a small-town high school stage into a stately old house and a "rest" home. He paused for a moment, looking back at Truman, who sat, clinging to the bench as if his ass were superglued to it.

"You coming? You're gonna do it, right?" Even though Mr. Wolcott only mouthed the words, Truman heard them in his head loud and clear. Mr. Wolcott nodded encouragingly.

In spite of his daring to wear makeup to school, in spite of his daring to dye his pale hair—or hanks of it—every color of the rainbow, and even in spite of his boldly and unabashedly donning some of Patsy's prettiest blouses for school, Truman felt his robin's heart just might fail at the thought of doing what Mr. Wolcott proposed.

No, really, he thought he might die.

He got up, and before Mr. Wolcott could smile with relief, Truman dashed into the closest restroom, which just by coincidence happened to be the girls' room. Ignoring Tammy Applegate, who was leaning against one of the sinks smoking a cigarette, Truman dashed into a stall and brought up the contents of his stomach in a dramatic, splattering fashion. He grunted on into the dry heaves, tears streaming down his face, his throat burning with acidic bile.

"Gross," Tammy remarked from outside the stall.

Heaving, Truman wiped his mouth with the back of a shaking hand. He slunk out of the stall, avoiding but feeling "Stretch's" stare on him.

"You okay, fella?" she asked on an exhalation of smoke.

But Truman didn't answer. He simply hurried from the restroom into the lobby, which he was relieved to find empty. If there had been anyone there, most especially Mr. Wolcott, he couldn't have done what every primal cell in his body told him to do—flee.

He dashed to the double glass doors and, holding his breath, pushed them open and ran off into the night. At that moment he felt a kinship to Stacy, certain he would never return.

WHEN HE got home, he found Patsy waiting, wrapped up in a big wool blanket, sitting on the steps of the front porch. Odd Thomas was curled up next to her, his head in her lap. Patsy idly played with one of his ears.

"What are you doing outside? You'll freeze that bony ass of yours off. I heard we're supposed to get snow tonight." Truman approached the porch. He couldn't think of a time when the sight of his mother was less welcome. He just wanted to get inside and into his room, where he could collapse on his bed and, yes, cry.

"Bony ass?" Patsy asked. "Anyway, Seth Wolcott called. He said you bolted out of rehearsal tonight. Just up and took off without a word. He wanted to know if you're okay."

Truman stood, shivering, in the dark. He didn't say a word.

"Are you?"

Odd raised his head, peered in his direction, then lay his head back down in Patsy's lap.

Truman toed some loose dirt. "I guess."

"Why'd you run away?"

"Can we talk about this later?" Truman tried to edge by her to get to the front door. "I'm so tired. I just want to crawl into bed and sleep forever."

But Patsy was having none of it. She grabbed on to one his calves and held fast. "Yeah. You're tired. But I didn't raise you to run out on people. He was worried. Tru, this isn't like you."

Truman looked down at Patsy's face. It was the very picture of determination. He knew that to fight her, to try to get away, would be an exercise in futility. He yanked his leg out of her grip. "Can we at least talk inside? It's freezing out here." Almost as though the universe wanted to prove his point, several snowflakes fluttered down.

Patsy stood. Wordlessly, they watched as Odd Thomas also got slowly to his feet, then descended the couple of steps into the yard and peed. He fairly trotted back. "I'll make us some cocoa," Truman said.

They went inside.

In the kitchen, Patsy slouched in one of the kitchen chairs while Truman busied himself making what they called cocoa—Nestlé's Quik stirred into a simmering pan of milk, bubbles just beginning to appear on the sides.

"We have baby marshmallows?" Truman poured the hot chocolate into mugs.

"No. And no Cool Whip either."

"Guess we'll have to make do." Truman set a mug before his mom before joining her at the table.

She sipped. "What happened tonight?"

Truman wasn't sure how—or even, really, what—to tell her. His first thought, unfair as it was, was that she'd laugh. That somehow his greatest champion and the person who loved him most in the world would laugh at him. It wasn't fair to her, and it was so off base that it was, well, laughable, but Truman couldn't help his fear, which he sensed came from a primitive place.

He started. "He wanted—" He couldn't continue. He lowered his face to his hands and cried.

Patsy was behind him, her hands on his shoulders, kneading. "C'mon, say the words—get it out. I know what he suggested. As a mom, I don't want to see you get hurt. As a person, though, I don't wanna see you ducking and hiding from challenges. You don't have to play this part, Tru, but you have to face that you handled things all wrong tonight. You can say no. And you can stick by your choice. Mr. Wolcott wouldn't fault you for that. And you know I'll support you, no matter what you wanna do."

Leave it to Patsy to speak the simple truth. Of course, she was right. He should have just marched right into the auditorium, pulled Mr. Wolcott aside, and told him he just wasn't gonna do it. Period. In fact, he could see himself doing it in his mind's eye. He could see the understanding—and the disappointment—on Mr. Wolcott's face. He knew he'd tell Truman it was okay. Even though it was last minute, they'd find someone.

Truman let that sink in. That his refusal would not be the end of the world. That the show would go on. That the cast, Mr. Wolcott, and everyone else associated with the play wouldn't hold it against Truman if he didn't want to make such a bold and daring move. They'd accept it graciously and move on.

But could *he*? Could he actually accept *not* playing that role? In a way, to not do what Mr. Wolcott wanted him to do felt very much like a betrayal. When he shoved his fear aside, Truman realized he'd be crushed if anyone else took over the part. It was his. It was him. He turned to look up at Patsy. "What do you think I should do?"

Patsy snorted. "When did you ever listen to me on that score?" She took her hands away from his shoulders and sat back down at their maple kitchen table. "I guess I'd answer that question with what I really believe—do what your heart tells you."

And a sudden thought intruded, jolting. *Mr. Wolcott could have recast that part a long time ago. He didn't because I was doing such a good job of it. Has this been his plan all along?*

Truman stared down at the varnished surface of the table. It had been here all his life; his high chair, once upon a time, had been pulled up to it. The legs were scratched, and one needed a matchbook under it to keep it level, but the table represented home to him. "That's so corny, Ma," Truman said, even though he knew, yes, in his heart, that she was right.

"Corny or not, one thing I've learned as I've become a wise old woman—" She chuckled. "—is that your heart, most of the time, is right."

Truman stood up from the table and grabbed his cup from it. "I'm gonna go to my room. Got some thinking to do."

"Okay. I'll be out here for a little while longer. Then I'm gonna do the crossword and turn in. I'm beat."

"No special visitor?" At the archway leading to the next room, Truman turned and significantly raised his eyebrows.

"Sweetie, it's not appropriate for boys to ask their mothers about things as delicate as their periods, for heaven's sakes." She took a gulp of hot chocolate, not looking at him.

"You know that's not what I meant. Is George coming over?"

Patsy shook her head. "He wanted to. But all I wanna do in that bed tonight is sleep… for hours and hours. I don't need some damn man keeping me from that."

"But things are good, right? Between you?"

She nodded.

"I told you I met his son, didn't I? Mike?"

"Maybe you mentioned it. I'm not sure. George says Mike's enrolled in the vocational school—wants to be a welder when he grows up or something. I assumed your two paths would never cross."

"He's on the stage crew for *Harvey*. Very good with his hands," Truman said and wished he knew more about that statement, despite Mike's silence.

He started toward his bedroom, and Patsy called, "Did he mention me?"

Truman paused, thinking. Should he tell her? He shook his head and shrugged, about to tell her she didn't come up in what little conversation they'd had, but instead he said, "Yeah. He told me his dad's nuts about you."

He turned to look at Patsy. She still had her face angled toward her cup, but she was smiling, and that made Truman feel good. "Good night, Mom."

"See you in the mornin'!" she said cheerfully. "You make sure you give Seth Wolcott a buzz or shoot him a text, let him know you're okay. Do it now."

"Yes, Mother." Truman went into his bedroom and closed the door behind him. He pulled his cell from his pocket, briefly fingering its face, considering. But in the end he tossed the phone on the bed.

He'd talk to Mr. Wolcott tomorrow.

And he knew exactly how to approach the conversation.

Smiling and chilled at the same time, Truman threw himself down on his back on the bed.

CHAPTER 12

MIKE FINISHED hammering the set's largest piece into place, a multicolumned flat that represented Chumley's Rest, where poor Elwood P. Dowd and his imaginary pooka/rabbit sidekick, Harvey, were supposed to be left. *Abandoned* was more like it, Mike thought. *Just because someone is a little different, people wanna shut 'em out.*

Mike leaned back on his haunches, looking up at the large black-and-white piece, proud of it and of his simple work on it—the painting, sawing, and hammering. It didn't look real but suggested the place in a kind of cool way.

He'd come in early to complete the piece. Most of the other set-building was done. The show was scheduled to go on in just two weeks. Mike had also come in early because he'd wanted to avoid the cast and his fellow stage-crew members. These days he just wasn't feeling sociable. Besides, it seemed that Tammy Applegate had developed a crush on him, and he felt like *Girl, you're barking up the wrong tree.* Still, even though he mostly ignored her, she'd follow him around like a puppy dog, always looking for ways to help. She smelled like an ashtray. Even if he *was* inclined toward her kind, that alone would stop him. His dad's secondhand smoke was enough for him to contend with.

And then there was Truman. Mike's heart hurt a little every time he saw him. He wanted to talk to him, to explain why he'd stood him up on that night not so long ago when it seemed like things just might be getting off the ground with the two of them.

But was there really an explanation? A good one? Mike wasn't sure himself why he'd blown Truman off—and not in a good way. He knew only his decision came from a deep place, one where shame and self-loathing grew.

Mike just couldn't see how knowing Truman could help him settle in and be accepted in this little backwater. He didn't need the shame and ridicule his interest would engender in this hateful place. He wished he could return to Washington. It seemed like people were more liberal there, more open-minded. Mike wasn't as afraid to be who he was.

He shut his eyes for just a moment, though, savoring the silence before all hell broke loose and all the other kids came trooping in. And when he did, Truman appeared there in the darkness behind Mike's eyelids. He smiled, and there was something both alluring and comforting in that smile. Mike wanted to look up to it, down on it, to see it next to him. Maybe on a pillow?

He wanted to touch that face, move it closer to his own. Closer....

He shook his head and opened his eyes. Tammy was just heading in, and Mike groaned inwardly.

"Hey, Stewart," she called cheerfully—she always used his last name—when she reached him. "You need some help with that?"

"It's done." *Can't you see that?* he wanted to add, but that would just be mean. From the smell of her, it appeared she'd just had her nicotine fix. "I think they need some help with the lights." Mike nodded toward Timmy Simms and Hal Obrecht, who were struggling to place a large spotlight on the grid above the stage.

"Sure," Tammy said, sounding both defeated and disappointed. Why did she care? Mike wondered. He'd offered her absolutely no encouragement.

He was sliding the piece he'd just finished into place on the stage when he noticed, behind him, all the laughter and talking among the cast and crew coming to an abrupt and sudden halt. Before he even looked, the hairs on his neck prickled as they rose up, and Mike felt a chill, the kind his grandma would ascribe to someone walking over his grave.

He turned slowly and was surprised to find his were not the only pair of eyes trained toward the back of the auditorium. No, the truth was everyone was looking toward the back.

Oh God. No.

There stood Truman, framed against the double oak doors. He was in full Myrtle Mae mode: belted black dress with tiny purple polka dots, white gloves, hat, and even heeled shoes. From as far away as the stage, Mike could see Truman's full makeup—lipstick, rouge, mascara, the whole nine yards.

Oh no, Truman. No.

Inside, Mike groaned. Outside, he knew he was staring, mouth open.

Someone whistled.

There was a catcall.

And through it all, Truman simply posed against those damn doors, one hand on his hip, the other on the door. It was as though someone had hit him with a spotlight. Mike noticed a lace hanky stuffed into the wrist of the left glove and rolled his eyes.

Mr. Wolcott was the first to speak. Mike expected admonishment or at least a reminder to Truman that dress rehearsal was still at least ten days away. *This just isn't right. Seriously, dude, what's wrong with you?*

Mike leaned back even farther, away from the stage proper. For some reason he couldn't readily explain to himself, he didn't want Truman to know he'd seen him.

Backstage, though, Mike could still hear.

And what Mr. Wolcott shouted back to Truman wasn't at all what he expected.

"Well, as I live and breathe! If it isn't Miss Myrtle Mae Simmons. In the flesh!" Laughter rippled through the auditorium, and Mike couldn't tell if it was mean-spirited and meant to ridicule or if it was good-natured.

Mike peeked out from the side of the stage, continuing to ensure he was hidden in the shadows.

Truman was sashaying—and that was the only word for it—down the center aisle, a big smile on his face, one hand, the one with the hanky, aloft, the other firmly on his hip. A couple of the kids applauded as he went by. From Truman's smile, he must have interpreted the laughter as benign, because he looked almost—what was the right word?—*proud* of himself.

Mike shook his head. The display turned his stomach.

Why would he do that? Does he want to get bashed?

He jumped at a light touch on his shoulder. He turned to see Tammy standing next to him, also looking out as Truman made his entrance. "Can you believe that freak?" she whispered to Mike, leaning close. The smell of cigarettes on her was almost overpowering.

Mike would have thought he'd agree with her assessment; after all, he was thinking practically the same thing. It was as though she'd yanked the question from his own tortured mind. And yet he felt this odd need rising up, not to agree with her, but to defend Truman.

"You're the freak," Mike spat out at her. "Get away from me."

She gasped and took a step back, almost as though he'd pushed her. Even in the dim light, Tammy's dark eyes shone. Her lower lip quivered just the tiniest bit.

And Mike felt like a complete and utter ass.

He reached a hand out to her. "Hey, man, I'm sorry…."

She just shook her head and ran in the opposite direction. In a couple of seconds, Mike heard the slam of the stage door.

Great. She's probably outside bawling her eyes out. You really know how to treat a person. Mike thought he should go after her but then reconsidered.

She was the one who started things—by calling Truman a freak.

What? Did she think she had found a sympathetic ear with Mike? That he was a bigot, a homophobe too? That he'd agree with her assessment? That they'd laugh about their shared hatred for the *freak* and then maybe share a smoke outside?

He turned and watched as the cast assembled around Truman—kind of an amazing thing. It was as though they were all taking their lead from the very friendly and appreciative Mr. Wolcott. One guy even patted Truman's back.

Breathless and a little sick to his stomach, Mike watched as the cast, as one, mounted the stage, ready for rehearsal.

Mike couldn't stand it. He bolted for the stage door.

Outside, the night air was cold, brisk. Just the slap in the face Mike needed.

Tammy leaned against Mike's pickup, smoking a cigarette. When she spied Mike, she started away.

"Hey, wait!" he called.

She stopped, keeping her back turned.

Mike was at a crossroads. One part of him was telling him to ask her if she could spare a smoke. Another told him to simply ignore the bigot. *Get in your truck and head up to the park, where you can think.*

He was leaning toward heading into the cool and shadowy embrace of the park when Tammy spoke. "What do you want?"

And Mike froze. What *did* he want?

He walked toward her. He got close enough to place one hand on her shoulder. She shrugged it off, flinging her cigarette to the ground. The smoke she exhaled burned Mike's eyes. He said again, very softly, "I'm sorry. I shouldn't have said that."

She turned to him, and the gratitude in her eyes shone out. A small smile turned up the corners of her lips. "Thanks."

Mike nodded. "Nobody should be called a freak," he said pointedly. "Everyone deserves respect."

The smile withered from her face.

Mike couldn't help himself. He went on. "He's not a freak, you know. He's different. That's all. You don't score points with me by making fun of other people or sitting in judgment."

She stared at him for only a moment. Then she directed her gaze downward, toward the ground. She moved one foot back and forth on the asphalt.

Finally, she looked back up at him. Mike hoped she'd maybe gotten a glimmer of understanding. But when she spoke, her words came out hard. "What? Are you sweet on him or something? I'm sure, if you want him to, he'll suck your dick. I heard he gives real good hummers."

"You need help." Mike turned from her mean face, her small eyes, and the grin she'd managed to plaster on, as though her comment somehow gave her an advantage.

He hopped inside and started the truck up much too hard. The engine roared and backfired.

As he drove away, he could see Tammy Applegate holding her sides and laughing at him. And he had a weird thought, not about himself, but about Truman.

He couldn't imagine what it must be like to live in Truman's world, day after day. He shut the thought out and simply drove through the night.

THE PARK was down the hill from the school, only a mile or so away. He needed the solitude he knew he'd find there among the shadows and the whispering sandpaper leaves of autumn. He wished he had a beer.

But the park wasn't empty. There was one other car parked there, an old red Mustang, and as Mike neared it, he saw someone in the driver's seat, just a black silhouette, really. He didn't think anything of it, and wouldn't have, but almost as soon as he noticed someone in the car, a head popped up from the driver's lap.

Even though it was very dark, Mike could tell it was two guys. He'd heard rumors—guys at school making fun, really—that the park was a cruising spot. As Art Hoyle put it, "It's where fags find other fags to suck cock and stuff. Lollipop Park, they call it!" Art's words had caused a queasy desire to rise up within Mike, even as he laughed it up with the other guys in woodshop class.

Art's dubious "recommendation" was one of the reasons Mike had started coming to the park at night. Hey, he was a teenage boy, and his hormones held sway over common sense.

Yet he'd never seen any evidence of cruising in the many nights he'd spent beyond the park's entrance fieldstone arches.

Until tonight.

Apparently, the rumors had some truth to back them up. Mike was tempted to shine his headlights in the car but knew how mean that would be, how disrespectful. He understood how he could send these dudes into panic mode, even though what they were doing was, well, kind of sick, even if Mike did have half a hard-on.

He parked as far away in the parking lot as he could from the Mustang, hoping, in a way, he hadn't ruined the encounter. What was the harm, anyway? There was no one else around—save for him. And he couldn't stop the thought that rose up, almost unbidden, yet powerful. *Maybe when that one guy shoots his load, I could cut in and get a little somethin' myself. God knows I could use it. I haven't had a mouth on my—* Mike's thought drifted back to Shoreline and to Aubry, his boyfriend back there. Aubry was a little guy, like Truman, but mixed race. His dark red hair clung tight to his skull, and right now Mike was imagining his hand on that coarse yet velvety-soft head as Aubry went down on him. It was magic. And Aubry would always let Mike come in his mouth because, as he said, he trusted him. And the trust was deserved. Aubry was Mike's first. First guy, anyway. He'd gone through the motions with a couple of girls at school, but he never found any real satisfaction. Whenever those clumsy and awkward encounters were over, Mike always felt like he'd passed some sort of test rather than feeling grateful or satisfied.

But Aubry, with his tight little body like Truman's, his green eyes full of mischief, and a sexual appetite that not only matched Mike's but exceeded it, was a revelation. Aubry taught him maybe not what love was, but that two guys together didn't have to be a shameful, dirty thing. It could be fun. A source of joy.

Mike undid the top button of his jeans and unzipped. He pulled out his dick, rock hard, through the fly of his plaid boxers and stroked himself. As he got more into it, he spat in his hand to make it slide more easily up and down the shaft, remembering Aubry and his smooth, almost hairless body, his uncut dick that curved to one side.

It was weird, though. Thoughts of Aubry morphed into thoughts of Truman. Truman naked. Truman going down on Mike. Mike, going down on Truman. In his mind's eye, Mike saw the alabaster smoothness of Truman's chest and torso and imagined his dick rising up from a thatch of wheat-colored pubic hair. He visualized the crack of Truman's ass as he got on all fours on a bed in some semidark room, looking back to Mike, inviting. Or perhaps Truman would be on his back, legs drawn up near his shoulders, with a look that was almost pleading.

Mike, breath quickening, was getting very close when he heard, dimly, the *thunk* of a car door slamming. He snatched his hand away from his dick as though someone had shined a flashlight on him and rapped on the window. *Caught.*

He looked to his right and saw someone emerge from the Mustang. An older guy, maybe his dad's age, stood near the passenger side of the car, zipping up. He had on a beat-up windbreaker and jeans. His hair was in a buzz cut, and he had a bit of a belly. He looked toward the truck, Mike thought guiltily, and then away. Mike slid down a little on his seat, not sure if the guy could see him.

He watched as the man lit a cigarette, exhaled, blowing a cloud of blue-gray smoke toward the star-studded sky. He seemed to look toward Mike once more. Then he started away from the car, toward the park entrance.

Mike sat for a few minutes, watching until the guy disappeared from view in Mike's rearview mirror.

And then Mike hazarded a glance toward the Mustang. He could tell, from the difference in the darkness, that the driver had rolled his window down. A hand, ghostly white, hung just outside the car.

And the hand was beckoning. *Come here*, it seemed to be saying.

Mike stared down at his dick, still standing at full attention, and was tempted. But he also felt paralyzed.

Really, dude, would you actually do something like that? What if a cop came by? What if the guy's some psycho?

Mike wasn't sure how to answer his own doubts and fears. Part of him felt almost sick to his stomach—with desire. That part was telling him to just hop out of the truck, walk over there, get what the other guy had just gotten. It'd be a relief....

Mike craned his neck a bit, leaning toward the passenger window. He cranked it down so he could see better.

A face neared the open window of the Mustang. Part of Mike hoped it would be the face of a creep— hideous, covered in sores, leering and toothless, with perhaps a line of drool leaking out of the corner of the guy's mouth. The image almost made him laugh.

He knew why he wanted the guy to be ugly. To make it easy to put his hands on the key, still in the ignition, start the truck up, and get the hell out of there.

But the guy wasn't ugly.

At least not from what he could tell from his admittedly compromised vantage point. One thing he was sure of—he didn't recognize him. Like his friend who'd just emerged from the passenger side only minutes ago, he was an older dude. It was difficult to say how much older, but at least forty. Mike could tell that much from the guy's dark but thinning hair, the glasses perched on his nose.

He motioned again for Mike to approach. A glimmer of a smile flitted across pale features.

Go ahead, a voice inside whispered seductively in Mike's ear.

And he had one hand on his key ring, poised between wanting to snatch the key out or giving it a turn to start the engine.

His eyes had adjusted much more to the dark as he sat here, and he watched in dumbfounded surprise as the guy raised his hips up from the seat. His dick, erect, came into view.

Mike tried to swallow, but his mouth was dry. He could actually hear the blood pounding in his ears.

The guy stroked his dick.

Mike's hand drifted off the key ring and down to his own cock. With only the slightest touch, he began spurting, covering his red Ohio State T-shirt with his seed.

He sat there watching his come pump out, as though the orgasm was happening to someone else. He felt a very strange combination of pleasure, release, guilt, and shame.

He waited until he was finished, then looked over again. The guy had gotten out of his car and leaned against it. His pants were open.

God, Mike thought, *could that be me someday?* He shook his head. His hands trembled as he groped around in the glove compartment for a tissue or rag to clean

himself up with. He found some napkins from McDon-
ald's and began the task, trying to ignore the guy.

Mike wanted to yell at him, to call him a freak.
But he said nothing. With a shaking hand, he started the car up and gave the engine too much gas. He
pulled out of his spot in a hurry, kicking up gravel and
dust.

And for the second time that night, he looked in
his rearview mirror to see someone laughing at him.

CHAPTER 13

ONCE AGAIN, Truman found himself walking home alone. He was in a jubilant mood. He'd met Mr. Wolcott's challenge head-on, "becoming" Myrtle Mae for that night's rehearsal. He'd been petrified as he changed in the restroom before, putting on the dress, stockings, and heels with shaking hands, questioning his own sanity, wondering if he was only making things worse for himself.

You should know better snaked through his thoughts more than once.

He was able to quell the trembling in his limbs enough to apply the makeup very successfully. When he stepped back and stared at himself in the mirror, Truman Reid did not gaze back, but a young lady of a certain social position did, a very pretty and believable one. He knew he'd need to get his hands on a wig at some point, but the white straw picture hat worked just fine for tonight.

When he went into the auditorium, he was afraid he'd pass out from fear, that his knees would simply buckle beneath him and he'd go facedown onto the linoleum floor.

He was afraid of a lot of things—that he'd be laughed out of the space. That there would be jeers and finger-pointing. That all the old bullying behavior would rise up once more, worse than ever. That there would be no taking back the plunge he was about to make.

Before he opened the doors, he was almost breathless with terror.

And yet he was determined to see things through.

One thing he'd learned as a studier of stagecraft was that they "didn't have to see you sweat." In other words, he knew he could go through the motions of whatever he wanted to project and could effectively hide his nerves, no matter how tied up in knots his gut was.

So he strode inside and struck a pose, praying for a good outcome. Patsy liked the old cliché *In for a penny, in for a pound*. Truman was never sure what she meant by it.

Until tonight.

He was prepared to be a laughingstock at best, to be the object of hatred and scorn at worst.

But the kids surprised him. Maybe it was because Mr. Wolcott pointed them in the right direction with his cheery call, "Well, as I live and breathe! If it isn't Miss Myrtle Mae Simmons. In the flesh!" But everyone, from what Truman could gauge, got what he was doing and were actually kind of tickled by it. And not in a bad way....

Had he crossed some bridge into a parallel universe where people simply accepted others at face value?

Were the kids, his castmates and classmates, simply too stunned to bring out their arsenal of teasing?

Or did they accept him? Not as Truman, but as the character he was bringing to life... as Mr. Wolcott said they might?

Truman decided he could go with any one of the scenarios coursing through his somewhat addled brain, but why not *choose* the one that made him happiest?

So he did. And his sashay down the center aisle was sheer feminine perfection.

He was not Truman Reid, he told himself as he met the eyes of his peers, but Myrtle Mae Simmons. And if that's what he believed, then so would everyone else.

Rehearsal went better than it ever had, now that a "real" Myrtle Mae was in place. The acceptance continued through both acts they rehearsed that night. Oh sure, there were a few whispers and giggles from the stage crew, but overall, Truman couldn't have asked for a better reception.

He felt a momentary sense of sadness when he thought of Stacy and how her misfortune had gotten him this part. He wondered how she was doing and wished, for the thousandth time, that she'd be in touch. Even a text would have been nice.

He looked for Mike to see what his reaction might be. But it appeared he'd left before Truman even made his entrance. And Truman, despite his glow of

self-acceptance, felt a measure of relief at Mike's not
being there. And a small measure of worry too. Had he
left because he'd seen Truman—and was disgusted?

Truman told himself he couldn't allow such
thinking, not if he wanted to continue to ride the high
of his performance. He'd been good. And he even
thought he'd made everyone around him a little better
too, as they reacted to his performance and not just
lines called from offstage. He'd transformed himself,
disappearing totally into his character. Wasn't that the
goal to which all actors aspired?

And now, as he neared the foot of the hill, Truman
realized he was smiling.

Right at the bottom of the parkway, there was an
old gas station that had been out of business for just
about as long as Truman could remember. The pumps
were gone but the ghost of the station remained, the
big windows long ago boarded up. White paint peeled
from its exterior. The lot it sat on was choked with
weeds coming up through broken concrete. Ghosts
of mechanics, Truman thought fancifully, worked on
engine parts inside, clad in grease-stained coveralls,
heavy metal music accompanying the sounds of drills
and the hydraulic lift.

Truman was surprised to see a pickup truck
parked in the lot.

He was even more surprised to see Mike, leaning
against the driver's side door, arms crossed over his
broad chest. When he saw Truman, he nodded.

Truman nodded back, both glad and a little ticked
at himself for being relieved he wore only a pair of
beat-up jeans, a Scooby-Doo T-shirt, and a red hoodie.

He'd even removed all the makeup in the boys' room before heading for home.

"I thought you might come along this way, if I only waited long enough," Mike said.

Truman wasn't sure how to take the statement. From his stance and expression, he couldn't feel confident that Mike was happy to see him. "Well, they say all good things come to those who wait." Truman, heart in his throat, ventured closer to Mike. When he was a foot or so away, he asked, "C'mon now. Were you really waiting for me?"

"I really was." Mike's voice was gruff, all gravel, sandpaper, and velvet. Truman knew it wasn't the gust of cold wind blowing off the Ohio River a few blocks over that made him shiver.

Truman cocked his head. "Why?"

Mike laughed. "Why was I waiting for you?"

"Uh-huh." Because, really, Truman couldn't imagine. The guy had stood him up and ignored him so totally he'd made Truman feel invisible for the past several weeks. He had to bite his tongue to not put these thoughts into words. The moment, right now, between them seemed charged with a kind of electricity Truman failed to understand, let alone describe.

Mike stared at him for a long time, and Truman felt he was being appraised. Instead of making him feel awkward and scrutinized, though, Mike's gaze made him feel appreciated.

Wishful think much, Tru?

"What? You don't believe you're worth waiting for? Because I have news for you, buddy—" And here, Mike gently poked Truman's chest. "You are."

Was this really happening? Truman wondered. *Here I was, just coming down the hill, pretty as you please, headed for home, some leftovers, homework, and maybe, if I could stay awake long enough, a little Chelsea Handler on Netflix.*

And then, bam, my Prince Charming shows up.

Truman smiled, knowing his grin was coming out sheepish, embarrassed, awkward, all those awful things a person doesn't want when what he really needs is to appear cool. He nodded and said, his voice barely above a whisper, "Thanks."

"I wanted to pick you up at the school, but my timing was off. So I came here and waited...."

"I'm glad."

"I know it's only half a mile or so to your place, but do you want a ride?"

Truman again questioned if this was a dream, if he'd awaken with the sun streaming in his bedroom window, Odd Thomas's smelly breath in his face.

"Yeah, that'd be cool." Truman grinned. "No skin off my ass."

Mike side-eyed him. "You makin' fun of me?"

Truman laughed, grateful Mike had gotten the reference. "Sweetie, I've cornered the market on being made fun of." Truman poked his own chest. "Me." He shook his head. "Not looking for pity, but I think I can safely claim that no one has been teased, taunted, and bullied more than yours truly... right here." Truman smiled sadly and raised his hand again, to touch not his chest, but his heart. "And while I can take just about anything those motherfuckers can dish out, I still wouldn't wish that kind of misery on anyone else.

So no, dear boy, I'm not making fun of you." He gave Mike a little bow. "Consider it an homage."

Truman stopped himself, realizing a couple things he'd just said, the endearments that tumbled effortlessly from his mouth. *Sweetie? Dear boy? Truman! Seriously? You looking to get your face punched in?*

But Mike looked serene, staring up a little at the night sky, which was clear and glistening with clusters of stars. All was quiet around them. If Mike had heard and not approved, he surely wasn't showing it.

"You're a nice guy." Mike laid a hand for just a moment on Truman's shoulder. "Kind. I like that."

The words of argument and dismissal were poised at Truman's lips. But then he thought, simply, *no*, and just said, "Thanks."

Mike rubbed his hands together, and for the first time, Truman noticed the mist, like smoke, coming out of his mouth when he spoke. "So, you want to go? It's freezing out here."

Truman moved around the front of the truck and climbed up into the passenger seat. He settled in, thinking *If I didn't know better, I'd say the cab of this thing smells like come*. Truman put the idea down to a flight of fancy, to simply being excited at being so near to Mike.

Mike hopped in and grinned at him. "Home, then?"

Truman nodded. "Home."

Mike started the truck but didn't pull forward toward the road. He simply sat there for what Truman thought was the longest time. Truman wondered if he'd changed his mind. After all, maybe the guy really didn't want to be seen with him. *Stop it!* Truman admonished himself.

Mike stared out the window, almost as though he was afraid of looking at Truman. Truman could tell he was poised to say something.

Go ahead. Say it. You just remembered you have to be somewhere. You have to get up extra early tomorrow. Your ma needs you to pick her up from the bar.

"Um, if it's not too late, and it's cool with you, maybe we could take a ride over by the river? Sit and talk?"

"Okay," Truman said, knowing how unsure he sounded. He wasn't tentative about the idea. No, not at all. He was tentative because Mike had just dangled a wonderful carrot in front of his face, and he feared that, if he reached for it too eagerly, it would be snatched away.

"I mean, it's cool if you don't wanna, it being a school night and all…."

"No. No. I wanna." Truman stared at Mike until Mike surrendered and looked back at him.

They smiled at each other.

Mike started the truck up. "Let's go, then."

River Road was a two-lane stretch of pockmarked and broken concrete. Once upon a time, it had been a busy thoroughfare between East End, where Truman lived, and Summitville's downtown. But since they built the new bridge into West Virginia, and the four-lane that entered and exited it, the old River Road was virtually abandoned.

The truck bounced over potholes, once sending Truman flying up so hard his head hit the ceiling. They both laughed.

Mike pulled over and parked under the great supporting beams of the bridge, dirt and pebbles flying up beneath the truck. They were in almost total darkness. Through Mike's cracked windshield, the river spread out before them like some kind of liquid black snake, reflecting that night's sliver of moon and even some of the stars. A tugboat, trailed by a barge piled high with gravel, cut through the dark water, heading up toward Pittsburgh.

They had an even better view of the river than they would have even two weeks ago, what with autumn's leaf attrition.

The two of them said nothing for a long time, simply staring out at the water and the clear night. Down here, so close to the river, they were virtually alone. On summer days people might be nearby, putting their speedboats in, swimming from the shore, feeding the ducks at the downtown wharf at the foot of the hill.

But the night and the chill kept everyone away. Truman could close his eyes and imagine he and Mike were the only people in the world right now.

And what a lovely world that would be.

He allowed himself, in the silence, to wonder why Mike was doing this. Was it just out of friendship? Or was there something more? Truman was savvy enough to know—and had had a little experience in this area too—that just because a guy came across as all macho, 100 percent man, it didn't really mean anything when it came to which way his bread was buttered, so to speak.

Could Mike… like me? he asked himself.

The thought, the dream, was almost too fanciful— and painful—to entertain. *Of course, he just wants to be friends. It makes sense. He's new in town, all alone. He's a little awkward. Shy. Quiet. He's probably just reaching out to me because my mom is dating his dad. We're like brothers. Yeah, right....*

"It's really beautiful tonight," Mike said. "The river, those hills over there in West Virginia. The lights here and there on the other side of the water. It's kind of magical."

Ah, he has a poet's heart! And Truman felt himself falling a little bit, maybe, in love with Mike. He was already in full-on, no-cure lust for him, and there was no way to deny that, but love? That was a new sensation, an addition that could either be a delight or the beginning of a broken heart. Ever the drama queen, Truman predicted the latter.

"Yeah," Truman said softly, wishing his brain would kick in gear and he could make even a little more intelligent conversation. But it was hard when there was one question that kept coming back, burning to be answered. Truman knew he was risking pain, but he had to ask, even if it meant putting Mike on the spot. "Why are you doing this?"

Mike turned to him in the dark. His eyebrows scrunched together a little, as though Truman's question stymied him. "Because I like you."

Truman felt a ripple of electricity course through him but said nothing more.

"Something happened earlier tonight," Mike said. "I don't wanna go into what or where. Those things aren't important. But what happened made me realize I shouldn't be ashamed of who I am." Truman watched Mike's Adam's apple bob up and down as he swallowed hard. "Or what I am."

Here it comes.

Mike went on. "I noticed you that very first day of school when I got on the bus."

You did? Truman still couldn't find the coordination in himself to unite tongue, lips, and teeth together to form coherent speech. He was buzzing—in a way he imagined a hit of cocaine would bring on.

Mike sighed. "I thought you were hot." He looked away from Truman. "Just my type." He snickered. "I like my guys small."

Truman asked what he knew was a dumbass question, but he had to be sure. "So you're, um, gay?"

Mike rolled his eyes. "Dude, seriously. Do you really have to ask after what I just said?"

"Well, I just wanted to be sure. You never know. I mean—" Truman could have gone on, said a lot more. A torrent of words just waited to emerge, born of nerves and excitement.

But Mike interrupted him by scooting across the seat, grabbing the back of his neck, and drawing him in for a kiss. Momentarily stunned, Truman began to pull away as though he was the one initiating the kiss, but he was able to stop himself in time. Mike's lips were surprisingly soft. When he gently parted Truman's lips with his tongue, he wasn't forceful about it, his tongue almost fluttering into Truman's mouth, where it drew out Truman's own tongue, initiating a kind of duel.

It was magic.

And Truman had to repeat to himself over and over—*This isn't a dream. This is real. This is really happening.* But gradually, or maybe not so gradually at all, coherent thought took a back seat to passion.

Mike pulled Truman even closer. Even though Mike's lips were soft, the sandpaper roughness of his stubble was all man, and Truman finally understood what people meant when they said something "hurt so good."

In no time Truman found himself on Mike's lap, straddling him and kissing him with a hunger he'd never experienced. Somehow, almost of their own accord, their shirts disappeared, pulled off heedlessly with no regard for which pair of hands was doing the pulling. And when Truman's chest came in total contact with Mike's, he was afraid this whole moment might crash to a very abrupt—and very messy—conclusion. He was that excited. Early tremors began to pulse through him at just the feel of Mike's hairy chest against his own smooth one.

Mike pulled away, staring at Truman in the darkness. Even though they were steeped in shadows, Mike's pale eyes sparkled like liquid. "Are we really doing this?" he asked a little breathlessly.

"I was just going to ask you the same thing. Never in a million years, when I left play practice tonight, could I have even imagined things would end this way."

Mike drew in a quick breath. "Things aren't ending, are they? I couldn't stand it."

"Oh, hell no," Truman answered and affixed his mouth to Mike's once more.

In a very short while, both of them were dissatisfied with the skin-on-skin sensations being limited to only their top halves.

"I want you naked," Mike gasped.

"I want to be naked—for you." Damn practicalities! As much as Truman hated to do it, he had to slide off Mike's lap. Things like shoes and pants were

simply too hard to remove when straddling a hot—
and big—guy's lap. Quickly he yanked off shoes and
socks, and then he leaned to one side to unzip and pull
down his jeans. In less than thirty seconds, it seemed
to Tru, he was naked. The air coming in through the
slightly cracked-open passenger window felt delightful on his heated flesh. He watched, feeling a little
dazed, a little high, a little breathless, as Mike struggled out of his own jeans. And he sucked in a breath
when he saw Mike's dick rising up from a thick dark
thatch of curly hair. A drop of precome oozed out of
the top and then dribbled down its veiny shaft. Truman
looked down at himself to find he was similarly situated, so to speak.

"What, um, what do you like to do?" Truman
asked, voice shaking, wanting this, all of this so bad,
and at the same time, desperately afraid he would
somehow screw things up.

Or Mike would have a change of heart.

Or a blinding spotlight would illuminate the
truck's cab as one of Summitville's finest pulled up.

"I want to, you know…." Mike was breathless,
barely able to speak, Truman thought. As some kind of
indicator, he grabbed his cock, pulled it forward, and
allowed it to slap back against his hairy belly.

The action almost made Truman come. He felt
those first tentative shivers and had to draw on some
very extreme will to stop himself.

"Do you wanna fuck me?" Truman asked. He
imagined himself sprawled across the seat, Mike
standing outside, between his legs, pounding away,
with Truman's calves on his shoulders. He wasn't sure
if he drew the scene from his own fevered imagination

of if he'd seen it on one of the porn sites he had book-marked on his laptop.

Either way, he wanted it to happen.

And happen now.

Mike tousled his hair. "Oh, buddy, I'd love that." He cocked his head. "You got a condom?"

"No. No, of course not. I don't carry them around. What do you think I am? A Boy Scout?" Truman popped open the glove box and rummaged around. "Don't you keep some in here?" He knew how desperate he sounded, and he didn't care. When he realized his search was futile, he said, "Maybe we could do bareback, just this once." He knew his libido was doing all his talking—and all his thinking—for him, but he felt he'd passed a point of no return. "It'll be okay. What are the odds either of us has anything?"

"You're right. But still…." Mike let his words trail off.

He didn't think it was possible, but for just a second or two, the voice of reason spoke up and Truman knew he shouldn't take the risk, no matter how experienced or inexperienced each of them were. After all, he imagined Stacy's line of thinking landed her where she was right at this very minute.

"Yeah, we should wait," he said, knowing how disappointed he sounded.

Mike nodded. "And not just for condoms."

"What do you mean?"

"Ah, if we're gonna do that, let's hold out until we have some privacy, a bedroom, and even a bed."

"Candles and soft music?" Truman asked, snickering.

"What are you laughing for? You don't think a big lug like me can be romantic?"

Oh God, he's romantic too. What did I do to deserve this? Truman thought the time for talking was over, and he got to his knees on the truck's bench seat, positioned his head over Mike's cock, and taking a deep breath, went down. He swallowed Mike in one magnificent gulp. If he could have smiled, he would have—at the gasp of sheer pleasure that came out of Mike.

Mike cried out again at the warmth and wet of Truman's mouth, his tongue.

And he came within a few seconds.

So did Truman, without even touching himself.

And, in the distance, a tugboat sounded its horn. It was as though it knew and was acknowledging their almost simultaneous orgasms.

CHAPTER 14

DESPITE POTHOLES and crooked brick streets, Mike felt like he was driving Truman home on a cloud. He didn't notice a single jolt or shimmy. He was aware only of Truman's head on his shoulder, his body pressed close.

He worried about the moment that was soon coming—when Truman would have to exit the truck and he'd go inside his own house, leaving Mike alone with his dick, which had risen again only minutes after his climax.

Maybe there's a way Truman can sneak me into his bedroom.

They pulled up in front of Truman's. Mike was surprised to see Truman's ma and his own dad, sitting side-by-side on the front stoop, a shared blanket thrown over their shoulders. Mike drew his gaze away from them and grinned at Truman. "So much for asking you to sneak me in for round two."

Truman sat up a little straighter. "Oh, ready for more?"

Mike grabbed Truman's hand and placed it on his crotch. "What do you think?"

Truman laughed, sliding away from Mike. "Stop! Our parents are right over there!"

"Oh, so now you're gonna go all Mary Poppins on me."

"C'mon, Mike." Truman turned his head to look at the two of them. His mom waved. And Mike's dad, true to form, took a drag off his ever-present cigarette. Mike supposed the cloud of smoke he blew out could be taken as a form of greeting.

"They'll probably spend the night together," Mike said. "It's not fair."

"They're old." Truman opened the door a little, more when Odd Thomas rose up and waddled over to the truck. "Do you want to come inside?"

"I thought I just did."

"Don't be crude. You can come in for a bit. I'm sure it'll be okay, if you keep your hands to yourself."

"You're no fun." Mike laughed.

Truman hopped out of the truck and squatted down to show Odd some love, scratching him behind the ears.

Mike got out of the truck, not sure he'd be able to abide by Truman's rules, especially if he got a moment alone with him. It was amazing how a little sex seemed to unleash all his inhibitions and longing. He had dreamed of Truman, fantasized about him, but reality was so much more, so much better.

Both Truman's mom and his dad sauntered over to the truck.

Truman's mother said hello to Mike and then said to Truman, "I didn't know you two were friends."

Truman stood up from his dog. "Fast friends." He grinned at Mike. "We met at play practice. Mike gave me a ride home."

His father eyed him. "Son, this is my lady friend, Patsy. Patsy Reid."

"I know her last name, Dad. Same as Truman's. How come you never said anything about dating before?"

George squeezed Patsy's shoulder. "Wanted to make sure she was a keeper."

Mike rolled his eyes. So did Patsy. "You sure you want to hang out with this jerk?"

"Hey!" George cautioned.

Patsy said, "I'm still deciding. It's nice to finally meet you, Mike. I've been telling your dad for weeks for him to bring you by. I'm glad you're getting to know Truman! And I'm also glad you got him home in one piece. I hate to think of him walking home by himself from the high school." She glanced at Truman. "It isn't safe. Too dark. And there are no sidewalks for most of the way! I don't want to see my little guy become roadkill."

"I'll take care of him," Mike said softly. He raised his hand, just a little, to place on Truman's shoulder. Then he thought better of it and dropped the hand back to his side.

He'd yet to come out to his dad, although back in Shoreline he'd often wondered if Dad suspected something going on between him and Aubry. Before the move, God knew the two of them were inseparable. Mike thought their relationship was pretty obvious. To everyone, that is, but parents in deep denial. He'd been going to tell his dad about a thousand times, but the words always seemed to stick in his throat. And his mom? Well, he didn't care so much about her, because she didn't appear to care so much about him.

"You guys want to hang out? There's some left-over chili in the kitchen if you're hungry."

Truman looked at him. "Sure. I can always eat."

With Truman in the lead, they headed for the front door.

Patsy called out, "We're gonna go sit out back. Holler if you need something."

"Oh, I need something, all right. I need to make *you* holler!" Mike whispered into Truman's ear as he pressed close at the front door.

"You're insatiable," Truman said. They, along with the dog, practically tumbled together through the front door and into the living room, where the TV was already going, tuned to the Food Network and an episode of *Chopped*. Truman snatched up a remote off the coffee table and turned the TV off.

"You want some of that chili? My mom makes a mean one. And even if she didn't, you can rest assured she brought some home from the diner. Theirs is pretty good, but not as good as Mom's. She puts a little cinnamon in hers, and it makes all the difference."

Mike grabbed Truman and gathered him up in his arms, kissed him. "All I want is you. You wanna show me your bedroom?"

Truman, disappointingly, edged away. "I better not." He laughed. "I might get raped."

"Can't rape the willing," Mike countered.

"Yeah, well, both of our parents are just beyond that wall." Truman pointed to the back wall of the house, which was also part of the kitchen. "Let me heat us up some supper. I'm starving—for food—even if you're not." Truman gestured toward the couch. "Make yourself at home."

Mike realized he needed to let go—at least for the moment—of his raging libido. Truman's house could certainly work as the place, but it definitely wasn't the time. He plopped down on the couch, put his feet on the coffee table, and snatched up the remote. He turned the TV back on. Scanning through the channels, Mike was amazed once again that there could be so many, yet so few he actually wanted to watch. When an old movie caught his eye, he set down the remote. A group of schoolchildren were running from a pack of attacking blackbirds.

"Oh my God," Truman said from the stove. "*The Birds*. I love this one."

Mike turned to look at him. Truman was busy stirring the chili in a battered white-speckled black pot, his face almost hidden by the steam rising up. There was something so homey about the image that it touched Mike's heart, and for just a second, he imagined the two of them alone… and that this humble little house was theirs.

And they were a couple.

He closed his eyes briefly, the feeling of contentment rising up as something not commonplace but wondrous, maybe even miraculous. Could he and Truman one day—

"Have you seen it before?" Truman asked, yanking Mike out of his playing-house bliss and reverie.

"Have I seen it? Only like a million times." Mike watched as the scene unfolded, chilled by it.

Truman came and sat next to him, perched on the edge of the couch. He watched with Mike in silence for a few minutes. Without taking his gaze from the screen, Truman said, "The first time I watched this, I was only about five years old, believe it or not. I had this crazy old babysitter, Gert Dalrymple, from down the street. She was a bit of a drunk but had a good heart. She'd let me watch whatever I wanted. Probably because she was already halfway through her first six-pack of the day by the time I started fiddling with the TV." Truman snorted. "I still remember watching this one rainy day…." Truman's voice drifted off, and his eyes went a little faraway as Mike watched him slip into memory. It made Mike smile.

"Patsy was going through her blonde phase then, and she had a fall."

"She fell?" Mike asked.

"No, silly, a fall, a hairpiece. Gert let me wear it that day, around the house." Truman smiled shyly at Mike. "I pretended I was Tippi Hedren."

At the admission, something went dark inside Mike. The smile vanished. He flashed on Truman at the back of the high school auditorium, in the dress and the big hat, and shuddered. He tried not to, but felt his lips turning down in a frown. He looked away not only from the TV, but from Truman as well, directing his gaze at a spot on the wall above the TV.

Truman must have picked up on his expression, and he laid a hand on Mike's knee. "What's the matter? Did I say something wrong?"

Mike suddenly didn't want to be touched. He worried that Patsy and his dad would walk in on them and see Truman sitting close, his hand practically on Mike's thigh. He moved his leg ever so slightly so Truman's hand would drop away.

"Nah. You're cool." Mike picked up the remote and turned the volume up a little. "Hey, you know what? That chili's gonna burn if you don't start paying attention."

Truman stared at him curiously for a moment, head cocked, and then jumped from the couch. He headed back into the kitchen area.

Mike listened as he took down bowls and opened a drawer. Spoons clanged against the ceramic tile counter.

In moments, Truman was back with a tray upon which were two bowls of chili, paper towels for napkins, two spoons, and two glasses of cola. Mike would have preferred a beer—in fact he longed for one—but couldn't ask.

"Thanks," Mike said. He let Truman set down the tray before them on the coffee table. Mike wasted no time to begin eating, eyes glued to the TV. Tippi Hedren herself was front and center in a new scene. Watching her, all Mike could think of was Truman in a blonde wig, or whatever he'd called the hairpiece, and prancing around this very room. He didn't see a little boy in his mind's eye, but Truman at the age he was right now, swinging his hips, holding one hand aloft, and gingerly patting a blonde bun at the back of his head. He squeezed his eyes shut, trying to banish the image from his head.

"It's good, isn't it? This is Patsy's own."

Mike didn't want to talk. He continued to stare at the screen, shoveling food in. He wondered if Truman was picking up on his sudden shift in mood.

You dick! Of course he is. Quit it.

The movie was almost over, the dishes were in the sink, and there was a sense of tension—palpable—in the air when Mike decided he needed to say something. The sentence was like some kind of animal inside him, burrowing and chewing its way out.

"Can I make a suggestion?" Mike aimed the remote at the TV, shut it off. He stood and cleared his throat.

Truman cocked his head. "Of course."

"Do you really need to be in that play?"

Truman paused as though taken aback, which he most likely was. "Well, yeah." He pushed some of his hair off his forehead and then reached down to finger the remote control lying between them. He yanked his hand away. "I'm not sure how we could go on." Truman glanced quickly at Mike. "You know Stacy left, and somebody had to fill the part."

"And it had to be you."

Truman, always pale, turned a little whiter. His voice was barely above a whisper. "I knew all the lines."

Mike nodded. "So that's why you have to do it? Because you, um, know all the lines? For this female character?" *Why are you doing this to him?*

"Well, there's that. Plus, I *want* to do it. I'm good at it. Don't you think?" He smiled.

Mike frowned. "I don't know. Who am I to judge? I don't know nothin' about acting, about—" Mike groped for the right words.

And Truman found them for him, it seemed. His face changed, hardened. "About parading around in women's clothes?"

"Well, no, not actually." Mike watched as the anger or hurt built up in Truman. His spine stiffened, and his arms moved up to cross his chest. Mike had to admit to himself that the right answer, the true one was, "Well, *yes*, actually." But Mike couldn't bring himself to say the words, knowing how much they'd hurt Truman.

But it didn't matter what Mike said, because Truman apparently heard an affirmative answer to his question regardless of Mike's actual words. "Does that scare you? Turn you off? Make you think… *less* of me?" Truman leaned back against the couch. And Mike hated to see the face he'd come to care so much about close like a flower, Truman's lips drawn together in a thin line, his eyes wary.

"No. No, no, of course not, Truman. I just think, you know, it's just gonna cause you more trouble in the long run. They're gonna tease you and bully you. I'm not pointing something out you don't already know." Mike sighed. "I'm sure there's some chick who'd love to take over that part. And then you'd be off the hook."

"Chick? Really, Mike?" Truman spat out the words. "Off the hook? I don't want to be *off the hook*! This little fish likes being *on* the hook." Truman shook his head, his features screwed up in anger. "Besides, we're only a few days away from opening night. I couldn't betray Mr. Wolcott, the rest of the cast, the crew—which, just in case you need reminding, in-cludes *you*—like that."

"I know. I know. But think of how people will look at you. And it wouldn't be so hard to get a re-placement. So what if a girl carries a script around on stage? You think anyone's gonna care? You and me both know the audience is all gonna be family and friends."

"You're missing the point."

"What's the point, then?" Mike sat back down on the couch. He wished he hadn't opened his big mouth. But now that the truth was out, he wanted Truman to use some common sense. He wanted to protect the guy. In his head Mike could hear the waves of laugh-ter in the audience when Truman came out, literally, all gussied up in women's clothes.

And Mike knew they'd be laughing *at* Truman, not *with* him.

"The point is, I *want* to do this. I've *dreamed* of doing it. I'm sorry I had to get the part the way I did, but hey, life works out that way sometimes." Truman smiled, but there was a glimmer of something cruel in it, and yes, something a little hurt. "You don't get it. And that makes me sad."

"What don't I get? Educate me."

Truman touched Mike's face briefly and then took his hand away. "I'm me. I like me. I don't want to be someone else. It hasn't always been easy, living in this little backwater town with its small minds, but I've kind of come to embrace who I am. I thought you got that about me." He stared off as though there were something projected on the wall across from them that only Truman could see. "I may not be your idea of what makes a normal boy, but normal for me and normal for you are different things."

"Not so different."

"What? Because you're gay?"

Mike nodded. He felt sad, knowing he was unable to grasp the point Truman was trying to make.

"That's not enough, Mike." Truman looked back at him, and Mike was shocked to see his eyes had welled with tears. "Tonight, for just a little while, I thought you liked me... *for* me. Just as I am."

Mike started to talk, but Truman put a finger on his lips, stopping him.

"No. What I'm hearing is you want me to be someone else. A *normal* boy. Whatever the hell that is. Maybe you're a *normal* boy, Mike. God knows, there was a time when I would have given anything to be just like you so all the bullying and hate would stop. But you know what? I could never be." He nodded. "And I've come to realize that's okay. It's okay to be me. And there's nobody, not even you, who can change that."

Mike felt terrible. But he didn't know what to say, so he leaned in and tried to kiss Truman, thinking a kiss would make everything better. His mouth was on Truman's when he heard the screech and slap of the screen door. He pulled himself away guiltily and looked up to see his father standing in the kitchen, taking the two of them in. His eyes were narrowed, his lips a thin, angry line.

"Dad!" Mike said, too bright, his voice too high, too nervous. "I didn't hear you come in."

"Apparently." His father glowered at him. And at Truman.

Mike hopped up from the couch and stood as far from Truman as he could. "I was just gonna head out, over to Grandma's. I, um, have some homework."

Mike hazarded a glance at Truman, who simply sat, arms and legs crossed, staring straight ahead as if neither Mike nor his father were in the room with him.

"I think that's a hell of an idea."

And Mike hurried out the front door, face burning and hands shaking. He paused at the edge of the yard, shoulders stiff. He waited for Truman to come out after him.

He wanted to talk more, get things ironed out. Back to good.

Someone did come out behind him. But it wasn't Truman.

It was his dad.

The old man stood next to him without saying anything for a couple of minutes. Then, "Listen, son, I don't know if this is such a good idea."

"Don't know if *what* is such a good idea?" Mike spat back, knowing perfectly well to what his dad was referring.

"You and Patsy's kid."

"What do you mean?" Mike asked, again knowing exactly what his dad meant, but maybe hoping if he just asked the question, he'd get a different answer from what he was assuming.

His dad moved some dirt around with his toe. Cleared his throat. It was like he didn't want to meet Mike's gaze. "You know what I mean, son. He's a—" His father seemed to be groping for just the right word.

Mike thought to fill in the blank for him. It was what a good son would do, right? So he said, "What,

Dad? A fag? A sissy? Queer? Pansy? Homo?" Mike stared off into the cold, cold darkness.

"Now, son…."

"It's what you meant, isn't it?"

His dad didn't answer for a while. And then, kind of sheepish, he said, "Yeah, I guess so." He breathed out, and Mike wondered if he was just dying for a cigarette. "My point is he's probably not a friend you want, not when you're just starting out here and trying to build a reputation for yourself. You hang out with those kind of folks and you get kind of, I don't know, guilt by association. He's a nice kid, don't get me wrong. But you're not like him, son. And you don't want folks thinkin' y'are. You need to find, you know, some normal boys, jocks. Guys we can go hunting with."

Mike felt chilled. It hadn't escaped his notice that Dad had used the word "normal" just as Truman had. There was a rage buzzing inside him, like a horde of bees, yet he felt stifled.

Now's the perfect time to come out. Just to see the look on his smug-ass face. It'd be awesome to see his mouth drop open when I tell him I'm a queer too. And that we come in all different sizes and shapes. Mike laughed bitterly, which caused Dad to stare.

And Mike had just opened his mouth to admit the truth, heedless and reckless as it might be, when he got interrupted.

"Those kind of folks?" Patsy stood just behind them.

Dad gasped and looked over at her. She stood not a foot away, arms crossed over her chest. "When did you come outside? I didn't even hear you."

"Clearly." Patsy narrowed her eyes. She raised her voice a little when she asked, again, "What did you mean, George, by 'those kind of folks' in reference to my son? Hmmm?" Patsy smiled, but there was nothing kind or warm in that smile.

"I just meant, uh—" George's voice trailed off as he stammered. Mike was certain his father's face was a bright shade of red, even though the dark prevented him from knowing for sure.

"He meant queers, Mrs. Reid, Fags, homos, you know," Mike said. His dad swiveled his head to stare at him, slack-jawed.

"It's Ms.," she corrected. She turned back to George. "So let me make sure I heard you right, George—" And on his dad's name, Patsy's voice broke a little, letting in some heartache with her anger. "Those kind of folks, gay people, I guess, are not the kind of folks you want your son hanging around? What was it you said? Guilt by association? Why guilt? Is it a crime to love?" She waved her hand at him. "Don't answer that. You don't want people thinking your Mike here is one of those people. God forbid!" Her mouth was set in a line once more. Mike thought she might have a good cry later, when she went back in the house—alone—but right now she was mad. He knew it for a fact, even though she never stopped smiling.

"Patsy," his dad whined, actually whined, pleading. "Don't go off like that. You got me all wrong." He reached out to touch her arm, and she stepped back.

"I don't think so, George. You made it clear that you think *my* son is less than. Less than yours. Less than all those regular guys out there, guys like you."

"Truman's a great kid."

"Just not great enough to be a friend to your son?"

"That's not what I said."

"It's exactly what you said." Patsy shook her head. In the wan light of the streetlamp above, Mike saw the glimmer of tears in her eyes. "And if you think my son is somehow not worthy of associating with your kid, then you and me, buddy, we're not gonna work out."

"Oh, honey, I know you don't mean that."

"Yes, *honey*, I do." Patsy stared down at the ground, breathing hard, as though she were trying to gain control over her emotions, which Mike was sure she was. When she looked up, her face was a mask of pain. "Let's not drag this out. I need you to get out of here. Okay? My son and I are gonna sit back, put up our feet, and watch an old movie. *All About Eve*, maybe. Or *Madame X* with Miss Lana Turner." Patsy laughed, but it was bitter. "I don't think you folks would be interested."

Don't include me with him! Mike wanted to shout, but somehow he couldn't get his lips to part.

Patsy turned away, leaving both of them standing there in the dark. George yelled after her, "I'll call you tomorrow!"

And Patsy paused only slightly to slowly raise her arm and flip him the bird over one shoulder.

Dad looked at Mike, sheepish. "She didn't mean that." He sighed and at last pulled out his Marlboros, lit one. "Women." He shook his head.

"Yeah," Mike said sadly. "And the gays."

"Fuck 'em."

Mike shook his head and moved wordlessly to his truck. He knew he should have told his father the truth about himself, but something inside was cowering and afraid.

Mike started the truck up and thought he'd lost a lot of people tonight. And he wasn't so sure he'd get any of them back.

CHAPTER 15

THE FRIDAY afternoon *Harvey* was set to open found Truman a hot mess of nerves, giddiness, eagerness, and out-and-out dread. He was due to be in the Summitville High School auditorium for a run-through in just under two hours.

And what was he doing? Well, certainly nothing useful or practical like running through his lines one final time. No, he'd secreted himself in his bedroom, holed up on his bed with Odd Thomas and working his way through a bag of Twizzlers. Everyone—except the one person he'd wanted to hear from the most—had given him encouragement. It was wonderful and uplifting to get the praise, confidence in him, and kindness—yet it filled Truman up with a crazy kind of terror because it seemed expectations were so high.

Mr. Wolcott had reminded him once more of all the males who'd portrayed females throughout thespian history. "Listen, Tru, in Shakespeare's time, none of the female roles were played by women—it was all men. So you're in good company, historically speaking." This was last night, at the end of rehearsal, as Truman walked with Mr. Wolcott to his car, a Nissan Leaf. "Same was true for theater in ancient Greece. And of course you know about people like Travolta—" Mr. Wolcott rolled his eyes, but still, he had a point. "And even Adam Sandler, Tyler Perry, Divine, Arsenio Hall, Eddie Murphy, the list goes on and on. There's nothing gay about you playing Myrtle Mae." He grinned. "Not that there's anything wrong with that. But you have nothing to worry about. I promise you. You're too good, kid. People will see that and be on their feet at the end of the show, and it'll be mainly for you. Because you do what all good actors do—inhabit a character." When he got to his car, "Did you watch *Kind Hearts and Coronets*?"

Truman nodded. Mr. Wolcott had loaned him the DVD the weekend before, just to show him how a real artist, as he said, plays female. Truman and Patsy thought the movie was kind of a snooze, but had to hand it to Alec Guinness, who'd played a multitude of roles in the movie, the highlight among them Lady Agatha D'Ascoyne, a suffragette with a feminist agenda.

"We'll see you at the show. You're gonna be amazing."

Truman remembered the conversation now as he snuggled closer to Odd Thomas. He wished he had the same confidence Mr. Wolcott had in him, the same fearlessness. If he did, maybe now he wouldn't be contemplating simply running out of the show, grabbing a bus to Pittsburgh or something, never coming back.

And what good would that do? It's your dream, Truman, to be an actor. So get over yourself and—act!

He thought of Patsy's encouraging words, despite her broken heart over losing George. "You'll make me proud," she'd said, emerging from her bedroom for the first time in days, eyes red and watery. "That's one thing I know I can count on. God knows there isn't much else these days."

"And you're sure you're gonna be up for coming to opening night?" Truman wondered. He asked because Patsy had taken losing George hard, even though she was the one who broke up with him. Yes, he'd revealed himself to be a real asshole—like his son? But Truman knew we couldn't always rationalize away a stomped-on heart. Even he had learned that lesson already. So he understood her grief—and empathized. She'd gone a long time without a man, real love, in her life. So long Truman had forgotten his mother would even need such a thing. When George had come along, he raised her hopes and joy up to a higher place, a very high place, one perhaps over the rainbow in Truman's vernacular, so that when the truth came out and love became impossible, Patsy had fallen farther and harder than she'd ever imagined she could. The crash hurt.

Yet she'd touched his face, looking at him like he was crazy for even asking such a question. "I wouldn't miss it for the world, sweetheart. I'll be in the front row, the proudest mama *ever*… don't you worry!"

How could Truman let her down?

Alicia, in her questionable wit, had left him a gift on the front porch—an old cast, probably from one of her brother's sports injuries, still bearing signatures and a big cut up one side. "Thought you could use this," her note read, "Because, honey, I know that tonight, you're going to break a leg! Har-har!"

Even Stacy had managed to get word to him. Just an hour ago, his phone had chirped, indicating he had a text message. He hoped/didn't hope the text would be from Mike, saying he'd had a change of heart and he supported Truman 100 percent. Hell, as long as he was fantasizing, Truman imagined that he voiced not only his support, but that he understood and was proud of Truman, who was "more of a man, in a way, than I could ever be."

Ah, if wishes were horses....

But still, even if it wasn't Mike, it was Stacy, a young woman Truman had come to care deeply about, even though he hadn't seen her in weeks. She never ventured far from his thoughts and his worries that she was doing okay. Just seeing her name on his phone screen prompted a tremendous sigh of relief to go through him.

Hey, honey, the text read, *I know you're gonna knock socks off tonight! And come hell or high water, I will be there to see it.*

The text brought tears to Truman's eyes and afforded him with yet another reason not to cop out. He quickly texted back *Oh I hope you can find a way to get there! It would touch my heart, really.*

But his phone, his email, his Facebook, had all remained mute these past several days when it came to Mike. Truman knew he shouldn't care, but he did.

The hurt was like something black and heavy inside, something he carried around invisible but always present, forever weighing him down.

His head told him he was better off without Mike. *Sure he's hot, gorgeous, super sexy and all that, but he's in the closet. He doesn't yet know how to love himself for who he really is.* And, as one of Truman's biggest drag heroes always said, "If you can't love yourself, how in the hell can you love somebody else?"

"Amen," Truman whispered to himself, and his head continued talking. *You need to find yourself a boy who not only loves you for you, but who's secure in who he is too. You can live quite well without Mike's self-loathing baggage, thank you very much.*

Truman closed his eyes. He didn't want to hear what his head had to say, logical as it was, as much sense as it was making. His head was urging him to go blissfully forward, to excise Mike from his brain and his life like a small tumor.

His heart knew the *truth*, difficult and wrong as it was. His heart said *I want Mike*.

His heart could see not only Mike's physical beauty, which was considerable, but also his kind heart, his confusion, and his feelings for Truman, which Truman knew were real. He knew because his own feelings were so acute, so poignant, so tender.

I want him back. I want to work things out. I want to show him that he can be him and I can me, and together, we can both be stronger. Just as we are.

But Mike had broadcast nothing but radio silence since that fateful night when he suggested Truman might want to try to be a little more *normal*. Truman hadn't even seen him around school or over by his grandma's. He'd stopped coming to rehearsals.

Mr. Wolcott told Truman Mike had quit.

And Truman's first thought was *Maybe he just can't bear seeing me in that dress! That makeup! Kitten heels! A straw hat!*

He sighed and got up from his bed. His makeup and costume were in his locker at school. Patsy had promised to get off work early to take him up so he wouldn't have to walk. He could now hear her old car pulling up in the gravel in front of the house, the little toot of her horn.

"Here goes nothing," he said to Odd Thomas, who'd jumped down from the bed when Truman rose. His tail thumped once, twice on the floor, and he looked up at Tru, seeming to grin.

But Truman knew he was only panting. Still, he imagined his dog wishing him luck, hoping for only the best.

The front door creaked open. "Tru? Honey? You ready?"

"Ready as I'll ever be," he said more to himself and went to open another door, the door on what felt like a new chapter in his life.

CHAPTER 16

Truman's mouth dropped open as they mounted the last small hill to get to the Summitville High School parking lot.

His breath abandoned him, even though his heart rate accelerated.

He couldn't quite make sense of what he saw. Dusk had just about finished its murky display of colors, but the light was still bright enough to show a small crowd of people milling around outside the high school auditorium. Truman blinked, wondering why they'd shown up so early for *Harvey*. The play wasn't set to begin for another three hours.

He'd been lulled into a sense of peace and calm by the colors of the night sky as Patsy drove up the hill toward the high school, her old car whining and coughing as it ascended. The sky, though, was perfect, a manifestation, maybe, of divine order. Dark midnight blue at the top, with just a few stars beginning to sparkle, and then layers as Truman looked down—lavender-gray, pale peach, and finally a burst of tangerine where the sky kissed the hilltops. It was easy for Truman to focus on the painting-like beauty before him and to put on hold, at least for a few minutes, his anxiety over his performance.

"What the fuck?" Patsy asked as she pulled into a parking space about a football field away from the small group that had formed outside the auditorium's doors.

When Truman had first caught sight of the few people outside, he'd simply thought they were a bunch of eager audience members waiting for the doors to open. You know, a good thing. But a quick reality check told him that couldn't be. It was just *too* early.

And then, with a sinking heart, he spotted the signs they carried as they milled about, back and forth on the sidewalk:

Truman = Tru-Woman
Boys will be Boys, EXCEPT for Truman Reid
No cross-dressers at our school
Let our kids be NORMAL! Don't see HARVEY!

Several people had the same sign—the word cross-dressing with a circle around it and a line through the circle, like a No Smoking sign.

"Oh God," Truman muttered, his stomach churning.

Patsy put a hand on his arm. "You okay?"

He looked over at his mom, tears in his eyes. "How can I be okay? I thought crap like this was over for me. Or at least lightened up some. Mr. Wolcott said people would understand, that there's a long history of men playing female in the theater." Truman hung his head, staring down at his feet. "I'm not *cross-dressing*. Don't they get it? I mean, cross-dressing is fine for some, but it's *not* what I'm doing in that part or even in my life. It's never been about that."

Patsy shut the ignition off, and silence filled the car. They were positioned away from the dozen or so streetlights in the parking lot.

Truman was breathing hard, trying to keep the sobbing at bay. He gripped the armrest with desperation. Would they never let up on him? Ever? He was so sick of it, he wondered if he should have just flung himself from the roof of the school all those years ago. Then everybody could just be happy....

"There really aren't that many of them," Patsy said. "One, two, three—there's only half a dozen."

Truman hazarded a glance. He didn't recognize most of the figures—maybe it was too dark, or maybe it was because his vision was blurred by tears. But one person stood out. A tall girl—some of the kids called her "Stretch."

"Tammy Applegate," Truman mumbled. He looked at his mom, but he was speaking to Tammy, "What did I ever do to you?"

"What?" Patsy asked. Her voice was a little high, excited, anxious. Truman knew she didn't know what to do or say. The plan had been simply for her to drop him off in the parking lot, and then she'd go home to get ready and come back just before the performance.

Who expected *this*?

Maybe I should have. Maybe I was being naïve when I thought people would understand, when I listened to folks telling me they'd applaud me for being good in the part, for being brave. Maybe I'm just the silliest boy in the world for expecting people to behave kindly, to celebrate differences rather than protest them. Truman snorted to himself. He didn't pay much attention to politics, but he wondered if these people would have dared attack a high school kid like this if it weren't for being emboldened by a president who sided with bigots and anti-LGBT forces.

Patsy tapped him. "What do you mean? I didn't do anything to you!"

Truman looked over at his mom, her lower lip quivering ever so slightly, and was confused for a moment, and then he recalled what he'd said. "Oh, Mom, I'm sorry. When I said, 'What did I ever do to you,' I was talking to her—" He pointed to Tammy Applegate, noticing an older man standing next to her with his hand on her shoulder. *How nice, Dad came along for the little hatefest! It's a family affair! Was she thinking crap about me all along?* "—Tammy Applegate. She's on the stage crew. I never had any idea she thought less of me for playing the part. She's sat through so many rehearsals without a word, without even giving me a side-eye." He thought he should just pull out his phone and text Alicia, get her up here. She'd kick these bigots' asses.

Why do you need her? The thought stood out, stark, in Truman's mind. *Why do you need any help at all?*

"Ah, people hide their true faces sometimes, Truman." Patsy blew out a sigh and then put one hand on the steering wheel and one hand on the shifter. "You want me to take you home? You don't need this."

And with her question, Truman found courage. It began to uncoil inside him like something alive—and so it was. "Home?" he asked.

"Sure. Of course. Sweetie, you don't have to go through those people. You don't have to deal with their shit. I don't care if the show gets canceled or whatever. I'm not gonna let them hurt *my* boy." Patsy was looking at him with such pain and such love that it nearly broke Truman's heart. For a split second, he wished he were a *normal* boy just so his mom didn't have to go through this, didn't have to ache vicariously for her son and the pain he knew she imagined him feeling.

He reached out a hand and tenderly touched Patsy's cheek. "I'm not going home."

"Well, what do you wanna do?" Patsy asked, befuddled, as if there were no other alternative than to simply flee.

What do I want to do? Or what do I have to do?

"I'm not going anywhere, Mommy," Truman said, reverting for some reason to what he called Patsy when he was little. "Those people aren't gonna stop me. They're just assholes, and I'll pay them no mind. I'll just walk on by, like in that old song. And if one of 'em dares to try and stop me—"

Patsy cut him off, at last smiling. "You'll kick their asses."

Truman let out a sheepish laugh. "Well, no. But I *will* scream real loud. And someone will come to my aid."

They both laughed. And then went quiet for several moments. Truman said, "We can't let them stop me. Then they win. And hate wins. I can't allow that, Mom."

Patsy took a deep breath, then leaned across the center console and the stick shift to grab Truman in a hard embrace. "I'm so proud of you right now."

"Ah, proud, schmoud," Truman said, pulling away and unfastening his seat belt. He opened the door and turned to his side to get out.

He tried not to let Patsy see it, but he was breathless with terror.

His back was turned to Patsy when he felt her hand on his shoulder. "You want me to come with? To walk you inside?"

"No. I have to do this myself." Even as the words spilled from his lips, Truman was questioning his own wisdom, his own sanity for turning her down. Having an escort was a good idea.

But his mom? He shook his head. Having her by his side as his protector would just add fuel to the fire—make him seem even weaker than the folks standing outside already thought him.

For a brief, shaky moment he did wish for an escort, a bodyguard. Mike would have been perfect.

Mike would have been so many things.

Patsy squeezed his shoulder. "Are you sure? One of those sons of bitches so much as touches you, and I swear to God, I'll kill 'em."

Truman laughed. "Oh now, you don't have to go all fierce-and-protective-mama!" He shrugged Patsy's hand off his shoulder and turned his head to look at her. "Like some kind of lioness." And Truman let out a little roar, which helped break the tension in the car and made them both laugh.

Truman took a few deep breaths. He thought the bravest thing—and the most stupid—would be to walk

through the crowd of protestors when Patsy left. Did
he have the courage to do such a thing? His shoulders
slumped. Walking all alone wouldn't be brave, only
foolhardy. So he asked Patsy, in a small voice, "Would
you mind just watching after me until I get inside? I'll
feel better."

"I'll come with you, honey. You don't have to do
this alone."

"No, Mom!" Truman whined. "I told you—I need
to do this by myself."

"Sure, kid. Again, sweetheart, I'm so, so proud.
Those people over there? They're the cowards... the
ones so scared of anything a little different, they have
to stamp it out."

"I know, Mom."

"I'll be right here. But I warn you—if one of them
even comes close to you, I'll be out of this car so fast
it'll make heads spin."

"À la Linda Blair?"

"I should have never let you watch that movie!"

Truman deepened his voice to a croak and said,
"Your mother sews socks that smell!"

"Get out of the car!" It sounded like Patsy was
both laughing and crying.

He exited. He stood by the car for a moment, his
hand on its cool metal surface to steady himself, and
drew in a deep breath. *You can do this. Just pretend
they're not there.*

He took his first step. Then another. Another.
Faster.

Soon he was close enough to look the protesters
in the eyes. But the funny thing was, not a single one
of them would look back at him. Truman wondered

why, why, when if they were simply demonstrating their convictions, following their beliefs, they didn't have the nerve to meet his gaze. Even Tammy Applegate turned her back on him, although her dad stood his ground, his face looking angry and screwed up with determination. There was something very much like a baby just before it bursts into tears in this man's face—and it almost made Truman want to laugh. Unbidden, a thought popped into Truman's head, directed toward the man he assumed was Mr. Applegate. *You're a weak little man, aren't you? With your thinning hair, worn-out warm-up jacket, and sweatpants? What difference does this make to you? How does this affect your life?*

It almost seemed like he and Truman made a telepathic connection, because he too turned his back, just like his daughter.

Coward. I'd have more respect for you if you stood your ground.

He passed by them, making sure he held his head high. *There's no shame here. At least not on my part.* He braced himself, shoulders up near his jawline, certain one of them would fling something at him, a piece of rotten food, an egg, maybe even a brick.

But nothing struck him.

Just as he neared the double glass doors, someone called out, "Faggot!"

There were a few titters.

At the doors, Truman turned to face them. Again, everyone standing there immediately seemed preoccupied with the concrete of the parking lot.

"Seriously? Is that the best you can do?" He shook his head and pulled open the door. Over his shoulder, he added, "You should be ashamed of yourselves. Even your cruelty is uninspired, stale."

That must have hit a nerve, because a female voice—young, yet the slightest bit gravelly—called out, "You're the one who should be ashamed, Truman Reid! You're an abomination!"

Truman wanted to smile and take a little bow. That was how he imagined brave Truman would act, but the truth was the epithet hurt. As Patsy had always told him, he was a child of God. And God didn't create "abominations."

Still, it all hurt.

The pain and the ostracism—the plain meanness—of it all threatened to crash down on his shoulders, sinking him right into the ground. A part of him wanted to release the flow of tears damming up behind his eyes—and his resolve. That same part wanted to dash back to the car and simply tell Patsy, "Go!"

He closed his eyes for a moment, listening to the murmurs of assent behind him, the soft titters. *Oh, they're enjoying this.*

He was halfway inside when the same voice, braver now, louder now, strident, called, "We're going to be in there, making sure this farce is an epic fail!"

Truman said, "Well, I hope you have tickets, because we're sold out."

He turned and walked over to Tammy. "Is this how you want things to go? After you worked so hard on the set?"

She stared at her dad and wouldn't look at him.

"Hard to talk, isn't it, Tammy? You know, face-to-face? Don't you wonder why you can't look at me?" He started away.

She screamed out something that caused his spine to stiffen and stopped him in his tracks. "Everybody knows you love Mike! He wouldn't be caught dead with a queer like you."

Truman clenched his jaw, wondering how to respond.

And then he rushed inside.

Mike? Mike? Really? What does she know about him? About them? Has he talked to her? The thought turned his stomach. He was pretty sure no one from the school had ever seen the two of them together.

So… why did she say that?

And then a thought seized him with so much pain it was almost like a cramp. *What if Mike joins this group of assholes? What if he knows what they're doing and doesn't care?*

Truman didn't know if he could endure the hurt that would accompany such a betrayal.

At the door he turned to look for Patsy, seriously contemplating just blowing this all off, as horrible as it would have been to everyone who'd worked so hard on the production. He'd learned about the fight-or-flight instinct in biology class. Right now his primal self was coming down on the side of fleeing.

But the choice was out of his hands. All he saw of Patsy was her taillights. And even they vanished as she descended the hill.

Truman went inside, feeling numb.

Alone.

CHAPTER 17

"FUCKERS," MIKE whispered to himself. "Fuckin' bigoted cowards."

He'd parked the pickup at the far end of the school parking lot, the end that looked down on the valley, the lights of Summitville, the dark snake of the Ohio as it wound through the town, separating it from West Virginia. It could have been a calming view, but what Mike was seeing in his rearview was making him see red.

Even though he faced away from them, the protestors in his rearview mirror, milling around outside the auditorium, were making his blood pressure skyrocket. He was about ready to hurl himself from the truck and kick some ass. It was getting close enough to showtime that people were arriving to see *Harvey*.

Classmates.

Family.

Friends of the families.

Proud parents.

Even from this distance, Mike could see they were taken aback by the protestors—and their hateful, crude messages written out on poster board—but at least none of the people who had tickets for the show turned away, which must have been disappointing for the protestors.

"Fuck them," he whispered to himself. He reached down toward the center console and lifted the can of Iron City and took a swig. "Narrow-minded dicks. What? This gives them a thrill? Picking on a high school kid?"

His heart ached for Truman.

He should have known this town would pull a stunt like this. Mike was only surprised they'd waited until now to do it. Why hadn't they gone to the school board early on, when it was generally known Truman was taking on the part of Myrtle Mae? *Because*, Mike answered himself, *they're too stupid and disorganized to use their poison in a rational way. A logical way. That would take planning, some thought.*

He wished he hadn't drunk the beer. He'd only had a couple from the six-pack bought by an older guy for him from the deli and party supply store downtown, but they were already making his head a little fuzzy, his body a little too relaxed.

He needed a clear head. He needed to help Truman.

He knew he'd been a shitheel, being out of touch since the night his dad told him not to associate with Truman. He'd been so furious at his dad, wanting to just do something to hurt him, punch his lights out, take a baseball bat to his prized Ford F-150.

But he'd done nothing. Was it because there was a small part of him that agreed with his father? A little self-loathing part that maybe saw the sense of what his father had said? It was true, after all, that Mike's high school life, of which he only had this year left, would be much easier if he simply stayed in the closet, passed for white, so to speak… and was just one of the guys. There were plenty of girls who wanted to go out with him, Tammy Applegate first among them. He could pretend for a while—pretend to like sports, girls, cars—all the things Truman would say *normal* boys liked.

It would be easy. He could skate by the next few months, not put himself out there, be one of the jocks, one of the motorheads. A dude.

He hazarded a glance in the rearview mirror and watched the people milling around outside the auditorium, placards held high, so sure of their purpose and of their hate. Dimly their chants floated over to him through his open window, along with the cold autumn night air. "Keep freaks out of our schools." "Boys *should* be boys." It made him sick. And he realized that for him to pretend to be someone or something he wasn't made him a lot like those people. Even if he didn't mean to take sides, he was.

Being silent on things that mattered—that put him on the wrong side of love too.

With them. The haters. The losers. The people who had nothing better to do than piss on someone, just because he was different.

Never mind that he was beautiful. Sexy as hell. Kind. Funny.

A boy I love. This last thought caught Mike up short. It caused a fluttering of both his heart and his gut, the places he realized his truest emotions were located.

Is that who I want to be, huh? Them? At least Truman has the courage to be himself. Hell, he's more of a man than I could ever hope to be. More of a man than my dad. Because he's a true man, true to himself, not backing down because somebody says who he is, is wrong. How could who he is be wrong when he was born that way? Just like I was….

Mike straightened up a little more in his seat. He finished the beer he was drinking in one long swallow. He set the rest of the six-pack in the space behind the front bench seat, knowing he would drink no more tonight.

Maybe it was the cold of the night air sobering him up. After all, there was a frost warning out, and temperatures were forecast to go below freezing.

But Mike thought the real thing clearing his head was simply realizing the truth.

He was a young gay man in love, maybe for the first time, with another young man. And what on earth could possibly be wrong with that?

By being silent, by avoiding Truman, he'd been avoiding himself and his own feelings. He'd been a discredit to his own self. And he'd been, in his quiet, do-nothing way, complicit with his dad, letting him set the tenor for Mike's own moral code.

And that was just wrong.

Mike crushed the beer can in one hand and flung it to the floor. He started the truck's engine with a roar and put it into gear.

Smiling, he made a U-turn and headed, at a pretty good clip, out of the parking lot. He hummed to himself as he headed down the hill and away from the school, toward the house he shared with his mother.

She, of course, wouldn't be home tonight. Wonder of wonders, she was actually out for dinner with his dad. They'd headed up to Boardman and the Olive Garden there to, as she said, see where they were at, see what could be "salvaged." Mike laughed at that.

It didn't matter if she was home. He was going to do what he was going to do. Whether his mom, dad, or those fucked-up protestors outside the school liked it or not.

CHAPTER 18

A COUPLE of stage crew members opened the two sets of double doors at the back of the auditorium, propping them open with the little kickstands at the bottom of each door.

It should have been a happy moment, one filled with promise.

Instead, the promise was usurped by despair as the protestors marched inside, hoisting their signs high. Sure, there were also clusters of family and friends who'd come to see their loved ones take to the stage. But they couldn't compete with the little group of haters and the threat they carried with them. There was a curious silence in the space when there should have been a hubbub of excited conversation.

Truman watched, peeking out from behind the curtain with a sinking heart. It felt as though his belly had slowly filled with lead.

He'd already dressed in the black-and-purple dot-ted-swiss dress, the kitten heels, the big straw hat. His makeup, self-applied, was flawless, his cheeks glow-ing rosy, his lips an alluring shade of crimson. Mas-cara. Fake lashes. Even a shoulder-length blonde wig.

He *was* Myrtle Mae Simmons.

But none of that was any comfort, because he realized the protestors must have all bought tickets. Otherwise they couldn't have gotten in. Could they be thrown out? They were gathering in the shadows at the rear of the theater. There was a subtle shift in the atmosphere as people began to give voice to either their consternation or their confusion. Whispering and laughing reached Truman's ears dimly from the stage.

What were they planning? Heckling and jeers? Would the cast have to shout their lines over them to be heard? Would they parade up and down the aisles with their signs, ruining everything?

Would the cast, at some point, have to concede defeat, shut the production down, and send everyone home? If they succeeded in something like that, Tru-man didn't know if he'd be horrified, enraged, or in despair. He supposed all three could coexist, but it wouldn't be comfortable.

A hand on his shoulder caused Truman to jump. He barely stifled a scream. He turned to take in Mr. Wolcott standing next to him.

Mr. Wolcott didn't look happy. There was a kind of fire in his eyes.

"I'm going to go talk to them," he told Truman, his tone more somber and grave than Truman had ever heard it. "They can't be a disruption. We've all worked so hard on this show. I won't let them ruin it."

"B-but they have tickets," Truman mumbled. *As if that changes anything....*

"They still can't disrupt our show. Part of the implied contract of the theater is that we put on the entertainment and the audience gives us their *respectful* attention. Everybody knows that. It's a cornerstone, a foundation."

Truman wondered if the rubes at the back of the auditorium had ever even heard of such a contract. And if they had, would they give it any credence?

"I don't know if talking to them's going to do any good."

Mr. Wolcott shook his head. "It can and it will. It has to. If they want to put down their signs and take their seats, they're just as welcome as anyone else, but I will *not* have them take over our show with their antics. Don't you worry—I won't let them take it away from us, all of us."

Truman watched him walk away. In seconds he appeared again out of the door at the foot of the stage. As he strode up the center aisle, Truman admired his courage and bravery. He could read both in his confident stride. Truman wished, though, he had more hope, could take more assurance in Mr. Wolcott's words. He felt a little sick, continuing to watch as Mr. Wolcott approached the protestors, whispering a nearly silent prayer that things wouldn't turn ugly.

Truman wasn't the only one observing either. People coming in were slowing to stare. At least half of those already seated had turned in their seats, craning their necks to get a view of the unexpected sideshow.

Braced for yelling, accusations, jeering, and slurs, Truman shrank away from the curtain. He stood in the stillness for a few moments. It was eerie how quiet it was backstage. The rest of the cast and crew were affected by the protestors, maybe just as much as he was.

Everyone seemed in a kind of trance.

Fortunately, he was deaf to what Mr. Wolcott was saying—and to how the protestors were responding. Maybe the lack of volume was a positive sign—maybe it meant Mr. Wolcott was making some sense to them. Maybe it meant there was some reasonable discourse going on. Truman knew how persuasive Mr. Wolcott could be.

But his hopes all shattered at once with the sound of a strident voice, shrieking loud enough for everyone backstage to hear her.

"No! No, sir! We have every right to peacefully protest! We will *not* sit down!"

He could at last hear Mr. Wolcott's voice too, placating, but a little louder.

A man, "The Constitution of these United States gives us the right to assemble!"

Then—a chorus of angry voices rising up.

No. This is getting out of hand. I've had enough.

Truman pulled the heavy red velvet curtain aside and started out and onto the stage.

"What the hell are you doing?" someone loudly whispered behind him.

Truman turned, only briefly. He opened his mouth to respond and then closed it when he realized the only words he wanted to utter, right at this very moment, were not toward his peers onstage but to the buffoons in the audience.

He headed for the stairs at the side of the stage, heels clicking on the stage's polished hardwood floor.

"Don't! You're in a dress, for God's sake. You're just gonna make them madder. It won't do any good! You'll just make things worse."

It wasn't one person saying the words, these cautions. It was a chorus of desperate voices, pleading.

Truman tried to shut them out, tried to believe his own bravery and courage meant more than a dress and a pair of heels. That what was going on in the back of the auditorium was because of him, and so it was up to him and not Mr. Wolcott or, God forbid, the police, to fix.

He stormed up the aisle filled with righteous indignation. Adrenaline, knowing he was right, stubbornness—whatever the reason, Truman suddenly found he was no longer afraid. And even as he acknowledged his fearlessness, he questioned it. Was he simply being stupid? Was he setting himself up to be hurt—emotionally *and* physically?

He didn't care. Everything in the past couple of months, he felt, had led him up to this point—*building, building, building.*

The only way to find relief was to speak up—and out.

As he approached, there were half a dozen furious voices raised in vehement disagreement.

Almost as one, they all stopped as Truman drew near.

Mr. Wolcott turned to look at him, and his jaw dropped. Then his eyebrows came together in confusion and concern. He started to open his mouth to speak, but someone beat him to it. He raised a hand as though to ward Truman off.

"Well, look," the man Truman assumed was Tammy Applegate's father sneered. "If it isn't Little Miss Mary Sunshine, come to toss pixie dust and wave her rainbow flag."

The protestors erupted in guffaws and titters.

Truman, trembling violently *inside* and on the verge of throwing up, forced himself to smile—and curtsy. "Truman Reid, actually, but I will answer to Mary Sunshine if the money's right. You can just call me Tru. And what should I call you, Mr.—?"

"Never you mind who I am. You need to get your faggot ass out of here before I kick it down that hill!" Fire blazed in the man's eyes suddenly, and Truman was honestly taken aback. So much so that he took a step or two backward, feeling as though he'd been sucker punched and the wind knocked out of him. It wasn't so much the words he'd put out there, but the sheer hatred with which he said them. Truman knew that this week's vocabulary word should be *zealot*.

Truman had been teased, bullied, stuffed into dumpsters, beaten up, had his lunch money taken from him repeated times, had his name besmirched in speech and print, had been called a girl too many times to count—as though being female was an insult!—but he thought that tonight, right here, with this man, he was facing unvarnished and unfettered hatred—a crazy kind of hate that knew no reason.

And that was scary. Truly terrifying.

The potential of such hatred, Truman thought, could be life-threatening.

Out of the corner of his eye, he saw Patsy slip into the auditorium. He wanted to run to her, push her back and out of harm's way. He knew how protective she could be, how riled up she could get when her boy was threatened. Right now, though, he could see she was stunned by what was going on. Her hand came up, clutching at her chest.

She looked beautiful, her hair pulled back and away from her face, in a simple black dress and heels, a rope of pearls—not real, of course—around her neck. A young Audrey Hepburn. There was something dignified about her, and for a moment Truman forgot his terror and simply felt proud of her.

Coming in behind her was another surprise—Stacy. Dressed in jeans and a loose red Ohio State hooded sweatshirt, presumably to conceal a swelling belly, she too radiated beauty, though in a different way from his mom. There was youth and vulnerability, but there was also a glow about her, a certain radiance. Her dark eyes sparkled.

Truman was jolted out of this small reverie.

"You gonna go or *what*? You filthy cocksucker…," the man spat. The words were like darts flung directly into Truman's heart.

Patsy strode forward. Her luminous features darkened even more with shock and rage. From past experience, Truman could tell she was about to launch into a tirade against this man—full of insults and righteous indignation and no shortage of cussing. He also knew she would not be above physically assaulting him.

And Truman felt a rush of love for this woman who cared so much about him that she'd risk her own safety to defend him.

But he wouldn't let her. Couldn't.

This was a battle he needed to fight for himself. *Wanted* to fight for himself....

So he held up a hand, stopping her. He met her eyes and shook his head. She stepped back a little.

He turned his attention back to the man. "I'm not going anywhere, Mr. Applegate." He paused for a moment, waiting to see if Tammy's father would try to deny his own identity, if he was that small a man.

He didn't. He simply stared at Truman, eyes focused into laser-thin pinpricks of pure hate.

"My place is here. I have a job to do. And I would appreciate if you would let me do it. If you have a problem with who I am, or what I am, or how I play this part, maybe we can meet up later and hash it out. Would you like that?" Truman made himself smile. He pointed over Mr. Applegate's shoulder at his mom.

"You know Patsy Reid, right?"

Mr. Applegate turned to look at her, then returned his gaze to Truman. Something had shifted in his expression, weakened perhaps. Or if not weakened, turned in a way. He didn't seem so sure of himself. He looked again at Patsy, then back to Truman, and nodded.

"She works down at the Elite Diner? Best fries in town. She'd be happy to find us a booth, rustle up some fries with gravy and a couple Cherry Cokes, and we could have ourselves a little chat, maybe. What do you think?"

Truman didn't wait for the man to answer. "We could talk about, I don't know, concepts like the Golden Rule—you know that one, don't you?—or maybe I could clue you in on *live and let live*, or maybe *turn the other cheek*. We could discuss things like equality and diversity and how the world is actually a better place because of *all* the colors in it. Wouldn't that be nice? Wouldn't that be *fun*?"

And as if on cue, something happened then that shocked not only Truman, but everyone watching—which was the entire audience now, who thought they'd come to see a high school production of a classic play and were now witnessing something far more important and far beyond their wildest imaginings.

The space behind Patsy darkened as a shadow fell. And—someone came in. Someone Truman didn't recognize at first, but when he did, he gasped and then laughed. His eyes widened.

As one, the protestors turned to see who'd entered the auditorium, who Truman was staring at, slack-jawed.

Truman would say that what they saw—at first—was a very tall, very ugly woman. Hell, he thought it was a big, not-so-attractive broad-shouldered, ungainly lass at first himself.

And then he latched on to those eyes—those crystalline blue, blue eyes. He'd know them anywhere.

Mike.

His dark hair was hidden under a black velvet hat, one that had a small bright red feather sticking out of the ribbon around its brim. His face, closely shaved, was nearly unrecognizable beneath a layer of foundation applied poorly—perhaps with a trowel? The eyeliner was too thick and as crooked as a politician's campaign promises. God love him, he'd tried to put lipstick on but wound up with more of a clown mouth than a lady's lips.

The aqua blouse with white pinstripes and—dear Lord—shoulder pads was a throwback to the heyday of 1980s fashion—or at least Truman supposed, based on what he'd seen in pictures. The blouse, along with the white palazzo pants, were way too tight. And the white sandals he'd managed to cram his size-twelve feet into? They had to be killing him.

The effect was almost comical. In fact, already, all around him, people were elbowing each other and giggling.

But Truman's heart didn't find Mike's gesture comical. He found it touching. He found a hand extended in solidarity. It had to have taken Mike a lot of courage, if not drag artistry, to do what he'd done, just to support him.

Mike smiled shyly at him, and for just one singular and magical moment, everything around them dissolved and they were alone in the room. "Hi, Tru," Mike said softly. Truman noticed that while Mike stood tall and proud, shoulders back and chin high, his hands were trembling.

"Hi." Truman smiled shyly. Truth be told, Mike looked awful, more a mockery of a woman than a woman. It was amazing to Truman how such a beautiful young man could morph into such a frighteningly unappetizing young lady.

Yet Truman loved him for it. His gesture was all at once kind, supportive, and genuine—he put his ass on the line for Truman. It *was* skin off his ass!

This was a moment he'd always remember. Because, by not saying a word, by not making some sort of political statement, but by sacrificing himself and his own reputation, Mike had shown such caring and love for Truman, it nearly took Truman's breath away. *So far in this life, I don't think anyone, other than Mom, has shown me such caring.*

Mike simply stood there, not saying anything, but the message was clear. *I'm with you, Truman Reid, and not ashamed of it.*

Truman eyed the protestors. Tammy Applegate had turned a deep shade of crimson and, of all of them, seemed the most aghast. Everyone gathered around her, earlier so vehement in their protests, were curiously quiet, eyeing Mike as one would a two-headed creature in a sideshow.

A *lovable* two-headed creature, Truman thought.

Even the signs the protestors carried drooped, now down near the floor. It was as though the wind had literally been sucked out of their sails. They seemed flabbergasted and tongue-tied.

Truman thought they weren't so much understanding as dumbfounded. And he knew it wouldn't take them too long to rev right back up to where they were before, so he used the shocked, hushed moment to his advantage.

He clapped his hands together. "Hey! Did everyone forget? We've got a show to put on here!" He glanced down at the white-gold bracelet watch Patsy had loaned him. "We're ten minutes past curtain already. Could everyone please take their seats?"

Mr. Wolcott stepped up to the plate then too. "Truman's right. It's time to start the show. Please—everyone—find a seat. There's plenty of room for all." He looked pointedly at the little cluster of protestors. "So no one should have to stand." This, Truman knew, was his subtle way of saying they needed to sit down.

As much as he would have loved to thank Mike for his gesture—perhaps giving him some tips on applying eyeliner—he knew this moment of quiet, of a kind of awe, wouldn't last forever. And he knew they needed to capitalize on it.

What he wanted to do, though, was give Mike *and* his mother a hug. He wanted to stare into Mike's eyes, offering up his thanks with a meaningful look. And maybe a kiss….

But what he *needed* to do, as both student director *and* Myrtle Mae Simmons, was turn around and march his ass back to the stage and get behind the curtain so things could start.

As he neared the stage, he glanced back over his shoulder. Almost everyone, save the protestors, had seated themselves. There was an expectant hush now in the room, where before there was an almost palpable sense of tension, almost like the hum of power lines.

Mike stood near the last pair of open doors, arms across his broad chest, eyeing each of the protestors with so much menace, Truman was a little chilled. Mike might have been dressed as the world's ugliest woman, but he was still imposing. In his stance and in his expression, he was daring any of them to step out of line.

Truman watched with a kind of bittersweet sadness as the protestors edged by Mike—and out of the auditorium. In a weird way, he'd hoped they would stay for the show. Maybe there was a chance they'd see he was just playing a part—and that he was good at it. Maybe they would have had a night of laughter, maybe shed a few tears—you know, the kind of pleasure good entertainment brings a person. Instead they'd probably go home and wallow in their self-righteous hate.

Truman shrugged. *It's their choice.*

After the last protestor was outside the set of double doors, Mike closed them. He smiled shyly at Truman, which just about made Truman gasp, and lumbered gracelessly down the aisle, wincing with every step. Those shoes! Those damn shoes! *They're three sizes too small*, Truman figured.

Mike took his seat, folded his hands in his lap, and waited for the show to start.

CHAPTER 19

"OH MY God," Truman whispered to Rex Lucas, who'd done such a wonderful job in the lead as the charming and whimsical Elwood P. Dowd. Truman thought Rex was easily just as good as Jimmy Stewart in his iconic film interpretation. He should have been, because he'd confided in Truman that he simply aped Stewart's film performance and had watched the movie version of *Harvey* more than a dozen times. Out of the corner of his mouth, Truman said, "We're getting a standing ovulation."

Max snickered. "And curtain call's not even over yet. Wait until they see—" Max stopped, Truman supposed because he noticed Mr. Wolcott in the wings, pressing a finger to his lips.

The crowd roared when the entire cast parted, their single line forming into two. The door at the back of the set opened mysteriously, as if by an invisible hand or paw. (Actually, the stage crew had rigged it to some fishing line so it could be pulled open from offstage.) The effect was that the last member of the cast—the rabbit, or pooka, more properly—Harvey, was entering the stage to take a bow.

They all waited as Harvey made his way to the front, and then each cast member bowed to him.

The crowd loved it. The applause was almost a deafening roar, seeming to go on for minutes. There were whoops and cheers. The accolades rose up in Truman's mind like a bunch of helium-filled balloons.

And Truman, with tears in his eyes, heard not a single catcall or anything derisive.

When they'd all taken a second and then a third bow, Truman squinted a bit to try to see out into the audience. It was too bright to see anything more than silhouettes or dim figures, but he was touched to know that there were several people he truly cared about among the nearly full house. It didn't matter whether he could see them or not. He knew they were there, cheering, and they were more than visible in his heart.

He could see Stacy in his mind's eye. He hoped she in particular was pleased with his performance and that she had no bitterness toward him, since the part was originally hers.

Alicia, of course, had shown up. He'd seen her earlier, and she was with her new boyfriend, an older guy who went to the Summitville branch of Youngstown State University. He was a dark-haired, brown-eyed Italian hottie from Wellsville, just down the river from them, and he seemed to adore her. The way he looked at her made Truman think of the term "puppy-dog eyes." She certainly dragged him around like he was her personal Yorkshire terrier, leashed by her clutching red-nailed hand. And maybe he was. And happy to be so....

And Truman pictured his bedrock, his best friend, his biggest supporter and protector—his mom, Patsy, grinning and clapping, her joy uncontained. He knew those wolf whistles were coming from her. She was a tiny woman, but she could make a big sound by putting just two fingers between her lips and blowing. He imagined the joy on her face, the vicarious pleasure and pride she must have witnessed in her son's artistry. He couldn't help being proud of his performance but knew Patsy was ten times prouder.

He was happy to add a little joy back into her life. She pretended like the breakup didn't matter, but he knew that, however justified it was, she still hurt. Although she'd never say it, he realized she wondered if it might be her last chance at love. The higher our hopes, the farther we fall when they don't work out.

Truman let out a little laugh as he thought of Mike, at last. Mike, dressed like a woman just to support him. He knew Mike, who passed under the radar with his deep voice, John Wayne gait, muscles, and stubble for days, had made a real sacrifice tonight. He'd effectively come out. Not so much by cross-dressing—that could have easily been done to make fun of Truman, rather than to support him—but by taking a chance and even kind of humiliating himself to underscore his caring for Truman and to make a point about how we're more than how we dress and, really, even more than our gender.

Just before the curtain went down, Truman closed his eyes for just a moment, allowing Mike's face, not the made-up one but the true one—with a shadow of stubble, full lips, eyes half-mast with a drowsy yet intense lust—to rise up before him.

Truman's pulse, already racing because of the postshow adrenaline and exhilaration coursing through him, jumped.

He opened his eyes just as the curtain closed.

All around him, his castmates and even the stage crew were jumping up and down, whooping and hollering. High-fiving each other.

They'd done it.

They had a hit on their hands. Truman thought, if not confined to the limits of a high school production that held them to two consecutive weekends, they might have run for years.

He took in everyone who'd pulled together to make the show such a success and felt a rush of affection for each and every person on the stage. Each for a different reason, Truman thought, they'd remember this night for the rest of their lives—this pure innocent joy, unfettered by judgment.

Mr. Wolcott slid up behind him. His strong hands grasped Truman's shoulders and gave him a quick little massage. The touch was momentary, but Truman felt swept up in it, a rush of warmth coursing through him. Mr. Wolcott spoke softly into Truman's ear. "You were terrific tonight. I mean it, really good. Above and beyond what I've seen high school kids do—and I've seen *a lot*. I think you have a real future as an actor. I really do." And then, just as suddenly, he drifted away.

Truman basked in the warmth for a moment. *How did he know what's in my heart? What my deepest dreams are? A real future on the stage? Really?* A sort of giddy joy rose up inside him.

Amber Wolfgang, who'd played his mother, Veta Louise, to comic matronly perfection, sidled up to him, smiling. "You did great."

"Thanks. So did you."

"You *are* coming to the cast party at my house tonight, right?"

Truman's breath caught.

He was as far from popular as probably anyone in the school. Although he'd never admit it to Amber, this was the first time in his whole high school career anyone had ever invited him to a party—or to anything social, really. There was a reason he considered Patsy and Odd Thomas his BFFs.

"So get your little butt over to my house, huh? My ma's ordering pizza and meatball subs from D'Angelo's. And there's a rumor Kirk's going to smuggle in some beer and wine." Amber giggled. "More than a rumor, actually, so you gotta come." She took off toward stage right but stopped to call over her shoulder, "And Tru? Wear whatever you want."

Truman laughed and gave her a thumbs-up. He knew she wasn't teasing him or making fun. And yet…. As excited as he was to go to his first high school party, he thought he just might have other plans.

He thought of Mike in the lobby, waiting. The notion of him, wearing not the feminine attire he'd donned for him tonight but nothing at all, left Truman with a delicious feeling of anticipation.

He slipped quietly backstage, where there were two crude dressing rooms set up with just a couple of stage flats separating the boys from the girls. One thing Truman appreciated—no one had ever given him shit about which one to use.

He entered the boys' dressing room and slipped out of the dress, the hat, the heels, and the white lace gloves. He rubbed at his face with cold cream and then used tissues to remove the makeup. He put his blonde wig on its Styrofoam head.

Behind him he could still hear everyone chattering excitedly onstage. He knew he had a moment alone—but only one or two—and he would use them to consider the young man staring back at him in the full-length mirror propped against the cinder block wall.

There he was, a skinny boy shivering in a pair of black boxers with yellow penguins. The outline of his ribs shone through his pale skin. His legs, if he were being honest, were little more than twigs, crowned with a little covering of golden hair.

He wondered what Mike saw in him, scrawny and runty as he was, and then immediately chastised himself. *It's just that kind of thinking that can hold a person back. It's just that kind of thinking that lets morons like the ones from earlier tonight get inside your head and your heart and make you believe you're less than. Don't.*

He looked back, turned a little in the mirror. Where before he saw scrawny, he now saw lithe. Skinny and bony morphed into trim and maybe even, if he would allow it, boyish. Yes, he was a pretty boy. But pretty boys can rock pretty—and they can be fierce.

He then considered the face looking back at him—with its silky, limp, straight blond hair tumbling down over his forehead, his oversized but penetrating eyes. And those full lips....

It was the same face he'd started the night with—and it wasn't. Maybe tonight, after all that had happened, there was change. Just maybe... there was something a little more mature in those features, something kinder and a little more compassionate, despite being hurt by others who seemed to lack those same qualities. Truman's face, in the mirror, reflected back the ability to rise above those who would seek to wound him.

And that, he thought, *is what will make me a fearless and uninhibited actor—not only on stage, but in life.*

He heard the patter of many footsteps, along with laughter, coming toward him and hurried to dress in his street clothes.

CHAPTER 20

MIKE LEANED against his truck outside, waiting for Truman. It was at moments like this one that he wished he smoked. There was something he couldn't deny in his mind's eye about a man waiting for the person he loved to arrive, leaning against a pickup truck, smoking a cigarette, eyes full of longing. It was sexy. Romantic.

Reality check! Think about your two-pack-a-day dad and his disgusting hacking every morning, right before he lights up. Consider the stink of him. The premature age lines, drawn by smoke, on his face. Mike shook his head at his thoughts. There was nothing sexy or romantic about smoking.

Still, he hoped that when Truman finally emerged from the field house, he would find Mike sexy and romantic.

Earlier, Mike had struggled out of that insane women's get-up (and the makeup! Lord, that was a whole 'nother story) he'd donned to show his love and support for Truman. Someone passing by the truck might have thought he was wrestling a bear in the cab, such were his contortions. He'd hoped a cop wouldn't happen by once he was naked! After all, he was in a school parking lot, even if it was at its outer edges.

But he'd changed quickly into the kind of comfy stuff he felt like himself in—a pair of jeans, so soft and pale they were almost white, with holes worn in the knees, and his favorite hoodie, back from when he lived in Washington State, gray and purple, with a University of Washington husky on its front, faded. The sweatshirt was also soft. The fleece inside felt good next to his skin, like a mother's touch. Not *his* mom, of course, but he could imagine. Someone like Patsy…. He had on a fleece Carhartt jacket handed down from his dad and a pair of old work boots. He didn't wear any of this crap because he thought it was sexy, but because he simply could forget the clothes on his back when he wore them. They were *him*—like a second skin.

He'd hopped down from the truck's cab into the cool night air and decided that, no matter how chilly he got, he wouldn't succumb to the temptation to get back inside. He wanted to be here for Truman when he exited through those doors. He wanted Truman to know that, even if the parking lot was empty, there was one person who couldn't, wouldn't go home until he'd had at least a glimpse of his favorite Myrtle Mae Simmons.

A few minutes before, Patsy had driven up to him in her belching beater and rolled down the window.

"You waitin' for the superstar?"

Mike grinned. "Yeah. Do you mind if I whisk him away for a couple of hours?" He nodded toward the truck. "I got wheels."

"That's up to him." She stared up at Mike, grinning, as though the two shared a secret. "He was amazing tonight, wasn't he? Just so funny, so real." She shook her head. "Sometimes I can't believe he's mine, that I raised him. Because Lord knows, I wasn't able to give him much!" She snorted. "You've seen our house."

Mike didn't know what to say. Or rather, he did know what to say but was unable to get the words out around the big tangerine-sized ball in his throat. He would have told her that Truman was lucky to have a mom like her, one who loved him unconditionally, one who'd always put him first, sometimes—often, Mike was sure—sacrificing her own happiness and well-being to ensure her son got the best she could give him. Mike sure would have liked to have had some of that kind of love. Never mind the material crap Patsy seemed convinced Truman needed. He put his hand on Patsy's car door and said, "You're a good mom. Anybody can see that."

Dark eyes shining, she stared at him for a moment. And in that moment, Mike felt the two of them became friends.

But he wanted to share a special moment right now with Truman and not Truman and his mom, so he broke the moment by stepping away from her car and said, "Yeah, he was something else. But then you and I aren't surprised, are we?"

"Not at all. We'll see you later, Mike. Come by the house if you guys want. Raid the fridge." She laughed and rolled up her window. She drove away, leaving Mike waving his hand in front of his face to dispel the exhaust fumes.

He watched the parade of headlights as everyone headed out—and home, or to wherever they were going afterward, Patsy's Elite Diner, or maybe the Mexican joint up in East End.

Now he was alone, shivering, and worried that he'd missed Truman exiting the field house. Wind blew out of the north, hard enough to moan like a howl. The moon had risen, almost orange, hanging like an impossibly big sphere near the tops of the Appalachian foothills. Mike wondered if this was what people meant when they referred to a harvest moon. He swore he could see a face in its cratered surface. Whatever. It sure was pretty, despite making a guy feel very alone.

The darkness all around him seemed to press in. Mike felt as though there were ghosts among the dark shadows, and they were whispering—knowing, as ghosts often do, what his fate was to be.

Did I really miss him? Am I standing here waiting for nothing? The thought chilled him even more than the wind out of the north. He had a six-pack of Iron City beer, a bag of Cool Ranch Doritos, and a bouquet of red roses waiting on the bench seat. His idea of an after-party. He hoped Truman would be surprised—and pleased.

He won't be much of anything if he already left.
Mike clutched the keys in his pocket, ready to de-
part. He could catch up with Truman later. That idea,
though, weighed heavy on his heart. A sad, self-de-
feating part of himself told him Truman wasn't coming. That his performance tonight was a triumph and
he would be too busy to find time for the likes of Mike.
And besides, why would Mike think Truman would
meet up with him when Mike had to admit that, in the
recent past anyway, all he'd done was ignore the guy.

But….

But….

But…. There was no need for those dark emotions because there *he* was, pushing through the heavy
glass doors to emerge into the night. Alone. The sight
of him, unaware of Mike for just this moment, made
Mike catch his breath.

What a handsome boy. The wind caught the hair
that was always coming down over his forehead and
lifted, revealing for a moment Truman's whole face.
Sexy. Vulnerable, yet strong. And yes, manly. Even
in a dress and long blonde wig, Truman was a man.
Because of his confidence, his unwillingness to bend
to convention, his willingness to love….

Truman Reid, will you be mine? Mike stepped
forward to make himself more visible in the pool of
light from one of the parking lot's tall lamps. He imagined himself as Truman might see him and flattered
himself with putting a kind of quiet joy—and lust—in
Truman's heart.

When their gazes connected, across the dark
sea of asphalt, Mike felt simultaneously chilled and
warmed—as though a shot of something hot had been

set loose in his veins, filling him with a heat like liquid sunshine. The temperature of that heat skyrocketed when Truman, spotting Mike, smiled. Truman's smile was megawatt, even in this dark, deserted parking lot. And it thrilled Mike beyond words because the smile was his and his alone.

Mike raised his hand in a shy wave. And grinned a bit as Truman hurried over to him.

Truman slowed as he neared Mike. "Hey, stranger," he said in a voice that was just a notch above a whisper.

"Hey yourself."

They stood in silence for a few moments, each shifting their weight from one foot to the other, considering the starry night sky, eyes meeting furtively, shyly.

Finally Truman broke the silence because Mike never knew what to say. "You make a shitty woman. I mean, if all the women in the world looked similar to what *you* put out there tonight, I'd have my pick of any man I wanted because, honey, all the men in the world would turn gay."

They both cracked up.

Mike wasn't insulted, not really, because he could see the warmth in Truman's body language and in his smile. Besides, Mike liked to believe, *had* to believe, that if all the men in the world turned gay, Truman would still pick him.

"So that's the thanks I get for going to all that trouble? You *dis* me? Fuck you." Mike turned as though he were going to hop back in the truck and drive away.

He knew exactly what would happen. He smiled as he felt Truman's hands grab at the back of his fleece jacket. He turned.

Truman's eyes shone. He shook his head. "I do thank you, Mike. I don't think anyone has ever done anything so selfless and so brave—for me. I can't tell you how much what you did means to me."

Mike felt heat rise to his face. "Ah, it was nothin'. All in a day's work, right?"

"You know that's not true. So, thank you." Truman hugged him tight, his face pressed against Mike's cheek. Mike felt like he could stay in the warmth of Truman's embrace—just like this—forever. But a voice from the south, from a different head, was stirring and begging for more. *Some parts of us are never satisfied....*

Embarrassed, Mike pulled away, hips first, the rest of him following. "You got plans?" he asked, knowing the hope in his voice was so apparent as to make him a pathetic creature, but he didn't care. He couldn't help it.

"Well, Amber Wolfgang is having an after-party at her house. She's rich—they even have an indoor pool! And there'll be pizza." He grinned. "And beer, or so I hear."

Mike said, "I got beer. Iron City. And Cool Ranch Doritos. And these—" He hurried around the side of the truck, opened the door, and came back to Truman holding out the dozen red roses he'd bought earlier at the Giant Eagle supermarket. "For my superstar."

Truman took them shyly, staring down at them as though they were something rare and precious. Voice choked, he managed to say, "No one ever gave me flowers before."

Mike grinned. "Get used to it, sweetheart."

They were just about to lean in for a kiss when the sound of a car starting up interrupted. Mike turned toward the sound, a little surprised because he thought he was the last one in the parking lot. Maybe he hadn't noticed the other vehicle because it was at the opposite end.

But as it neared, Mike got a chill because he recognized the car—a beat-up old red Mustang. It came close, the headlights blinding Mike for a second, but when the car turned toward the exit, Mike recognized the face behind the wheel, maybe because it was a face he'd seen previously in darkness. He put two and two together once he saw the guy with the glasses and thinning hair coupled with the old red Mustang.

His mouth dropped open. And something queasy and dread-like woke up in his gut, making him feel a little sick.

Truman looked after the car, watching it, Mike guessed, to make sure it disappeared down the hill. He turned back to Mike. "I'm surprised they just drove on by. I mean, without calling us fags or something. Or maybe telling us we were on the highway to hell. Or worst of all, that they'd pray for us. I don't need their sanctimonious prayers. And neither do you." He shook his head and rolled his eyes. "You do know who that was, don't you?"

Mike knew.

Mike knew all too well. His recent night at the park rose up in memory like one of those old 70s porn movies he'd discovered online. He didn't know, though, if he wanted to admit that association to Truman. He tried to swallow and discovered he had no spit. With a shaking voice, he asked, "Who?"

"Tammy Applegate and that homophobe dad of hers!" He laughed. "By themselves, they were probably too cowardly to say anything to me, or to us."

Mike turned, staring off into the darkness. The lights of Summitville glowed down below, warm yellow. He imagined everyone in the world safe and sound, snug in their homes, free of memories like the one torturing him at this very moment. How could a moment go from magical to sick with one swift turn? "Shit," he whispered.

He turned to find Truman staring at him, arms crossed, head cocked. "Is something wrong?"

"No." Mike had to look away from Truman's inquiring eyes. He felt vulnerable, like he'd been under the rock Truman had just lifted.

"Yes," Mike said, turning back to face Truman. He let loose a big sigh, almost a moan.

Truman took a step closer. "What is it?"

"That guy. Mr. Applegate. I've seen him before."

Truman shrugged. "It's a small town."

"No. You don't get it." *It's time to tell him. So what? You didn't do anything with him. You just happened to see something.* The thought was cold comfort when Mike put it in the context of how he'd reacted to what he'd seen—the arousal, the temptation. *You don't have to tell Truman everything. You have a right to some privacy. How your body responded to something it saw is not cause for shame or guilt. Neither is it cause for confession.* "You know the park?"

Truman nodded.

Mike didn't need to name it because there was only one.

"You know what, uh, sometimes goes on up there, after it gets dark?"

Truman eyed him warily. And Mike could imagine where his mind was going. "No!" Mike cried. "I just go there to think, to be alone. But one night—"

And he told Truman what he'd seen.

He was surprised when Truman snickered. "Really?"

"Yeah."

"And you're sure it was him?"

"Oh yeah. Positive. Even though it was dark, no one else in town has a Mustang like that one. Vintage."

Truman shook his head, and then he burst into renewed laughter, so hard he was eventually holding his sides.

"It's not funny!"

"The hell it isn't," Truman said. "Mr. Holier than Thou up there on the hill giving hum jobs to the local men. It's priceless!" He doubled over. Suddenly Mike saw the humor in the situation—and the hypocrisy.

What could a guy do but laugh?

And he realized there was no reason for him to feel guilty. So what if he'd experienced a little vulnerability, a little temptation that night? He didn't act on it. He gave himself some credit for that. He couldn't help being tempted, but he could help how he reacted to that temptation.

When they had reined in their laughter—and their tears, because, yes, it was *that* funny—Truman grabbed Mike in an embrace and kissed him. Long and hard. When they pulled away, a little breathless,

Truman said, "I don't want you going to that park at night alone."

Mike bristled—but for only an instant. His first thought was about what right Truman had to tell him where he could or couldn't go. It wasn't like they'd made a commitment to one another. Not yet, anyway.

But that feeling, that indignation, was fleeting. Mike actually *did* want Truman to tell him where he could and couldn't go. He cared. Mike wanted that concern, that jealousy, even. Hell, no one else in his life gave a shit where he was at any given hour or day.

So he just said, "Okay." A lightbulb went off above Mike's head. "Should we hop in my truck and chase 'em down?" Mike took some malicious glee in imagining Mr. Applegate's face when he "outed" him, especially with his daughter sitting beside him. Talk about priceless! "He doesn't have much of a lead. I could catch up."

"And then what?" Truman asked.

"Well, we could let Tammy know what a hypocrite her father is. Hell, we could let the whole town know." Mike shook his head. "That asshole. Bad enough he's sucking cock when he has a wife—she does my ma's nails every other week. But okay, so he likes a bit of cock…." He grinned at Tru. "Who doesn't? But then, does he have to try and be all self-righteous about any-one who's different? We should shine a light on that motherfucker."

He fully expected Truman to chime in with agree-ment. But Truman surprised him. "Nah. I don't think we want to do that, Mike. You and I both know that man's tortured. He's leading a double life. And after what you just told me, it kind of makes me feel different about him."

"How? Why?"

"Because I know now that all this crap about me wearing a dress in a high school play is just camouflage for how he feels about *himself*. See, he doesn't hate me, he hates himself. And in his own twisted way, what he did tonight was a bad attempt to deal with that."

Mike felt a little abashed when he thought of Truman's wisdom—and his kindness. "Yeah, you're probably right." Mike didn't say it, but he thought if he'd acted on his own temptation that night in the park, it wouldn't have been as much out of lust as it was out of a kind of self-loathing.

He knew he had a lot to learn from Truman.

He also realized he had a few other things he hoped Truman could teach him. And this latter thought caused a sly, lascivious grin to cross his face.

He leaned close to Truman. "It's fucking cold out here. What do you say we get in the cab, take a drive down by the river... and warm each other up?" His eyebrows wiggled.

"I can't imagine what you have in mind, mister, but I'm willing to trust you," said Truman, smiling and then turning toward the driver's side of the pickup truck. "But only if you let me drive. Tonight I feel like driving."

"Are you saying—?"

"Just shut up and get in the damn truck."

CHAPTER 21

IT HAD gotten even colder by the time they reached what Truman thought of as their trysting spot down by the river, in the shadows on the big bridge crossing over into West Virginia. The wind had picked up, and it had begun raining—hard. It pounded on the metal roof of the truck like hoofbeats—a whole team of tiny horses cantered up there. The rain smeared the glass all around them. And if the smearing wasn't enough, their own breath further isolated them.

Mike had left the heater on for a good ten minutes after they'd parked but then told Tru he was low on gas so they'd have to conserve, turning the engine off and on as necessary. With a nervous grin, he told Truman he'd need to do his best to keep him warm, and that if he was successful, they wouldn't need to start the truck up again until they were ready to leave.

Mike leered when he said, "Which I hope is hours and hours from now."

Truman hoped so too. For the last half hour or so, they had been locked in a passionate embrace, their bodies melded to one another's as though they were one being. It made Truman think of a phrase he'd run across in some bodice-ripper novel Patsy had left lying around—*making the beast with two backs*. Their lips and tongues left each other's only long enough to explore the nape of the other's neck, an earlobe, even an eyebrow. All of Mike tasted good. And Truman hadn't even gotten to the best parts of him yet.

It was surprising to Truman that they'd never managed to get out of each other's arms. Seriously, it seemed like they were clinging to one another every single second. And the thing that had Truman in a state of wonder? How they'd managed to accomplish the feat of staying together while at the same time getting undressed.

They were both stark naked now.

And Truman was grateful they were cocooned inside the truck in their own little world of raindrops and fog. If someone was standing on the running board outside his window, Truman believed they still wouldn't have a clue as to what was going on inside.

And what was going on inside was lovemaking, passion, down-and-dirty, the kind of raw sex that takes your breath and your ability for conscious thought away. Truman felt he'd become an animal, a desperate, wanting animal that knew no satisfaction but only lusted for more, more, more.

He moved his lips away from Mike's and started downward, licking and tonguing his ears, his neck, his chest, pausing to shower his nipples with pointed attention. From his moans and cries, Truman knew Mike was loving what he was doing to him. Truman had never had the experience of sucking a man's nipples before, and he discovered a new joy. The light growth of dark hair around Mike's broad nipples tickled his face—and he realized how those two pieces of salmon-colored flesh were hot-wired to Mike's dick, which he was thrusting upward into Truman's belly.

Things could turn very serious, very soon.

Or very messy....

Which was why, Truman supposed, Mike pulled him back up, grasping him under the armpits as Truman began to head farther south.

"No. If you get down there," Mike said, panting, "I won't be able to last a minute. And I want all of this to last much longer."

Truman was glad Mike had faith in Truman's powers of longevity, faith he didn't have in himself.

"I wanna suck you," Mike said. And then he did.

Mike was so hungry, so perfect at what he was doing, Truman flailed his head back against the truck's bench seat and buried a hand in Mike's dark hair. He thrust into Mike's mouth, faster, faster, thinking this was *it*.

But Mike obviously had other ideas. Because just as Truman was about to shoot and, he thought, experience his most volcanic and delicious orgasm ever, Mike pulled away, grasping the base of Truman's throbbing dick and squeezing. Truman thought the effort was too little and too late to interrupt the geyser of seed about to erupt.

But somehow—a miracle—the pressure worked, and it stemmed the flow.

For the moment.

Mike looked up at him, chin wet and breathing hard. "I want you to fuck me."

Now that's not what I expected. Maybe it was what I wanted—deep down—but I never thought he'd want me to. I thought he was going to say he wanted to fuck me.

Good God, I've never fucked anybody before. What if I'm terrible at it? I'm supposed to be the bottom here. I've always been the bottom boy. Aren't all sissies?

Maybe not....

His thoughts, more than a little frantic, came to a screeching halt when Mike pleaded, "Please! I need you inside me."

What do you do when a lover makes such demands?

You comply if there's any way you can.

And Truman, staring down at the long, pale rod of steel that was his dick, knew compliance would be no problem. Staying power might be another story, but he'd cross that bridge when he came to it.

"Got condoms?"

Mike reached over to fling open the glove compartment. "There." He pointed to a box of Trojans.

Truman was grateful to see they were lubricated, because he didn't see any lube in the glove box or anywhere nearby. With a trembling hand, Truman reached out to grab the box. He held it for a moment, looking down to see it contained a dozen condoms, wondering if they'd use them all tonight.

Wondering if they had enough….

Mike slid off him, sitting restlessly in the passenger seat, watching.

Truman removed one of the condoms, his hands shaking so badly he couldn't open the foil packet. He tried once, twice, three times… and even the third time wasn't the charm. "Damn it," he whispered. "Why do they make 'em so hard to open?"

Mike said, "Fuck it." And Truman thought they were going to bareback, which, at this point in the fever of his passion, would have been just fine. The odds were good there was little risk for either of them. But Mike snatched the packet out of his hand, tore it open with his teeth, and then proceeded to roll it onto Truman's dick. When it was in place, he smiled up at Truman, proud. Breathlessly he said, "Trade places."

They exchanged places on the bench seat, Truman sliding over to the passenger seat. He sat back, legs splayed, dick sticking up as though to point the way to heaven. Mike grabbed Truman's dick and climbed on board his lap. And slid down, an inch at a time, a little bit faster with each inch….

In just a few seconds, Truman felt the wonder— for the first time—of being deeply inside another man, that embracing, clutching warmth. "Oh God," he moaned. "I want to stay this way forever." *What do you know? I might be a top after all. Because, damn, this feels amazing.*

Mike gripped Tru's shoulders and then started to move, sliding up and down. Truman grabbed his hips to stop him, holding him down, impaled. "Don't fucking move." It seemed like his whole body was twitching. The prospect for this being over in less than a second was very likely. He breathed rapidly through his mouth, willing himself not to come. *Please no. Please no. Not yet.*

And yet another miracle occurred. The spasms coursing through him slowed just enough to reassure Truman he wasn't going to come. At least not for the next minute or so.

He thrust upward and into Mike slowly, smoothly. Back out, up again. He started to establish a rhythm. Mike was doing a sort of groaning, humming thing, so Truman knew he was pleasing him, delighting him, leading him to the edge of ecstasy. He smiled.

"I'm doin' okay?" Truman managed to ask.

"Better. Much better than okay." Mike's eyes were beginning to roll back in his head. His mouth was open, and Truman could feel Mike's ass tightening down on his dick.

Heaven is right here on earth.

Of course, as Truman had known they would be from the moment he'd slid inside Mike, things were over all too soon. With one mighty thrust upward, Truman cried out as the first gush of semen jetted out of him, filling the tight rubber to capacity. Mike groaned, guttural, and within a second, hot splashes of come landed on Truman's cheek, chin, and chest.

They collapsed against each other, shuddering. Truman couldn't help it—he started laughing almost hysterically, with relief, with joy. Mike followed in the laughter after a second.

When he could get his breath back, Mike asked, "What the hell are we laughing about?"

Truman squeezed him, still buried deep inside. He wondered if he'd stay hard enough for round two without having to pull out. This top thing, he thought, agreed with him. "We're laughing because we're happy. We're laughing because we're together—and that brings us joy. Right?"

Mike inclined his head so his forehead rested against Truman's. "Right," he agreed breathlessly.

"Where do we go from here?" Mike asked after a while, when their bodies began to relax, their muscles to at last loosen a bit, their blood to redistribute, maybe a bit, to the more regular places. He softly planted a small kiss on Truman's neck, just below his earlobe.

"What do you mean?" Truman grinned. He was beginning to get hard again.

"Sexually. Geographically. Us," Mike said.

"Sexually, I want to try fucking you on your back, with your legs on my shoulders." He gazed into Mike's eyes, serious as a heart attack.

"In this cramped little cab? I mean, I like the idea, but—"

"Hush. You can lay across the seat, and I'll stand outside on the running board."

Mike snickered. "You have it all figured out, don't you?"

Truman nodded. "The little head down south helped me put all the puzzle pieces in place."

"Won't you get cold?"

"With your ass around my dick? I doubt it. No, I know I won't. No matter if a fucking monsoon is pounding down on my back and Arctic winds are blowing."

"Well then, maybe we should see how this little plan of yours works out."

Truman nodded eagerly. "Maybe we should."

Mike slid off him.

"But before we get started again, I think I need to answer your other questions—you know, about where we're going. *Geographically*, I want to bring you home. I want to fall asleep in your arms. No worries—I think I can sneak you in, even if Patsy's up late listening to her namesake, Patsy Cline, and doing a crossword puzzle. I have my ways of getting you in undetected." He winked. "I've done it before."

Mike frowned. "Really?"

Truman gave him a tap on the arm. "Don't get the wrong idea. With Stacy. Never with a guy."

Mike's long exhale indicated he was both appeased and relieved. Maybe relieved because he was appeased. Was he going to be the jealous type? Truman wondered.

Mike said, "Well shit, man, if we have a bed, wouldn't you rather have me on my back there… where it's warm and cozy?"

"Maybe later. Right now I want to play out this fantasy. Hot guy. Pickup truck. You know the drill."

"Honestly, I don't. Not really." Mike reached over Truman to push open the truck's passenger door. Cold night air rushed in, an assault, almost like a third presence in the cab, causing goose bumps to rise on both their skins.

Rain pattered against the truck's interior. Mike shoved Truman, laughing, out of the truck.

Truman watched Mike, his heart rate accelerating, get into position on his back. He drew his legs up near his ears, and Truman regarded his ass with wonder, with lust, with a small sense of ownership. He marveled—even Mike's ass was crowned with a mat of dark hair. Truman thought he could come just looking at it.

But he didn't want to come from just looking at it.

He leaned to reach into the glove box, undeterred by the rain sliding down his back, the cold wind blowing. He pulled out another condom, and this one he opened like an accomplished pro. He slid it onto his upward-pointing dick and maneuvered himself into position between Mike's spread thighs.

Before he plunged in, though, he said, "There's one more area you asked where we're headed to, and I wanted to answer that"—he grinned—"before we completely lose our minds. You asked about *us*—where *we're* going."

And with simply saying those words, Truman's mind and heart shifted a little. Tears sprung to his eyes. A different kind of warmth seized his heart. A happy future began to take shape in his head, like a flower opening in time-lapse photography. As he looked down at this man-feast laid out before him, he realized Mike was someone he could love, really love—maybe for a very long time. Maybe forever. That his dreams and Mike's could be compatible. That they could be there for one another, as support and refuge. From the way Mike gazed back at him, with adoration and expectation, he was certain Mike felt the same.

"*Us*. We're a thing now. And I hope for a long time."

"Me too," Mike said. "You're my heart."

"And you're mine. I love you, Mike."

"And I love you, Truman Reid. You *are* a true man." He smiled. "And you need to fuck me again before I completely go crazy."

And Truman did.

EPILOGUE

IN A small house, just above the winding brown snake of the Ohio River, two boys slumber together in a twin bed, arms and legs entwined. Moonlight slips in, slatted and silver, to lie upon the floor and cast the pair in grayish light.

One of the boys—who cares which one—snores softly, a resonant rhythm born of complete exhaustion. The snore accompanies a similar rattling intake and outtake of breath coming from the dog on the floor who lies near the bed, content in the knowledge that his master is deeply happy. The dog dreams of being a puppy again, in filtered sunlight on the pebbled bank of the Ohio River. He chases a stick that dances over the sun-dappled water, and when he catches it, it magically throws itself again. But he never tires, and the joy he knows is boundless. For Odd Thomas, the aches and pains of old age exist no longer.

One of the boys turns, the one with the dark hair and the stubble he's too young to have on such a baby face, and murmurs in his slumber, perhaps in response to a dream he's having, one in which he and his own true love, Truman, inhabit a small apartment somewhere vast and bustling. Outside, a cityscape rises up to illuminate the night sky, blotting out the stars, but no matter; the windows of all the skyscrapers are stars themselves. In his dream, he and Truman sleep wrapped in each other's arms on an old couch, a beaten-up and frayed quilt thrown over their naked bodies.

The other boy dreams too. And perhaps the three of them, together so close in this room, have synced their dream cycles. Truman dreams of a city too, of rows of lighted marquees and crowds emerging under bright lights. He steps backstage after taking his curtain call to fall into the overjoyed and loving embrace of Mike, who is somehow years and years older yet still the same. They look into each other's eyes, and all the backstage machinery and magic-making, along with dozens of other castmates and crew members, vanish for just a moment as the two hold their gazes steady, knowing that real success lies not in the trappings of what's around them but what's in their hearts—and their eyes.

One room over, a woman sleeps fitfully, the smell of white wine perfuming her every exhalation. She doesn't dream, not anymore. But in those moments when she tosses and turns and her eyes flutter open, she hopes.

In the living room, a young girl with dark hair cocoons herself on the couch, one hand on her belly to perhaps reassure the life growing within her. She dreams of the soft, fat cheeks of a baby, downy to her touch.

IN THE morning Truman jerked awake, staring over at Mike, who still slept, mouth open, a line of drool dribbling out of the corner. "How cute." Truman rolled his eyes.

He woke Mike with a kiss. When Mike opened those incredible baby blues, Truman forgot for a moment what had panicked him a moment ago—the fear of being caught with a guy in his room by Patsy. He wasn't quite sure how she'd take it. It was one thing to have Stacy here—who was now couch-surfing in the living room after refusing Patsy's offer to give up her own bed—quite another to have Mike.

A boy I just had sex with. Four times. A boy, more importantly, with whom I'm falling more deeply in love with every breath I take.

"You need to get out of here," he whispered in Mike's ear, much as he hated to say the words. They were still, after all, high school kids. Was this even proper?

"Really?" Mike reached down to give Truman's dick, at full mast, a playful squeeze. "Maybe one more? For the road?"

"Later, Tiger." Truman felt even a little more panicked. He'd just heard the toilet flush. What time was it, anyway? The way the sun was shining in, he would guess it was *not* super early.

A knock at the door made both of them tense. Truman, mouth open, looked wildly to Mike. Perhaps he could slip out the same window he'd come in the night before.

But then they both relaxed as they heard Patsy, laughing, say, "There's a man in your room. I can smell him."

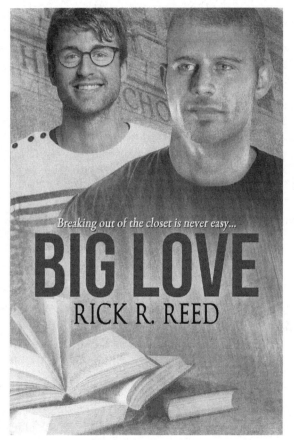

Breaking out of the closet is never easy...

BIG LOVE
RICK R. REED

Teacher Dane Bernard is a gentle giant, loved by all at Summitville High School. He has a beautiful wife, two kids, and an easy rapport with staff and students alike. But Dane has a secret, one he expects to keep hidden for the rest of his life—he's gay.

But when he loses his wife, Dane finally confronts his attraction to men. And a new teacher, Seth Wolcott, immediately catches his eye. Seth himself is starting over, licking his wounds from a breakup. The last thing Seth wants is another relationship—but when he spies Dane on his first day at Summitville High, his attraction is immediate and electric.

As the two men enter into a dance of discovery and new love, they're called upon to come to the aid of bullied gay student Truman Reid. Truman is out and proud, which not everyone at his small-town high school approves of. As the two men work to help Truman ignore the bullies and love himself without reservation, they all learn life-changing lessons about coming out, coming to terms, acceptance, heartbreak, and falling in love.

PROLOGUE

Dane Bernard, a big, gentle man, a teacher, would always look at that particular first day of school at Summitville High School as the one that changed his life forever.

Three things happened in that one momentous day that made returning to his old, comfortable life impossible—he rescued a boy from bullies, he lost his wife of twenty years, and… he began a journey to find himself.

How these three events, seemingly so disparate, tie together is our story. Let's begin with the first.

CHAPTER 1

TRUMAN REID was white as a stick of chalk—skin so pale it was nearly translucent. His blue eyes were fashioned from icy spring water. His hair—platinum blond—lay in curls across his forehead and spilled down his neck. He was the kind of boy for whom adjectives like "lovely" and "pretty" would most definitely apply. More than once in his life, he was mistaken for a girl.

When he was a very little boy, well-meaning strangers (and some not so well-meaning) would ask if he was a boy or a girl. Truman was never offended by the question, because he could see no shame in being mistaken for a girl. It wasn't until later that he realized there were some who would think the question offensive.

But this boy, who, on the first day of school, boldly and some might say unwisely wore a T-shirt that proclaimed "It Gets Better" beneath an image of a rainbow flag, didn't seem to possess the pride the T-shirt proclaimed. At Summitville High School, even though it was 2015, one did not shout out one's sexual orientation, not in word, not in fashion, and certainly not in deed.

Who knew what caused Truman to break with convention that morning when he made up his mind to wear that T-shirt on the first day of school? It wasn't like he needed to proclaim *anything*—after all, the slight, effeminate boy had been the object of bullies and torturers since, oh, about second grade. Truman could never "pass."

He was a big sissy. It was a fact and one Truman had no choice but to accept.

His shoulders, perpetually hunched, hunched farther during his grade school and junior high years, when such epithets as "sissy," "fag," "pansy," and "queer" were hurled at him in school corridors and playgrounds on a daily basis. Truman knew the old schoolyard chant wasn't true at all—words could and did hurt. And so, occasionally, did fists and hands.

And yet, despite the teasing—or maybe it's more apt to say *because* of it—Truman was not ashamed of who and what he was. His single mom, Patsy, his most vocal supporter and defender, often told him the same thing. "God made you just the way you are, honey. Beautiful. And if you're one of his creations, there's nothing wrong in who you are. You just hold your head up and be proud." The sad truth was, Patsy would often tell her boy stuff like this as she brushed tears away from his face.

It wasn't only tears she brushed away, though. Her unconditional love also brushed away any doubt Truman might have had that he was anything other than a normal boy, even though he was not like most of the boys his age in Summitville, Ohio, that backward little burg situated on the Ohio River and in the foothills of the Appalachian Mountains. In spite of the teasing and the bullying—and the pain they caused— Truman wasn't ashamed of who he was, which was what led him to wearing the fated T-shirt that got him in so much trouble his first day as a freshman at Summitville High School.

The incident occurred near the end of the day, when everyone was filing into the school gymnasium for an orientation assembly and a speech from the school's principal, Doug Calhoun, on what the returning students and incoming freshmen could expect that year.

Truman was in the crush of kids making their way toward the bleachers. High school was no different than grade school or junior high in that Truman was alone. And even though this was the first day of school, Truman already had a large three-ring binder tucked under his arm, along with English Composition, Biology, and Algebra I textbooks. Tucked into the notebook and books were papers—class schedules of assignments and the copious notes the studious Truman had already taken.

Kirk Samson, a senior and starting quarterback on the football team, knew the laughs he could get if he tripped this little fag in his pride-parade T-shirt, so he held back a little in the crowd, waiting for just the right moment to thrust out a leg in front of the unsuspecting Truman, whose eyes were cast down to the polished gymnasium floor.

Truman didn't see the quarterback's leg until it was too late, and he stumbled, going down hard on one knee. That sight was *not* the funniest thing the crowd had seen, although the pratfall garnered a roar of appreciative laughter at Truman's expense. But what was funnier was when Truman's notebook, books, and papers all flew out from under his arm, landing in a mess on the floor.

Kirk, watching from nearby with a smirk on his face, whispered two words to the kids passing by: "Kick 'em. Kick 'em."

And the kids complied, sending Truman's notes, schedules, and texts across the gym floor, as Truman, on his knees, struggled to gather everything up, even as more and more students got in on the fun of sending them farther and farther out of his reach.

Now, *that* was the funniest thing the crowd had seen.

Who knows how long the hilarity would have gone on if an authority figure had not intervened?

DANE BERNARD, English teacher, gentle giant, cross-country track coach, and indisputably one of the most well-liked teachers at the school, saw what was happening to Truman and rushed over. He only wished he could have been quicker to act—the boy's books and papers were now kicked out almost to the middle of the gym floor.

Dane knelt down by Truman, though, and helped him pick everything up as the kids behind, their laughter dying to a few isolated giggles, scrammed for their seats among the bleachers. It took a long time for the titters and whispering to die down.

Once the papers had been haphazardly gathered and even more haphazardly stuffed back inside notebook and textbooks, Dane put what he hoped was a calming hand on Truman's shoulder and gave it a little squeeze.

"You okay, son?" he asked.

The boy didn't have to respond. Dane frowned as he took in the tears standing in the boy's eyes. "What's your name?"

"Truman. Truman Reid." As befitting his name, the slight boy's voice came out reedy, a little high, still cracking, the bane of adolescent males since time immemorial.

"I'm Mr. Bernard."

Truman stared up at Dane, and as he did, a tear dribbled down his cheek, across a couple of acne bumps, to land on the floor. "Thanks. Thanks for helping me." Truman wiped away any remaining tears with the back of his hand. "I should get to my seat."

Dane looked over at the crowd, many of whom were watching, giggles ready to burst forth from their mean little faces. Dane thought there was no creature crueler on God's green earth than the teenage boy or girl. He squeezed Truman's shoulder. "Listen, the assembly's no biggie. Rules and regulations. Making sure you have 'an attitude that will determine your altitude.' Crap like that. You wanna skip it?" With a gentle smile, Dane tried to convey he cared. "We could go sit together someplace quiet for a bit and just chat." Dane shrugged. "No pressure."

"I don't know." The boy looked toward the crowd. Dane was disheartened when he followed his gaze. He didn't see one welcoming face.

"Come on," Dane said. "I've got Starburst in my homeroom."

"Well then, if you've got Starburst, how can I possibly say no?" And at last Truman smiled.

That smile was the kind of thing that made Dane get up every morning and come to work.

"Follow me."

Dane led the boy along the school corridor— green tile floors bracketed on either side by rows and rows of lockers in the same shade of industrial green. The boy, Truman, stopped at one of the lockers and began trying to work its combination lock. Dane paused to watch, figuring the boy wanted to divest himself of the load of books and papers he lugged around. Who had so much *stuff* on the first day of the semester?

Truman whispered what sounded like a curse to Dane as he did battle with the lock. He couldn't get it. He tried several times, spinning and spinning to no good effect. His books and papers once more tumbled to the floor. The situation was so sad, so pathetic, it almost made Dane want to laugh. Not at the boy, no, but at the absurdity of life and how it could simply be so plain cruel as to kick this harmless-looking boy when he was so down.

Dane didn't laugh. He neared Truman as the boy crumpled to the floor, sobbing.

Dane squatted next to him and patted his back. "It's okay. It's okay. Get your things together. We can get your combination from the janitor. No prob. Come on. Pick your stuff up and come back to my office."

Dane's heart just about broke as the boy looked up at him, cheeks damp and snot on his upper lip. What a way to start the year! He took in the shirt the boy was wearing and thought he might as well have affixed one of those "Kick Me" signs to his back before starting school this morning. *Why ask for trouble?* Dane wondered. Maybe he could figure the kid out once he got him to his office. Maybe he could let him know that some things that were personal should remain that way.

Truman stood, unsteady, a colt getting to its feet for the first time. He looked wildly around, like he was trapped there in the corridor. "I wanna go home," Truman said, voice barely above a whisper.

"Don't you wanna talk?" Dane asked, his eyebrows coming together with concern. "You'll find my homeroom is a judgment-free zone."

"I want to go home," Truman repeated, his voice a little louder.

"Do you walk to school?"

Truman shook his head.

"Buses won't be here for—" Dane glanced down at his watch, a Fossil timepiece with an orange band his wife, Katy, had gotten him last Christmas. "—another forty-five minutes. Come on. We'll wait in my homeroom." To repeat the offer of Starburst seemed like a silly incentive now. "Let's just go there and chill a little. You're a freshman, right?"

Truman nodded.

Dane grinned. "Come on. How many chances will you get to skip out on an assembly with a *teacher*? You like books?"

Truman nodded.

"Good. I teach English. You'd be surprised how many kids don't, how the only things they read are text messages, tweets, and status updates on Facebook. Who do you like to read?" Dane started walking toward his homeroom, hoping to coax Truman along.

"I like Stephen King and Dean Koontz," Truman said, not moving. "And I wanna go home."

"I like them too. I read my first King when I was about your age. *Christine*, I think it was. You read that one? About the possessed car? Sick!"

"Look, sir, you're being really nice and all, but I need to get home. I know the final bell hasn't rung yet, but do you think you could let me slide? I don't have to tell you I've had a rotten day, and I just need to get home, where I can hide."

Dane shook his head, not to refuse Truman's request but at the sadness of how the boy viewed home. "Where do you live?"

"Little England. It's only a mile or so from here."

Dane scratched his chin. Little England was one of the poorest neighborhoods in Summitville, bordered by the Ohio River on one side and railroad tracks on the other. The neighborhood, sitting just below river level, was regularly flooded. The houses there were mostly adorned with rusting aluminum siding. Or they were wooden frame in need of paint. Little England was poor. Dirty. And for Truman, Dane supposed, it was home.

"I can walk. Can you just look the other way? Please? Just for today?" Tears sprung up in Truman's eyes again. "I could use a break."

Dane so wanted to say yes, but there would be consequences if something should happen to the boy on his way home. Serious consequences, the kind where he could lose his job. And with twenty years here at the school, two kids and a wife to support, he couldn't let that happen. Yet the terror and pain on this boy's face rent his heart in two. "Tell you what," Dane said finally. "If you can call someone to come get you—your mom or your dad—I can let you go with them. Otherwise—" Dane stopped himself as he watched Truman pull a phone out of his pocket. His fingers flew over the tiny screen. Dane was amazed how even the poorest of kids these days managed to have cell phones.

Truman didn't look at him. Instead he stared at the screen as if willing it to life. After a minute or so, Truman breathed a sigh of relief. He held the screen of the flip phone up so Dane could see. Dane read the shorthand texts, which basically confirmed that Mom could get off from work and pick him up in ten minutes, but she wanted to know what was wrong.

What *wasn't* wrong? Dane imagined Truman thinking.

"Can I go wait outside?" Truman asked.

Dane sighed. "Sure you don't want to come talk to me? Just for a few minutes? We'll see your mom pull up from my window."

"You just have to make this as hard as you can, don't you?" Truman snapped.

Dane's smile faltered. "I was trying to do just the opposite," he said.

Truman's face reddened. "I'm sorry, man. I just need to get home."

Dane nodded. "I get it. Go ahead. Wait outside for your mom."

Truman started away, walking quickly, books still stuffed under one matchstick arm.

Dane called after him, "Come talk to me tomorrow. We'll get your locker combination figured out." *Among other things*, Dane thought as he turned to head back to his homeroom.

Once there, Dane plopped down in his imitation-leather desk chair and sighed. He rubbed his hands over his face. Seeing kids teased and bullied was, unfortunately, part of the job, and over two decades, Dane had lost count of the number of times he had witnessed cruelty. Sometimes he thought high school students had cornered the market on unkindness.

But Truman Reid bothered him more than most. It was that damn T-shirt he wore, one that might as well have proclaimed "I'm a big old fag" on the front, instead of its message of hope and the pride of the rainbow flag. Kids here just looked for any excuse to tease, to belittle. The jocks especially seemed to feel that someone's being gay was as good a reason as any to make their life a living hell.

Dane was just about to reflect on the relevance being gay had on his own life when his phone rang. For a moment he was grateful for the ringtone, because it saved him from some of his darkest ruminations, thoughts he shared with no one, but which Truman—with his damnable and enviable pride—had brought out in him.

He pulled his iPhone from his pocket and glanced down at the screen. Unknown, Caller ID taunted him. Dane was tempted not to answer, to just let it go to voice mail and head for the student assembly so he could at least say he'd been there, but instead he pressed Accept.

"Dane Bernard here." He fully expected a telemarketer.

"Mr. Bernard." A male voice came over the line. "Is this the husband of Katherine Bernard?"

A chill coursed through him. "Yup." He tried to swallow, but the sudden dryness in his mouth nearly prevented it. "Is everything all right?"

"I'm sorry to tell you this, Mr. Bernard, but there's been an accident involving your wife. This is Bill Rogers, by the way, with the State Highway Patrol."

Dane could feel his whole body go cold, as if dipped in ice water. "But she's okay, right?" he managed to gasp.

The man responded, "Do you think you could come down to City Hospital? I'll meet you at the ER. Just ask for Bill Rogers. I'll wait."

"Is she okay?" Dane repeated, gripping the phone—hard. But the patrolman had already hung up.

CHAPTER 2

TRUMAN HELD his hand up to his eyes to shield them from the sun as he watched for his mother's car—a rusting Dodge Neon that was older than he was. Patsy called it "Herman," although Truman had no idea why. Truman would hear its grumbling muffler before he actually saw the car. But right now, seeing the car was the most welcome sight Truman could imagine.

He tried to hold it together, the tears and the sobs inside threatening to break free like an itch needing to be scratched.

He closed his eyes with a kind of relief as he saw the little gray car coming down the street, a plume of exhaust belching out of its back end. The car swung rapidly to the curb, front wheels going up on it, and screeched to a stop right in front of Truman.

He was used to his mother's driving. He rushed to get in the car, ignoring the whine it made when he opened the passenger door.

His mother sat across from him, looking glamorous as always. Today Patsy had on dark jeans, a blue lace crop top, and strappy rhinestone sandals that matched her dangling earrings. Her dyed black hair hung in loose curls to her shoulders. Truman thought she could waltz right into the school and fit in perfectly with the other teenage girls—no problem—even though Patsy was the ripe old age of thirty-one.

All his life, it had just been the two of them against the world. Truman didn't know who his father was and, in darker moments, figured Patsy didn't either. She took her hand off the shifter and looked over with concern.

"What happened? What's wrong?"

Truman had never been able to keep a secret from Patsy. He sniffed once and said, "How'd you know?"

She touched his cheek, which had the paradoxical effect of making Truman want both to flinch and to bask in the warmth and comfort of her hand.

"Honey, that sad face is lower than a snake's belly."

"We were at an assembly, and I dropped my books and paper, and—" He could barely go on, getting his humiliation out in fits and starts between gasps for breath. He lowered his head and released the real sobs he'd been holding in since the kids had been so mean to him in the gym. His shoulders shook. His eyes burned. His nose ran. He felt like a baby, and at the same time experienced relief at finally letting his grief go. The worst part, he thought, was that jock who had tripped him telling everyone over and over to kick his stuff. And they all did what he said. And thought it was hysterical!

Patsy had the sense to drive away from the school as Truman sobbed into his hands. He felt like there was a tennis ball in his throat. He just wanted to get home, where he could curl up in bed with his dog at his side. The dog, a mix of bulldog and dachshund that everyone but Truman thought was hideous, was named Odd Thomas, or Odd for short, after a character from a series of Dean Koontz books that Truman adored. The name, though, fit the mutt.

Patsy also had the sense not to say a word until they pulled up in front of their house, a little two-bedroom cottage sided with some kind of tarpaper that was supposed to look like brick but just looked like shit. The front porch appeared as though it could fall off at any time. But Truman never complained—he knew Patsy was providing the best home she could for the two of them on her waitress's salary and tips.

She put a gentle hand on his shoulder that felt as good as a hug.

Truman, able to speak at last, said, "And don't say I shouldn't have worn this shirt to school! You bought it for me!"

"I wasn't gonna say that, sweetie. I think it's a cute shirt, and you have every right to wear it."

Truman should have known. His mother had found the shirt at Goodwill last month. Truman had thought how lucky he was to have a mom like Patsy when she brought it home to him. It was a kind of tribute to Patsy that he had worn it today. He knew he'd probably catch shit for it, but as Patsy always told him, there was no shame in being who he was. If someone had a problem with it, the problem was theirs, not his.

It all sounded good when they were curled up in front of the TV watching *Grey's Anatomy* together or something, but in the real world? Truman was not only gay, he was a very sensitive boy whose feelings were easily crushed. What was he supposed to do with that?

"Come on. I brought home some fries and gravy from the diner, and if they get too cold, they're gonna taste like crap." Patsy got out of the car and waited for him to follow.

Truman wanted to simply dash from the car and hole up in his room with Odd, but he knew Patsy wouldn't leave him alone. He loved her and hated her for it.

So he shuffled in behind his mother, snuffling and rubbing at his burning eyes. Odd jumped off the couch and ran up to him. Truman stooped and let the dog lick his face hungrily. Truman wasn't kidding himself—he knew the dog's extra kisses weren't meant to be a sign of joy at his homecoming or a comfort, but simply a way to taste the saltiness that was so delicious on Truman's skin.

Truman endured the facial tongue bath for several seconds, then scratched Odd behind the ear and patted him on the head.

"I'll go in and heat these up and make us some burgers while you run him out, okay?" Patsy smiled and nodded toward the leash hanging on a hook by the door.

Truman set his school stuff down on the table and headed out with the dog.

"Don't be long," Patsy called after him.

Outside, it still felt like summer. The quality of light, so bright, promised forever day. The breezes were still warm. And those clouds, puffy cotton-ball affairs, seemed painted on the bright blue sky. Insect life hummed as a soundtrack.

Odd urged him on, down toward the banks of the Ohio River where he was happiest. Truman was happy there too. The river was muddy brown and smelled fishy, but the low-hanging trees, willows and maples mostly, shielded Truman from the world, made him feel blissfully alone. And alone was not such a bad thing to be when the world seemed to take every opportunity to kick him in the teeth.

Truman released Odd from his leash and let him run on the riverbank, sniffing at the detritus the river had thrown up. There were old tires, tree branches, cans, and other stuff so worn down by the water it was impossible to identify. Truman sat down on a log while the dog splashed at the water's edge.

Maybe Patsy would say he could just stay home from high school. Was fourteen too young to drop out? Or—wait—maybe she could homeschool him? Right! Like she had extra hours on her hands for that.

Truman stood and skipped a rock across the water's surface, wondering how it would feel to just walk into the brown current until it swallowed him up and carried him away, erasing all his woes. He imagined the cool green surrounding him, his blond hair flowing in the current, those last final bubbles from his nose and mouth ascending toward the sunlight above the water….

But then he thought of his mother. He could imagine her grief, her utter devastation if he was gone. She'd be alone. He couldn't do that to her.

He sighed.

He trudged home, knowing what Patsy would say—how he had to be strong, how he had to be proud of who he was and not take shit from anyone. He'd heard the same speech a thousand times over the course of his short and sissified life. It was cool that his mom was so in his corner, that she was so accepting, but sometimes Truman just wished he wasn't one of the misfit toys, that he was just a normal boy, playing Little League or whatever it was that normal boys did. One of the guys. His mother would tell him that what he wished for was to be common, to be unremarkable, and that someday he'd be glad he was different. It was easy for her to say, or at least so he thought, since she was beautiful, and the worst she had to deal with was being hit on by the truckers and traveling salesmen who came into the diner.

As he neared the porch, he called for Odd to come and, when he did, squatted down to reattach the leash to his collar. Patsy didn't allow the dog to roam free outside. She said it was because she was afraid he'd run away.

Truman wondered if it was really Odd Thomas she feared running away.

He turned and faced the house. Through the screen door, he could hear and smell the ground beef sizzling in its cast-iron skillet and could smell the brown gravy as it surely bubbled on the stove, and the aromas made him, surprisingly, hungry.

Home was a good place.

And tomorrow was another day. Maybe things would be different.

"Yeah, right," he whispered to Odd as he fol-lowed him through the door.

Real Men. True Love.

RICK R. REED draws inspiration from the lives of gay men to craft stories that quicken the heartbeat, engage emotions, and keep the pages turning. Although he dabbles in horror, dark suspense, and comedy, his attention always returns to the power of love. He's the award-winning and bestselling author of more than fifty works of published fiction and is forever at work on yet another book. Lambda Literary has called him: "A writer that doesn't disappoint…"

Rick lives in Palm Springs, CA with his beloved husband and their Boston terrier.

Website: www.rickrreed.com

Blog: www.rickrreedreality.blogspot.com

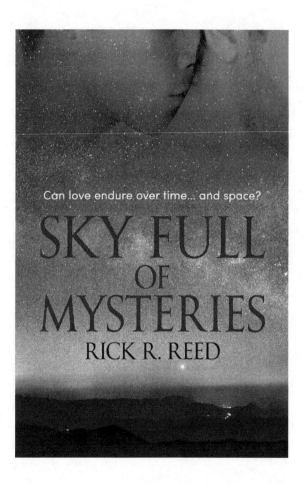

Can love endure over time... and space?

SKY FULL
OF
MYSTERIES

RICK R. REED

What if your first love was abducted and presumed dead—but returned twenty years later?

That's the dilemma Cole Weston faces. Now happily married to Tommy D'Amico, he's suddenly thrown into a surreal world when his first love, Rory Schneidmiller, unexpectedly reappears.

Where has Rory been all this time? Has he time-traveled? What happened to him two decades ago, when a strange mass appeared in the night sky and lifted him into outer space? Rory has no memory of those years. For him, it's as though only a day or two has passed.

Rory still loves Cole with the passion unique to young first love. Cole has never forgotten Rory, yet Tommy has been his rock, by his side since Rory disappeared.

Cole is forced to choose between an idealized and passionate first love and the comfort of a long-term marriage. How can he decide? Who faces this kind of quandary, anyway? The answers might lie among the stars….

www.dreamspinnerpress.com

THE PERILS OF INTIMACY

RICK R. REED

Jimmy and Marc make an adorable couple. Jimmy's kindness and clean-cut cuteness radiate out of him like light. Marc, although a bit older, complements Jimmy with his humor and his openness to love.

But between them, a dark secret lurks, one with the power to destroy.

See, when Marc believes he's meeting Jimmy for the first time in the diner where he works, he's wrong.

Marc has no recollection of their original encounter because the wholesome Jimmy of today couldn't be more different than he was two years ago. Back then, Jimmy sported multiple piercings, long bleached dreadlocks, and facial hair. He was painfully skinny—and a meth addict. The drug transformed him into a different person—a lying, conniving thief who robbed Mark blind during their one-night stand.

Marc doesn't associate the memory of a hookup gone horribly wrong with this fresh-faced, smiling twentysomething… but Jimmy knows. As they begin a dance of love and attraction, will Jimmy be brave enough to reveal the truth? And if he does, will Marc be able to forgive him? Can he see Jimmy for the man he is now and not the addict he was? The answers will depend on whether true love holds enough light to shine through the darkness of past mistakes.

www.dreamspinnerpress.com

LOST AND FOUND

RICK R. REED

The way to a man's heart is through his dog.

On a bright autumn day, Flynn Marlowe lost his best friend, a beagle named Barley, while out on a hike in Seattle's Discovery Park.

On a cold winter day, Mac Bowersox found his best friend, a lost, scared, and emaciated beagle, on the streets of Seattle.

Two men. One dog. When Flynn and Mac meet by chance in a park the next summer, there's a problem—who does Barley really belong to? Flynn wants him back, but he can see that Mac rescued him and loves him just as much as he does. Mac wants to keep the dog, and he can imagine how heartbreaking losing him would be—but that's just what Flynn experienced.

A "shared custody" compromise might be just the way to work things out. But will the arrangement be successful? Mac and Flynn are willing to try it—and along the way, they just might fall in love.

www.dreamspinnerpress.com

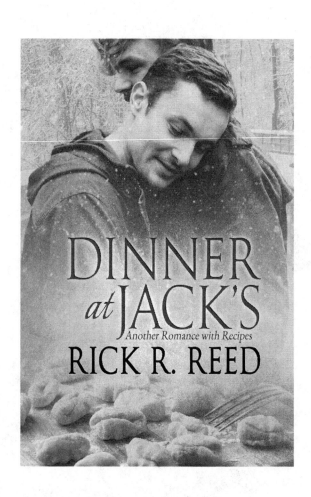

DINNER
at JACK'S
Another Romance with Recipes
RICK R. REED

Personal chef Beau St. Clair, recently divorced from his cheating husband, returns to the small Ohio River town where he grew up to lick his wounds. Jack Rogers lives with his mother, Maisie, in that same small town, angry at and frightened of the world. Jack has a gap in his memory that hides something he dares not face, and he's probably suffering from post-traumatic stress disorder.

Maisie, seeking relief from her housebound and often surly son, hires Beau to cook for Jack, hoping the change might help bring Jack, once a handsome and vibrant attorney, back to his former self. But can a new face and comfort food compensate for the terror lurking in Jack's past?

Slowly the two men begin a dance of revelation and healing. Food and compassion build a bridge between Beau and Jack, a bridge that might lead to love.

But will Jack's demons allow it? His history could just as easily tear them apart as bring them together.

www.dreamspinnerpress.com

STRANDED
WITH DESIRE

Vivien Dean and Rick R. Reed

*When their plane crashed,
their desire took flight.*

When their plane crashed, their desire took flight.

CEO Maine Braxton and his invaluable assistant, Colby, don't realize they share a deep secret: they're in love—with each other. That secret may have never come to light but for a terrifying plane crash in the Cascade Mountains that changes everything.

In a struggle for survival, the two men brave bears, storms, and a life-threatening flood to make it out of the wilderness alive. The proximity to death makes them realize the importance of love over propriety. Confessions emerge. Passions ignite. They escape the wilds renewed and openly in love.

When they return to civilization, though, forces are already plotting to snuff out their short-lived romance and ruin everything both have worked so hard to achieve.

www.dreamspinnerpress.com

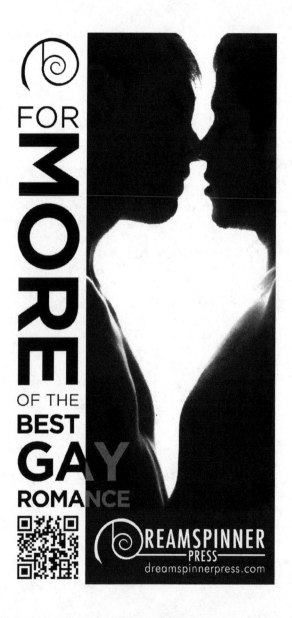